ONE MORE LAST TIME

THE GOOD GUYS BOOK 1

ERIC UGLAND

AIR QUOTES PUBLISHING, INC.

Air Quotes Publishing

Cover by Sarah Anderson/No Synonym

This is a work of Fiction. All of the characters in this novel and series are fictional and any resemblance to people living, dead, or undead is purely coincidental and surprising. And let's not even begin to talk about the fact that it's all in a fantastical world in some other universe. There may be mentions of real places in this book, and while these passing mentions of real locations might have passing resemblance to said real locations, that's really just incidental, as these locations are all used fictitiously. The science in this book is only accidentally accurate, and no medical or scientific value should be attached to any of the ideas espoused within.

Except that Kent is a jerk.

ALSO BY ERIC UGLAND

The Good Guys LitRPG Series

Heir Today Pawn Tomorrow

Dungeon Mauling

Four: The Loot

Dukes and Ladders

Home Siege Home

Bare Hunt

Eastbound & Town

Four Beheadings and a Funeral

The Bad Guys LitRPG Series

Scamps & Scoundrels

Second Story Man

Skull & Thrones

War of the Posers

To Kristen,
Thanks for reading everything and helping me figure out all this beautiful nonsense. Rock on, yo.

1

Like any good story, it began with a girl. It was supposed to end with a bullet.

The gun was on my desk, and I was in the midst of writing a lengthy and rambling note explaining my reasons for using the bullet to make a delicate hole in one side of my skull and blow out the other in a glorious, gruesome display of Pollockian gore. But something interrupted my attempts at apartment redecoration.

I lived on the third floor of a building that was too expensive for me, too nice for me, and about to evict me. I heard the rumble of an engine downstairs. I limped over to the window from the desk, and peeked out through the drapes. A van had pulled up. It was white and impressively ordinary, specifically chosen to be like every other white van you've ever seen. But on this particular evening, it was filled with men coming to kill me. They were related to the girl. Everything was. Well, most everything. One thing wasn't.

The phone rang.

An unknown number.

Normally I'd pass, but considering the killers outside,

the gangrenous wound inside, and my pseudo-suicidal state, what was the worst a telemarketer could do? I figured, at the least, I could ruin someone else's day.

"Hello?" I asked as an answer.

"Nils?" a voice from my past replied.

"Yeah, is this—"

"Normand. No last names, I'd venture." My former boss. A friend. Perhaps the last friend I had. Eccentric millionaire and all-around good guy. I highly recommend eccentric millionaires as friends — they're almost always worth it.

"They're probably listening, yes," I said. They being the police. Or the FBI. Or both. As far as I knew, I was being investigated by multiple agencies.

"I've heard a few things about you."

"Some might be true."

"Not everything, I hope."

I didn't answer, but I think he knew what I would have said.

"In that case," he said, understanding me, "I think I have something for you."

I took a chance at peeking out the window once again. The men were outside the van now, talking to each other. One at the back was loading bullets into a clip. Up and down the street, it was deserted. As if the rest of the neighborhood knew to avoid the area on this night.

"Normand, I appreciate the call," I said, "I really do, but I'm not sure—"

"I am offering a way out."

"Better get here in the next thirty seconds, or it's too late."

"Should be there now."

"Uh, Normand—"

"Check your email."

"Seriously?"

"Seriously."

I limped back over to the desk and sat down with a grunt. Something definitely oozed out of my stomach wound. A quick few clicks, and I had my email up. Sure enough, first in the inbox was from Normand. A few more clicks and I was confused.

"It's a link," I said.

"Click it."

"I—"

"I thought you had mere seconds."

"Seconds might be pushing it."

"Then trust me, and click it."

I sighed. I had very little to lose at this point, and almost hoped it was going to lead me to something like blue waffles or lemonade party so I could have one last laugh.

The link took me to a webpage for a game with a rather silly title, iNcarn8. There wasn't a ton of information about the game, just a lot of marketing talk hyping the game up. All about changing lives. Living in a new world and being free. A game with total freedom. More than a game, a life.

"What the fuck is this?" I asked.

"It's, I mean, it is what I, it is a way out. A way for you to live. Or continue to live."

"I don't get it."

"Unfortunately, I don't think I have time to explain further, do I?"

I stood up and looked out the window just in time to see the street light get shot out.

"Nope," I said.

"So you will have to trust me. It's something I've been investing in. Bringing this, uh, opportunity to, well, to us. To people whom I find worthy, and there's really not many who are going to be given the chance to join, and be a part of this, I mean, I guess, experiment."

"So I'm a guinea pig?"

"To an extent."

"What extent?"

"Does it matter? From what I understand, you're about to die anyway—"

"How much do you know about me, Normand?"

"Enough," he said. "Enough to spend a lot of time, money, and other things in order to give you this chance."

I took as deep a breath as my wounds would allow, then exhaled slowly, giving my brain a moment to consider. It promptly spat back that this seemed the only option for continued existence.

"What do I do?" I finally asked.

"Fill out the forms, press accept, live your new life like you told me you wished you had lived this one."

"I don't get what this is going to do, old man."

"Give it a try."

The phone started to crackle, and I took a peek at it. Down from full bars to one.

"I think they've got a cell phone jammer," I said.

"Good luck. I hope to see you the next time around," Normand said.

"Thank you," I said, but I have no idea if he heard it, the phone cut out.

I stared at the screen.

"Fuck it," I said, and I started typing.

It was the usual rigamarole for an RPG. Name, sex, race, distribute attribute points, choose starting location, stuff that normally, you know, if I was going to be playing a game, I'd have relished taking my time with. If I'd had time, I'd have been effusive with my praise for the developers giving so many options to the players — the list of races and places was seemingly endless. Instead, I cursed at them, clicking through as fast as I could, selecting random anytime I could. Finally, I clicked submit.

Which pulled up a huge list of questions.

Fuck.

The questionnaire was more along the lines of a psych eval. At least, that's what it seemed like to me.

The front doorknob jiggled.

I pulled my gun from the desk to my lap.

I answered the questions just like any internet poll — as quickly as possible, not giving a fuck about veracity. Being done was more important than being right. I flew through the questions, then clicked the damn button at the bottom of the page.

A fucking pop-up.

But this seemed like the end.

Whispers outside my door.

I scanned the pop-up briefly. It was asking if I was really ready to submit. I clicked yes.

Another pop-up asking me to accept the terms and liabilities.

I clicked accept.

Another fucking pop up asking if I was sure.

Yes, dammit, I'm fucking sure.

Then two things happened.

First, another pop-up window, a last notice making sure that I knew everything was final, that there was no chance to remake my character after I pushed this button.

Second, the window next to me exploded inward as a man in black tactical gear came flying into the room, assault carbine aimed near me.

I clicked the yes button just as the man's feet collided

with me. Training kicked in, and, thank God for that. I swept his feet to one side, doing my best to push him into the chair as I came out of it. It might have been a cool move if not for the second dude coming in behind the first asshole.

He smashed me over the back with two hands together, and I dropped to my knees, my gun clattering across the floor and disappearing into the black hole underneath the fridge.

With only the shit that had fallen around my desk as an option, I took a half second to search for any semblance of a weapon, and saw a fork. As they say, any fork in a storm.

I used said fork to stab Asshole Two through the foot. He screamed, and I had the barest of moments before Asshole One grabbed me and pulled me up by the neck, squeezing hard.

My innards were screaming at me, my homemade stitches having torn out. Blood poured out of my flabby abdomen. Flabdomen. There might have been pus too. Likely a lot of it. It was gross, okay? Let's leave it at that.

Black seeped around the edges of my vision, and I knew my end was coming soon. I snuck a glance at the computer screen: it was processing something.

Asshole One's fingernails dug into my neck. My lungs burned, desperate for a quick breath. I snapped my head back hard, and sure enough, Asshole One had missed the lesson on don't-keep-your-face-right-against-the-fucking-skull-of-your-opponent. I did a number on his nose — I could feel the hot rush of blood from his ruined schnozzola soaking my neck. His grip loosened, and I took in a huge gulp of air.

Asshole Two had his gun up and trained on me. I'm sure he was desperate to fire. So desperate, in fact, that he hadn't taken the safety off, and the gun just kinda did nothing when Asshole Two pulled the trigger.

I stomped on the fork, driving it all the way through the man's foot into the previously unblemished hard wood floors below. So much for getting my security deposit back.

Then, I stomped on Asshole One's insole, and bit his hand. I grabbed Asshole Two's hair and pulled him towards me.

He punched me, absolutely perfectly, his fist going through my newly re-opened wound, and actually into my intestines.

There was quite a bit of screaming from everyone involved. We were all in solid amounts of pain, and conjoined in a seriously unpleasant way. I was barely holding on, the only thing keeping me going was that, at least I was going to go out in style. Then, a telltale terrible noise: the *tink tink tink* of a metallic object bouncing across the floor. The grenade came to a gentle stop on my fucking foot.

A sharp *bong* rang out from the computer, and everything went black.

2

I thought I'd died.

Everything was black.

Everything.

Not like your-eyes-are-closed black, but like a ceaseless, unending void of darkness. Besides, as far as I could tell in that moment, my eyes were open and there was nothing to see. An absence of light and matter and everything. I felt and saw and tasted nothing. All my senses reached out as far and as hard as they could. They all stopped at me.

I mean, given that I'd heard a grenade bounce across my floor and seen it wind up balanced neatly on my boot, I figured this was what death was.

A void.

Awesome.

And wrong. I mean, obviously.

"Welcome, Hero!" a deep and melodious voice boomed out from the nothingness. "You have been summoned to the world of Vuldranni, to be a noble—"

There was a bit of a pause. A very obvious unplanned pause.

The voice continued, much quieter, as if speaking to someone off stage. "This can't be right — it says—" then there was muttering. People talking off mic.

"Yeah, and there's also three of them," the deep voice snapped angrily. "Three. Yeah... Because I can see them, numbnuts."

I looked around. Still nothing. Blackness. But for the first time, I could feel something near me, that vague sort of vibration surrounding living beings. Someone, perhaps, was almost touching me.

"This isn't supposed to, you know, I was told this was a professional operation, and—" there was a loud click as the mic got turned off, and lights flicked on. Bright, sterile lights illuminated a blank white room. A large window to one side revealed an empty recording studio.

To my right, Asshole One.

To my left, Asshole Two.

Which left me — Asshole Three, I suppose — in the middle.

Just a bunch of assholes.

They still had all their gear on. We were all dressed as we were in my apartment. It meant I had no weapons on my person, which was a minor minus in my book, but, you know, plus side, I was also no longer bleeding out of my gangrenous wound. Which, oddly, didn't seem open or gangrenous anymore.

Asshole Two, for the record, still had the fork stuck through his foot. Below that, a very large section of hardwood floor had come too. Termites were already spreading out, and as soon as the lights shot on, one brave cockroach had made a scurry for a wall he'd never find.

Things were still for a moment. Finally, an elegant man in a three-piece suit walked out of a door that wasn't there until he came through it. He sat down at a desk that appeared between blinks. Right around the time chairs appeared and I realized that I was sitting down. Maybe I'd been sitting the entire time. I was pretty sure I'd been standing.

The man pulled out a pair of platinum rimmed glasses and perched them on his nose. He looked down at the desk, and flipped through a sheaf of papers that came into existence.

"This is some Alice In Wonderland shit," I said softly.

The man seemed to smile ever so slightly while reading over the papers.

We three assholes sat there in silence for a moment, completely caught off guard and unable to process a damn thing we were seeing or experiencing, which, you know, was a bit weird. Because, well, they'd been quite actively killing me mere moments before, and now we were sitting in front of a man at a desk like we were truculent teens hauled before a tweedy vice principal of a second-rate middle school.

"So," the man said, plucking a manila folder from midair and laying it on the desk. He put all the papers in it, and then looked at us slowly, making eye contact with each of us before continuing. "There are a few things I'm confused upon. First of all, which one of you is actually supposed to be here, and which are—"

"Dude, what the fuck is all this supposed to be?" Asshole One yelled.

Asshole Two chose a more proactive route, and launched himself across the desk at the man with glasses.

I was going to raise my hand, but, instead, I grabbed Asshole Two by his tactical webbing, and pulled him back down to his seat.

"Well," the man said with smile, clicking his pen and making a note in the folder, "that makes it quite clear."

There was a bright popping sound, and the assholes simply disappeared. Now it was just me and the elegant dude.

"We've got a number of," the man paused and looked around, trying to find his words, "well, questions for you. You managed to break our system quite soundly."

"I'm a little confused," I replied, "because I have no clue, in the least, what's going on."

"Did you not read the EULA?"

"Does anyone read that shit?"

"I do."

"I just ran out of time."

His eyebrows went up, and he snapped his fingers. "Time, right. Must remember the time," he made a note. "See, I thought you'd read it because you brought a lot to trade."

"Trade?"

"Yes. All the goods and creatures which aren't you."

The man opened the folder and spread out a huge variety of photos. All the things that had come along with me, that weren't, well, me. The two men, the cockroaches, the termites, the guns, the grenade, the fucking floorboards, the fork. All photographed and catalogued.

"Uh, I guess I just try to be prepared? Because I was a Boy Scout?"

"A Boy Scout?"

"Yeah, uh, this group of—"

"I know what the Boy Scouts are. What rank were you?"

"Eagle."

"Ah, congratulations." He made a note in the folder.

"Thanks?"

"With what you've brought, I should think you'll be quite prepared for your new adventure."

"About that—"

"Oh time. I nearly forgot. I've just got so much on my mind lately, I've been late for almost everything." He glanced down at his wrist, where there was now a nice watch. "Gods, just one moment—"

He gestured at the wall, and a clock popped up. Not a small little thing either, but something I imagine was equitable to Big Ben, with a massive second hand clicking along.

"Apologies for the disgusting decor, but I simply must keep an eye on the exact time. Vitally important to get you processed before time is up. Or, you know."

"Actually, I don't."

"You don't get to play if you don't get in the game on time."

"Oh. Shit."

"Yes, my fault, entirely. I do apologize, and promise I will make it up to you. But, for the moment, perhaps you'll tell me if you were actually serious with your choices.""

"I, uh—"

"Honesty is the best policy here today, because you have disrupted quite a lot of things, and we are in uncharted waters. Which, I do say, is beneficial for us as we can do some work on our end, clarify this and ensure this type of foolishness doesn't happen again. Now. That said, if you really wanted to be a sentient rock lobster named *Asdfjkl* in a land-locked sand desert, that can still be arranged. But I have a feeling there was an error somewhere. So, perhaps you might tell me if the error was on your end, or ours."

"I hit random for, like, everything."

"Ah. Interesting tactic. Still, it shouldn't be possible for that particular combination to happen. I'll have to speak to Q and A. Questions for me?"

"What is this?"

"Did you not read *any* of the information about this product prior to purchasing?"

"Uh, it was a gift."

The little man turned his head to the side, frowning in confusion. He took his glasses off, wiped them, and then checked his watch again.

"Unexpected," he said, "but let me see if I can do this on the quick. You have the opportunity to live a new life."

"I think, I mean, didn't the big voice at the beginning say something about being a hero?"

"Yes, well, that's the typical path your kind likes to take."

"My kind?"

"Humans. From Earth. In this, well, verse."

"Verse?"

"Let's not focus on the cosmology, and instead, answer your question. This is a new life. Should you want to be a hero, sure. Do it. We'd love it. It'd be better for us and you. But it is your choice."

"So I'm supposed to—"

"Ah, don't go along that line of thinking. Stop imagining you are supposed to do anything. Instead, try imagining what you'll be able to do."

"Which is?"

"Whatever you like."

"Fish at a lake?"

"Totally possible."

"Build a house."

"Rather advisable."

"Not be a hero?"

"Sure. Be a villain. Dig ditches. Bake bread. Steal cookies

from children or save infants from fires. Do something. Or nothing. But be aware, if what you are doing is awesome and wonderful, you'll find that more viewers tune in to watch, and that those viewers will find ways to send you things. Presents, and coincidences, and—"

"Whoa, take it back one second there. Viewers?"

"Of course. This is largely free to you, but we must fund our operation somehow. So many of the many universes find this entertaining. Hugely popular, I might say. Hence, why everything is done in a gamified way."

"I'm really not getting this."

"One, I'm sorry. Two, usually that's why we don't do this sort of interaction. We've got a lovely video that explains most of it, plus a brief tutorial to introduce the concepts to you, play the game and understand how it works, give the chance to view the world and make educated choices. But unfortunately, due to time constraints, well, you were on the fast track already, and now, you are on the even faster track. So the day is getting away from us, and we have run out of time for questions. You will simply have to learn as you go."

"But—"

"Right, Trade goods. Bother, and your character. So much to do, and we are so very late, character or trading?"

"I—"

"Character might a good start, because you might be able to make better choices with your trades. But, if you trade for something which opens up character options, you'll be irritated you didn't wait. Pluses and minuses all over the place, all the time. Such is the world in which you will live in. Now. Choose."

I thought for a second. I've played games. A lot. I mean, I used to. Up until the bad times, with all the violence and the crime and the exceedingly poor choices, games were a primary hobby for me. The whole reason I did the Eagle Scout thing was because it let me go on camping trips where we'd play D&D, and I got good grades so my parents wouldn't bug me when I spent 18 hours on a Saturday grinding out characters in WoW. I had experience both min-maxing and roleplaying, and though this was supposedly real, it certainly seemed like the best idea would be to go with making myself as overpowered as I could. This time around, I wanted an easy life.

"Do you mind if I ask your name?" I asked.

"Mister Paul will work," he replied with a smile.

"Mister Paul, I'm—"

"I'm assuming your name will be changed, so perhaps you'd like to give me your in game name."

"Oh," I said, thinking. I'd never been particularly pleased with my name. It was fine — it was who I'd been. But now that I had the chance to change everything about myself, I couldn't make a decision. Options ran through my mind, but nothing stuck out. "Well, what's the naming convention like, on, you know, uh,—"

"Vuldranni?"

"Yeah, that's the one."

"You mean, the planet that has many sentient races, each with multiple competing cultures, spread out across a planet that makes your Jupiter pale in comparison? How long have we got to sit here?"

"I—"

"Trick question, we are out of time. Name, or I'll pick one for you. And, minor spoiler, it will be Betty."

I didn't want a lifetime as Betty — no offense, Ms. White — but my mind blanked. It's always easy to speculate on naming, and I never had problems when I'd played games. I'd just do something silly, like I. P. Freely. But in games you never really get called your character name. Having to actually introduce myself as I.P.? That bothered me. I wanted something simple, strong, evocative of who I am, or who I wanted to be. I could name myself after my favorite football player. And yet, my favorite fictional character was a well-known archaeologist named after a state. Maybe there was a happy medium if I just—

"Time is up," Mister Paul said softly, "please give me a name."

I had nothing else.

"Montana."

"Lovely," he said, jotting it down on a piece of paper. "Race?"

"I remember seeing a ton of choices—"

"Truly a staggering amount," Mister Paul replied. "But perhaps you'd consider an alternative--"

"Letting you choose?"

"You would let me?"

"Fuck it, man, sure."

"Just for the rule mongers, let me clarify: you are allowing me to choose your race."

"Yes."

"And you're human now, correct?"

"Far as I know."

"That's fine. Want to stick with being male?"

"Sure."

"Moving right along. Do you understand attributes and traits and—"

"I think so, yes."

"Perfect. Done with character. Trading.

"Uh, how does it normally happen?"

"Normally, if someone has brought along a thing or two, it happens automatically. You just find some bonuses in your inventory when you begin. You get a small bonus by making some choices."

"Let's do this."

"My sentiments exactly," Paul said with a big smile. "You managed to bring two humans with you. For that, you'll get, say, what they would have received, points wise. "

"Sounds fair." And by fair I meant that it sounded like I'd get an overpowered start, which I was totally fine with. I wanted to be overpowered.

"The other animals, well, how about—"

"—I can talk to animals?"

"Some bonus attributes and a bonus to handling animals."

"Uh, sure."

"On to weapons. You've brought seven firearms, two knives, and one grenade. Rather impressive. For all that, I *can* give you a magical weapon—"

"Which kind of weapon?"

"You'll choose at embark. Now, Nightvision goggles, easy translation—"

"Darkvision?"

"Instead of Nightvision? I suppose that's doable. Body armor, how about a shield?"

"How about magic armor?"

"How about a magic shield? This is trading, not dreaming."

"Fine."

"I will also grant you a boon, just a little thing that deals with language, usually reserved for VIPs who buy the upgraded package, but here we'll give it a trade for the wood floor."

"Okay—"

"Now, penultimate, as we are running out of time," he

looked up at the clock, "really quite late. Do you have particular concerns about your appearance in your new life?"

"Not really, just, you know—"

"Perhaps you could just trust me?"

"That's a lot of trust."

"Then we might not finish in time, and—"

"Okay, if I'm letting you design me, I'm doing you a favor by getting you out of here on time, right? So, as a favor to you, I'll say yes, just make me muscular, handsome, and with the capacity for a big bushy beard. And no balding. And not fat."

He smiled, like a genuine smile. I swear I saw a twinkle in his eye. "Deal."

He wrote a bunch of things on the paper very quickly. Then he stacked all the pages up and slid them neatly into the folder.

"I am ready to let you embark," he said, "but I do have a question."

"Hit me."

"I have always wanted to see someone get down off this particular peak. If I were to give you a boon, would you be willing to start there?"

"What's a boon again?"

"A special gift from a higher power."

I narrowed my eyes. *Now* it was negation time. "Two boons."

"Two boons of my choice."

"Two boons of your choice that are useful to me and my long-term survival in this new world."

"Agreed, and you'll do well remembering that specificity in what is said matters in your new life and this new world."

"So my spawn point is the top of a mountain," I said, hoping I hadn't gotten myself into some shit.

"For the moment, though it can be changed."

"How many respawns do I have?"

"I'm not sure. There is sort of a limit, but it also depends on your rank and popularity with the viewers."

"Can I see my rank?"

"No. And you cannot speak about it in the world. It's very gauche, and ruins the verisimilitude we value. Most of your kind don't know they're being viewed, and we would appreciate keeping it that way. So once you leave here, you won't remember any of this portion of our conversation."

"You can wipe my memory?"

"We have immense access to you, as we are putting you in a whole new world. So—"

"What kind of world is it?"

"Vuldranni is a Medieval Fantasy."

"Can I get a baseline of what average attributes are?"

Mister Paul smiled, just a tiny bit, and tapped his head. "Smart boy. For a human, average strength is around 13. A truly gifted athlete, 20. Enough?"

"Sure. Let's play ball."

"Beautiful," Mister Paul said "We are truly getting you in right under the wire."

He scribbled a few things on a sheet of paper, and slipped it into the folder, pulled an envelope out of the air, and put the folder and the papers into the envelope. The envelope poofed out of existence.

Mister Paul stood up and extended his hand.

I stood too, and we shook.

"Enjoy your new life, Montana."

3

I entered my new world falling.

Not far — maybe six feet — but a sudden fall is always disconcerting. Luckily, I had a soft landing, almost disappearing into deep snow.

I sat up shivering, and looked at my surroundings. My first peek at Vuldranni.

Mountains and snow. As promised, I was on top of a fucking mountain. One of the highest peaks around. I was above clouds, my breath coming out in white puffs of steam.

And I'd be freezing my new balls off if I wasn't covered almost completely in fur. Thick white fur. It took me a second to realize that I was wearing it, not growing the fur. I had pants, boots, gloves, and a hooded jacket, all covered in ridiculously thick, heavy white fur. I even had a half-mask of fur that snapped onto the front of the hood, keeping my face toasty warm.

It was cold and windy, but quite beautiful in an extreme sort of way. Deep blue skies above, fluffy white trails below, and basically any which way I looked, peaks of other mountains. If I wanted to get out of the mountains, I only had one direction to travel. My starting position was less than ideal for anything other than aesthetic reasons. Also troubling: the sun was high in the sky, pretty much straight above me. Noon. So I had half the day to get off the mountain before I'd freeze to death at night, no matter how many awesome fur-clothes I had.

I could almost hear Paul chuckling above me. I stared at the snow and the rocks and the rugged world all around me, wondering how the hell I'd survive this nonsense.

Something nagged at the corner of my vision, and that made me think about points and abilities and all that, at which point my vision was completely filled with various prompts and menus and options, to the point that I was overwhelmed. I took a step back, tripped over my own feet in the snow, and fell on my butt, which did absolutely nothing for all the crap blocking my vision. I waved my hands around my face, and, after a moment, I realized that I could move the prompts about space, and, for the most part, the prompts would stay there. I put things where I could in order to get a handle on the situation.

The attributes seemed to be the normal gaming affair:

Attributes

Strength: 10
Agility: 10
Dexterity: 10
Constitution: 10
Wisdom: 10
Intelligence: 10

Charisma: 10
Luck: 10

Unassigned points: 54

At the bottom flashed a grim warning that I had 36 hours to allocate my points or lose them forever.

I didn't bother standing — I needed to do some quick thinking before starting my hike down the mountain. If I got triple points for the assholes with me, that meant a normal person new to the game would get 18 points. So if you split your points evenly across all attributes, you'd be just below average in everything at level one with, maybe, one attribute just above. Interesting mechanics. That means the starting character needs to grind right away in order to approach heroics. But I'd start ahead of the pack, which was perfect because I wanted to live a life of quietude, not spend my time embroiled in combat or courtly intrigue. In that regard, dumping points into charisma seemed unnecessary. I put ten points in strength immediately. Given that Vuldranni was a medieval fantasy world, Strength would be something to keep me out of trouble. Five points into Dexterity to be nimble and avoid trouble, five points into Agility so I could run away from trouble. Ten points into Constitution so I might survive unavoidable trouble. I put three into Intelligence, three into Wisdom, and three into Charisma. Then, because I felt a bit like I'd had a crap first life, I tossed the rest into luck.

My finger hovered over the okay button. I wasn't exactly

sure how Intelligence as a stat worked here. Or Charisma for that matter. I still seemed to have all my memories and learning from my previous life, and people had liked me well enough there. I guess I'd just need to figure it out.

I pushed okay.

I checked the list again.

Attributes

Strength: 20
Agility: 15
Dexterity: 15
Constitution: 20
Wisdom: 13
Intelligence: 13
Charisma: 13
Luck: 25

Unassigned points: 0

I pushed okay and stood up. I felt different. My body responded faster, better. I could breathe deeper, feel more. My muscles felt big, robust. I felt powerful, and smiled. I flexed, and my muscles responded, feeling taut and hard and awesome. I was big and beefy and not fat or balding. Maybe this was going to be all right.

The next set of notifications concerned the boons from Mister Paul. The first was:

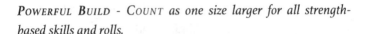

Powerful Build - Count as one size larger for all strength-based skills and rolls.

Dope boon. Meant my strength of 20 would count as a lot more than a normal human. Might be super useful in this world. And offered me a slight surprise should anyone get a look at my attributes.

Regeneration - Outside of combat, your body will repair rather quickly. Given enough time, it's possible you will heal from nearly any wound.

Now that was useful. Probably the most useful thing I could have received as a boon. As long as I could hide for a bit, I'd get better. And, it meant I could be pretty cavalier in combat, provided I could win.

The final one was the thing he'd said was usually reserved for VIPs or something.

Gift of Gab (Mister Paul) - Should you encounter a language you do not understand, as long as you hear at least three words of it, you will understand it, and speak it, perfectly.

SEEMED to be the ideal thing to have as a tourist in an entirely new universe. I always wanted to speak another language, now it looked like I was going to be speaking all of them.

I needed to start down the mountain — this was taking a bit longer than I wanted. But I figured if I started down now, I'd end up paying too much attention to reading my notifications and walk right into a crevasse. Then, who knows? I'd be stuck there forever, regenerating my health as fast as starvation depleted it.

I sped through the welcome notices, mostly things about being in the World of Vuldranni and how the mountain that I was on was my respawn point. Then I saw the little tab marked equipment. I pushed on that, and saw that I had some equipment gifts.

YOU HAVE FOUND ***SWORD OF THE GODS***

SWORD of the Gods

Item Type: Legendary

Item Class: One-handed Melee, Two-handed Melee

Material: Celestial Admantium

Damage: 390-420 (Slashing)

Durability: 20000/20000

Weight: 4.8 lbs

Requirements: Str 8

Description: A straight-bladed sword having a cruciform hilt with a grip for one or two handed use. Made for and by the Gods for the purposes of smiting everything.

~

YOU HAVE FOUND ***SHIELD OF THE GODS***

~

SHIELD ***of the Gods***

Item Type: Legendary

Material: Celestial Admantium

Armor: +120, 100% immunity to Fire

Durability: 20000/20000

Weight: 18 lbs

Requirements: Str 18

Description: A massive shield designed to protect from everything.

~

THE SWORD WAS your standard fantasy long sword, kinda big but well done. The pommel was solid gold, and had a nice glow about it, and the blade was balanced perfectly. I mean, I had very little experience with swords, so everything seemed fine to me, but what the fuck did I know? The shield was a giant gold saucer with a bevy of runes etched across the front, all of which had a light blue glow to them. It was heavy, but holdable.

I swung the sword around, doing this and that with the blade, totally thinking *snicker-snack* as I chopped off the heads of imaginary enemies. I maybe just recreated a few of my favorite movie fight sequences, and perhaps even let out a few lightsaber noises, even though those had absolutely nothing to do with real swords. Or fantasy swords. And it wasn't a saber. I also announced I was Inigo Montoya.

I pulled up the inventory screen, thinking to see how much I could carry, and if there was some sweet gamification concept that allowed me to carry a ton of shit even though I didn't really have a bag or anything.

~

Inventory

Worn: Furs

On Person: Sword of the Gods, Shield of the Gods, starting gear.

~

STARTING GEAR?

I felt around myself, and maybe felt a bit of myself, which, you know, check, still there and, uh, proportional. That's also when I discovered that I had pockets around the belly area of my stupid huge furs. And, from said pocket, I pulled out an orb. As I held it front of my face, a message popped up, pointing at the orb.

~

*Do you wish to open your **starting gear**?*

Yes/No

~

"YES," I said, and immediately wondered why I was talking out loud to myself when I could just think the yes.

The orb seemed to shiver out of sight, and a list of gear popped up, differing starting packages.

PLEASE PICK ONE.

THE GAME WAS POLITE, a welcome change. Mister Paul had been pretty damn snarky, and I figured the game would continue in that vein.

There were five different sets to chose from, obviously geared to differing play styles. A dagger and a bow and some lock picks for the nefarious types. A sword, a shield, and a piece of leather armor for the fighter. And what I figured was for crafters, a hammer, a saw, and a carving knife. The final kit, that one was all mine. A fishing pole, a pick, and a hatchet.

Easy choice.

*YOU HAVE FOUND the starting kit: **Gathering***

Fishing Pole.

Bronze Pick.

Bronze Hatchet.

Harvesting Skillbook.

Rations.

Rope.

Knapsack.

Bandage.
Money Pouch.
Lifeform Identification Spellbook.
Basic Object Identification Spellbook.

ALL OF THE stuff just dropped out of the sky, and half of it disappeared into the snow. And then I had a bunch of crap I had to put about my person. I had no, like, bag of holding or anything. The inventory system here could use some work, considering it was, more or less, just reality. I wrapped the rope around my torso, and got it tight enough that I could tuck the hatchet across my chest. The pick went in my belt opposite my sword. I put everything else into the knapsack. I then slid the sheath onto my belt, put the sword away, slung the shield over my back, and was ready to hike down the fucking mountain. I took a single step, and a little text bubble popped up.

YOU HAVE AN UNACCEPTED QUEST. Do you wish to read the quest?

WELL, sure. Sounded like a good idea.

YOU HAVE BEEN OFFERED a quest by Mister Paul:
Descend from the Peak!

Get down from the peak of the mountain. Preferably with verve and excitement. And alive.

Failure: If you refuse to ever leave the peak and/or if you die too many times before making it down safely.

Reward for success: XP!

Penalty for failure (or refusal): none.

Yes/No

I ACCEPTED MY FIRST QUEST. I felt a bit of a thrill. For the first time, this game maybe seemed fun.

Then I got an idea. A terrible, amazing, fantastic idea.

4

Spoiler alert: terrible idea.

Believe it or not, sledding down a mountain on a large round medieval magic shield turned out to be a bad idea.

At first, I made great time while having a great time, zooming down the mountain, the golden shield sending up sprays of snow behind me. And the snow was pretty close to perfect for sledding: deep, fresh untouched powder. But the thing with snow saucers is, there's not exactly a ton of steering or stopping capability. You're really just hoping you end up on a line down a hill with no bumps and a nice flat spot at the end to run out the speed. Oddly enough, that's not what I found on the top of a mountain. I found mostly steep bits and rocks. So many rocks.

I was nearing take-off speed at the end of one particularly gruesome pitch, holding onto the shield straps as tightly as I could, when I hit the first big rock. I jolted skyward. It was exhilarating, the wind whipping against my face, the ground zipping under me. I landed with a hard thump. My vision flashed red, and I got a notification, but things were happening too fast for me to pay attention to it.

I tried to steer as best I could, pulling this way and that, doing a minimal amount yet avoiding major obstacles. Maybe if I'd been on something with real turning ability, I'd have missed the crevasse.

Nope.

Right off the edge, soaring across the gap. I *almost* made it to the other side. Instead, the shield, with me on top of it, clanged straight into a wall of ice.

I, naturally, continued forward until my face impacted against the same ice wall, and I had the distinct and memorable feeling of my nose breaking and my cheekbones shattering. Red flared in my vision, and a number floated up. Hit points. I thought about looking at my total HP, seeing how wounded I was, but then I had my very own Wile E. Coyote moment.

For the barest of moments, the shield stuck in the ice, and then, well, it didn't. I went down.

Straight down.

I scrabbled at the ice and rock desperately, ripping out my fingernails, screaming in pain and desperation. My leg caught an outcropping of some sort, and I flipped end over end, twirling though the air like a coked-out cheerleader.

Blackness crept into my vision, and then washed over me as I lost consciousness.

5

Plus side: I was not awake for the impact at the bottom of what turned out to be a massive ravine in the midst of some sort of cave system. Downside: I was awake for what happened next.

I came to in vague darkness. With a slight mental push, I activated dark vision, and could mostly see. Pretty much the definition of dark vision I suppose. It was a little brighter than comfortable, due to the line of light waaaaaaaay above, the opening I'd fallen through. Nothing of me worked, everything just sort of refused my brain's commands.

There was a teensy-tiny little icon flashing in the lower right of my vision. A red circle with a slash across it over a running man.

Great, I thought, *paralyzed.* Thought instead of said, because I couldn't quite get my face to work since it was smashed to fucking pieces.

I brought up my status page, and I was down to two hit points. Two. At this point, if I accidentally sneezed, I'd kill myself. I also had a prodigious list of broken bones, so many that I just dismissed the status page. I couldn't be bothered reading names of bones I didn't even know existed.

That would have been terrible except for regeneration. As long as I could stay out of combat and not get seriously wounded, I would heal. My flesh was already starting to knit back together and my bones were starting to inch back towards each other. Which, thanks to my paralysis debuff, I barely felt. I laid there patiently, waiting for the moment when I could move again. But then this thing came along.

A creature.

I counted eight legs coming off a long, straight body. It was somewhere between a lizard and a wolf. And, well, a nightmare. It sniffed me.

Despite my attempts at screaming, the creature didn't seem to care in the slightest, and, instead, took a rather large bite out of me.

And then there were other bites taken out of me. Something I could only really feel because of the way my body was being pulled from one side to the other. Lots of chewing and hearing my own bones snap. I got a great view of its teeth at the end. They were big and sharp, and I managed to scream out a hearty "FUCK YOU" before I died. Didn't seem to faze the creature.

Finally, thankfully, everything went black.

6

A great banner popped up in front of me as I hung in nothingness.

WAAAH-WAAAH. You have died.

Kicked the bucket. Shuffled off the ol' mortal coil. You have been weighed and measured and found wanting. But, good news! You have at least one respawn left. Maybe you've got more. Who knows?

Would you like to respawn?

YES/NO

I TOOK A MOMENT TO THINK. This new world was brutal. The pain was intense, and there were big weird creatures that ate humans. Still, what was the alternative?

Yes.

7

I popped into existence in the same spot I had at the beginning, falling the few feet until I plopped into the snow. I jumped to my feet, my fur covered feet, and I did a little dance, feeling good, because all of me worked again. I willed my status page up.

Montana - lvl 1 ***nothing***

Statistics

HP: 110

STAM: 320

MP: 172

Level 1 nothing? Well fuck you too, game.

It did make me wonder if there was some sort of class system I'd yet to discover.

I was back to where I started from. Sweet.

Slight disappointment in that my weapons were gone. My god-tier weapons, down in a cavern beneath a crevasse on the top of a fucking mountain likely inside a creature with lot of teeth and a hankering for human flesh. I did have my starting gear, so it was nice to know that if I died over and over again, I could slowly accumulate a massive assortment of picks, fishing poles, and hatchets. I could make my fortune starting the first REI outpost on Vuldranni.

The sun sat low on the horizon, meaning there'd been a time-lapse between death and rebirth. Good to know. But it was going to be dark soon, and I had a long climb down. A small, dark purple light blinked slowly in the corner of my vision, letting me know I had notifications to go through and decisions to make.

Still, I needed to book it or freeze to death in darkness.

I started walking, being safe this time. I hoped I'd given Mister Paul enough of a show, because I was going to be absurdly boring this time. I spent some time slipping down steep inclines, and doing some minimal climbing when I'd gotten to a point I couldn't jump or crawl down. It wasn't the most challenging of hikes, but there was an endless quality to it. The snow fields just seemed to go on forever. Had I been a skier, with skis, or one of those people who develop ski resorts, this would have been a hell of find.

With the sun down below the mountain ridge to the west, the temperature began to drop. The sky darkened into something I had never experienced. The stars were bizarre and, obviously, otherworldly. It was a joy to behold, as I could see things I had never before seen, whole galaxies up above. Great swaths of glittering lights right overhead. A moon rose shortly after the sun fell below the horizon. Then a second, and a third, and a fourth. Four different moons, four different colors, four different sizes. They forced a panoply of moonlight across the landscape, transforming the bare white snow in to a kaleidoscope of colors. On a steep slope, I stopped to just take in the beauty around me, calm and unreal as it may have been.

But the sharp cold got me moving again. I didn't want to experience freezing to death. Sure, I'd respawn, but there were certain experiences I didn't need to live through.

So I dipped into my Eagle Scout knowledge, and I made a snow cave as soon as I reached a flat spot. Then I hunkered down in the darkness, and fell asleep.

8

I slept for a while. Not sure how long — in a land without clocks, time becomes more fluid. I dreamt of my life. Of the short good bit, the slice of paradise I'd found and fucked up somehow. I saw her, and we were together, and happy in our stupid little apartment surrounded by construction and mud. The empty fridge, the lack of furniture, and the bliss that comes from living with someone you truly love. A dream, because the bad stuff never kicked in.

I woke with a start, unsure of what caused me to wake. I looked around for the girl, and then I remembered everything that happened.

Snow cave. No flabdomen keeping me stuck to the bed. Despite the initial death, I appreciated what Mister Paul had done for me.

I got on my knees, and wiped the sweat from my brow.

Shit, I thought. *Sweat.*

Sweating is just a bit dangerous in super-cold locales, but I had no real options to combat it. I didn't have layers to take off. I had layer. Singular. And that layer was fur. Worst case, well, I'd just die again, I suppose.

I snagged some of the 'rations' out my knapsack and gave them a look, hoping I had something approaching breakfast. They weren't much to look at, and even less to eat. I had my choice of very tough, very dry mystery meat or very hard, very dry mystery biscuit-type thingies. I ate a bit of each, and they were gross.

Breakfast over, I pulled up my character sheet.

Montana - Lvl 1 Nothing

Traits

Race: Fallen

Height: 6'2"

Weight: 220 lbs

Eye Color: Hazel

Hair Color: Blonde

Renown: 0 - No one even knows you exist.

Statistics

HP: 110

STAM: 320

MP: 172

Armor: +3 vs Piercing

Active Effects:

Attributes

Strength: 20
Agility: 15
Dexterity: 15
Constitution: 20
Wisdom: 13
Intelligence: 13
Charisma: 13
Luck: 25

UNASSIGNED POINTS: 0

SKILLS

Riding - improvised (LVL 1): You can now ride improvised devices. +5% to handling.

Falling (LVL 1): You can flail through the air with the best of them. Watch for the sudden stop at the end.

Animal Handling (LVL 5): You can calm down a domesticated animal, keep a mount from getting spooked, intuit an animal's intentions, or, if you're really lucky, tame a wild best.

Abilities

None

FEATS

None

Boons

Powerful Build (Mister Paul) - You are bigger than you look. For all strength roles, you are counted as one size category larger than you actually are.

Regeneration (Mister Paul) - Outside of combat, your body will repair rather quickly. Given enough time, it's possible you will heal from nearly any wound.

Gift of Gab (Mister Paul) - Should you encounter a language you do not understand, as long as you hear at least three words of it, you will understand it, and speak it, perfectly.

Indicium

None

THE LEVEL One Nothing thing really bugged me. It just seemed overtly cruel. And, I mean, a rather apt reflection of my past life.

While chewing a piece of the mystery meat — it required a substantial investment in chewing — I pulled up the notifications from the previous day and began going through them.

Most were damage notifications. Hitpoints lost by bashing into a rock, hitting a branch, hitting the ground, fall damage, bite damage, that sort of thing. Then there was the paralysis and death. A lovely trip down memory lane.

I pushed through the snow cave and stepped out into something almost like morning. The sun was at the edge of the horizon, but there was enough wind to whip up the loose top snow, swirling it all around me, and making it difficult to see.

A small box wrapped with a red ribbon sat right outside my snow cave, precisely where I would see it upon exiting.

It had to be a trap. This was a game, after all. Thing was, I could see my footprints going back up the mountain, and I could see where I'd walked around to make my shelter, but I couldn't see any prints around the box.

I looked up to the sky.

Nothing.

I knelt down and felt around the base of the box. Snow. There was a small tag tucked into the ribbon on the far side of the box. Without touching it, I laid down in the snow next to the tag so I could read it.

Montana,

Forgot this.

MP

Well shit. I bet he was laughing at my display of paranoia.

*Cool Beans, you've learned the skill **Investigate**. Now, when you don't know, try and figure it out! +5% to find the hidden. +5% passive perception.*

WELL, thank you paranoia.

I picked up the present, pulled the bow, and the box just poofed out of existence. Instead I held a small vial of iridescent green liquid with a delicate little tag tied onto the stopper. It said *Attribute Points.* As soon as I read that, a note popped up in front of me.

YOU HAVE FOUND ***Bonus Attribute Potion***

ITEM TYPE: Potion

Item Class: Rare

Item Quality: Exquisite

Durability: 4/4

Weight: 1 lb

Requirements: the ability to drink

Description: This rare potion gives you some additional attribute points (6) to spend as you see fit. Beware, as soon as it is exposed to the sun, it begins to degrade.

"SHIIIIT!" I cried, watching the durability drop by one.

I flicked the stopper off, and chugged the whole damn thing.

There was a loud *bing*, and then a notification came up.

Wowza, you've got Six (6) additional attributes to assign. Do it in 36 hours or lose them forever.

I sighed and pulled up by attributes.

Attributes

Strength: 20
Agility: 15
Dexterity: 15
Constitution: 20
Wisdom: 13
Intelligence: 13
Charisma: 13
Luck: 25

Unassigned points: 6

I had to wonder, had my agility or dexterity been higher, could I have grabbed the rocky outcroppings and avoided becoming lunch? Would increased constitution have staved off the paralyzation? What would I need to stop making stupid mistakes?

I put the points into Intelligence, but then my finger hovered over the 'okay' button. But I couldn't push it. I put two points into Luck, and then four into Charisma. I'd have to meet people eventually, and, maybe, if they liked me, they'd leave me alone.

~

Attributes

Strength: 20
Agility: 15
Dexterity: 15
Constitution: 20
Wisdom: 13
Intelligence: 13
Charisma: 17
Luck: 27

~

Unassigned points: 0

~

With the admin crap taken care of, it was time to return to living life. Only one direction to go. I started downhill.

Unlike the previous day, the clouds were sparse, so I could see the lands below me. There were verdant deciduous forests ringing the mountains, undulating hills between rising peaks, rivers and lakes. All of it was beautiful, in a John Denver way. Oh, and pretty fucking far away. I was still in a world of snow and ice and nothing nice. Nothing living, that's for sure.

As exciting as my first descent happened to be, the second was exactly the opposite. The damn mountain just kept going. And going. And going. All the time alone with my thoughts meant too much thinking about the girl, and I didn't need that shit. I started sliding down on my belly for stretches, just to give myself a break.

Though a bit scary, it was fun and quick, and I managed to make up some time. I messed up once by rolling down the slope instead, which left me really fucking dizzy and led to me puking up the little breakfast I'd had. Still, better than becoming something else's breakfast.

The sun was already high in the sky by the time I hit another large flat spot. I took a momentary break there. Slogging through snow without snowshoes was exhausting and unpleasant at best. At worst, well, I think I'd discovered worst my first attempt. I sat down, the thick snow providing a bit of padding. The furs covering me were mostly white, as if taken from a polar bear with an excessive hair condition. Since the snow was caked around the fur, and it was white, I figured I'd be able to lay down on the snow and basically be invisible. Which, you know, if there had been any life around me, would keep me safe.

Naturally, that's when I caught a sign of life.

Above me and to the left, a large form floated lazily in the air. Well in the distance, mind you, but it was there. Something huge flying around. I wouldn't say it was the size of a 747, but it was definitely up there, easily besting a regional jet.

My brain screamed at me, begging me to figure out what was happening because something that big shouldn't be flying. A good reminder that the laws of physics might be different in Vuldranni.

I laid flat and closed my eyes. Perfect camouflage.

As soon as my heart rate came back to normal, I sat up and looked for the flying thing.

Gone.

I mean, it was pretty far away, so there'd be little chance of it seeing me, or even wanting to cross the distance to see if I was something edible. Still, better to be moving, better to get away from whatever it might be.

And a solid reminder I could no longer be sure of what I'd encounter.

9

Somewhere close to mid-afternoon, I took my next break, sitting down in the snow and tucking into the rations once again. Dried mystery meat isn't quite as bad the second time around. I took mouthfuls of snow to drink, what with not having a waterskin or canteen or anything to hold liquids. It had gotten overcast above and below me, but the clouds parted in front of me, and I could see a bit more of where I was going. A flat area, thank God (or gods), with a number of large, rounded protrusions all over the place. Something like a boulder-strewn plateau, maybe it was a spot a glacier came through. I have no real idea. I spent geology class getting my rocks off, if you know what I mean. Thanks, Chelsea.

The landscape dipped hard after that, but a steep slope started up again, up and up leading to another peak. The dip had to be a pass between these two mountains, and that'd be my next goal, especially because I could see just few wisps of smoke coming from that area. If I could get there, I might find civilization. At the very least, I could choose which side of the mountains I wanted to go down.

Most likely, I'd want to see if I could figure out which way the weather came from, and go that way. Much better chance of finding fertile and verdant land that way. And that meant more food. More food meant happier people and fewer things that eat you in caves and shit.

With that small decision made, I got to my feet, brushed off my butt, and started hiking again.

It didn't take long to get to the flats. Curiosity got the better of me, and I dug out one of the round protrusions. It actually was just a boulder. Maybe I did learn something in Geology after all.

The flat, though, was much rougher than I thought. I had to walk up slight inclines, and then into mini-valleys that were filled with snow. Like, up past my hips deep. For the first up and down, it was kind of fun, but then it got annoying. Up, down, up, down, burning through my stamina.

Each up, I watched my stamina bar nearly bottom out. Definitely a bizarre feeling to have a visual representation of stamina, watching the bar fill up and feeling better. I took a short break when the bar dropped, breathing hard in the cold and watching the world around me to let the stamina fill all the way back up. The slog seemed interminable.

As I finally neared the pass, I heard noises coming from behind a boulder. It sounded a bit like a group of somethings squabbling. An argument. Then, I heard the scratching noise of metal on metal, and everything went quiet again.

This was exciting — I was about to come into contact with actual sentient beings for the first time in this world. Still, given my first experience interacting with the beings of the world, I figured it might be better to err on the side of caution, so I edged along the boulder and peeked over.

I saw small green-skinned creatures, wearing mismatched armor and home-made snow shoes, chewing on sticks of meat. I counted six of them. They all had miniature bows on their backs, and small quivers of arrows at their hips. Maybe three feet tall or so, but they had outsized heads with large ears flopping off the sides, very large mouths filled with sharp pointy teeth. Their hands and feet didn't fit their body either, to the point that I wasn't exactly sure they even needed snow shoes. A seventh creature, slightly larger than the rest, knelt at the top of the next crest, looking sharply down and watching something. It had to be the pass.

Every once in a while, one of the six would snap, make some offhand comment or throw something. There'd be a retaliation and escalation until they made enough noise the big guy on the ridge would turn around and shush them.

I wondered what they were, trying hard to concentrate on them, to see if there was some way I could get some information on the creatures. Like a pop up or something. Species name. Level.

Nothing happened.

Something finally clicked, and I remembered the books I got with my starting gear.

I pulled them out and gave them a look. The first, and smallest, was a green book with an embossed sparkly leaf on the front. As soon as I made to open the book, I got a prompt, floating up between me and the book.

Would you like to learn the skill: ***Harvesting****?*

Yes/No

OBVIOUSLY, yes.

The book vibrated for a moment, pulsing in and out of existence. I felt a pressure around my head, and my impulse was to fight back, not let anything in. But I made a snap judgement, thinking that I was trying to get knowledge, so it probably needed to be in my head. I let it in.

Thoughts swirled around, and my brain immediately raged in pain. New pathways were forced open, and suddenly I knew a whole hell of a lot about the plants of Vuldranni.

COOL BEANS, you've learned the skill ***Harvesting (Lvl 5)****. You can pick plants, you can grab fruit, you can cut neat things out of creatures you slaughter. That'll save the world, right? At Level 5, you are able to harvest common elements with no penalties. +10% successful gathering chance*

SWEET.

Next book.

Small with a black cover and a gold magnifying glass.

As soon as I tried to open the book, I got the prompt:

WOULD you like to attempt to learn the spell: ***Lifeform Identification****?*

Yes/No

I NOTICED THE WORD ATTEMPT, which meant it was possible I'd fail to learn the spell. I wondered if that meant I'd lose the book, and the chance to learn the spell.

Still, I had to take the chance.

Yes.

The book did the same as the previous: a bit of vibration, some pulsing in and out of reality, and then head pressure and pain.

A feeling in my head of newness, and I *knew* the spell.

LOOK AT THAT, you've learned the spell: ***Lifeform Identification***

Lifeform Identification allows you to examine creatures and know certain traits. At higher spell levels, you will gain access to additional information.

I HAD MAGIC. Boss.

I also had one more book.

Object Identification.

Same deal: got the prompt, said yes, book did its thing, head hurt, knew the spell.

LOOK AT THAT, you've learned the spell: ***Basic Object Identification***

Basic Object Identification allows you to examine objects and identify certain traits. At higher spell levels, you will gain access to additional information.

I WAS on my way to opening my own pawnshop.

With a bit of intense thought and a whispered word, I cast *Identify Lifeforms.*

A little bubble appeared above the creature I was looking at, moving along with the creature.

GOBLIN

Level 2 Scout

NOT A TON OF INFORMATION, but better than nothin.' Plus, I could see that it wasn't a much higher level than me. Goblins are usually evil creatures in games and literature, worthless shock troops of the dark lords to let noobs grind up until they're actually useful characters. But was that the case here? Were they evil? I mean, they weren't really doing anything evil. They were just having a bite to eat, and spying on someone.

I took a deep breath and let it out real slow, doing my best to release my nerves and get my thinking cap on. I had to make a choice: either assume I knew everything about this world and go in with violence, or, the more dangerous choice, be open-minded. Try to be friendly.

Maybe this was a nice world, cave-beasts not included.

I pulled my gloves off, tucked them into my belt, and

folded my hood down. Now, I figured I just looked like an ordinary dude out for a stroll in the arctic. Totally normal and non-threatening.

"Hiya," I said, taking a step around the boulder.

I had seven sets of yellow eyes on me immediately. Four whipped bows out, their arrows pointed in my direction. Two had spears I hadn't noticed. Those were out and ready, pointy end towards me. The de facto leader, the dude spying on the ridge, had a sword of sorts out. It was a large curving blade that looked like something between a cutlass and a scimitar, with several holes cut in it along the non-sharpened side. Thick rings hung from the holes, giving it a bit of a jingle jangle when moved.

"Uh," I said, holding my hands up, "I come in peace?"

We held that tableau for a moment, and I figured I needed to let them make the first move.

The leader eyed me up and down. He said something I didn't understand, but apparently it was enough for my boon to kick in:

~

SMASHING! *You've learned a new language,* ***Goblin.***

~

"YOU NEED ANSWER: where you come from?" he barked at me, his voice somehow both high-pitched and guttural, like a toddler with a six-pack a day habit suckling from bottles of whisky.

I pointed over my shoulder at the mountain.

"With Queen?" he asked.

My first impulse was to lie, to gauge what it was he

wanted to hear and feed it to him. But this was a new life. Why start it off on the wrong foot?

"No sir," I answered.

A really nasty smile came over the leader's giant mouth, his wicked teeth coming into view. "Kill him," he said with a sneer.

10

Apparently goblins *were* evil in this world. Or at least just really big supporters of the monarchy. I've heard it both ways.

Four small goblin arrows snapped through the air, all of which slammed into me.

I prepped for serious pain.

Which was unnecessary. A bit of pressure as each hit me, but no pain. No red flashing.

"Hey," I said, "look at that."

My buddy's smile disappeared, and he barked out: "CHARGE!!"

One of the spear men ducked his head and sprinted towards me, seeming to float across the surface of the snow on his little snow shoes.

I fumbled with the hatchet, trying to pull it out of my belt, but as soon as it came free, it tumbled and then disappeared into the snow.

"Well shit," I said, but looked up just in time to see the spear coming right towards me.

There was no dodging it — I just watched the ragged point jam directly into my thigh.

I screamed in pain as red numbers floated up into my vision. I took a deep breath and willed the numbers to go the fuck away and let me fight. The familiar cold came over me and the world slowed down just a little bit. The focus of rage that comes from a lifetime of fighting and being embroiled in violence.

Seeing how effective the spear had been, the rest of the goblins all dropped their bows in favor of melee weapons.

My initial attacker tried to push harder, to get his spear deeper in, but I stopped him. I pulled the spear out of me, the spearhead coming out with a rather revolting sucking sound and a depressing amount of pain. The little goblin had his mouth open in surprise, but was still gripping the spear. He only weighed, like, twenty pounds, so I just used the spear to pick him up, and slammed him as hard as I could into the boulder, leaving a green-black splotch behind.

GG! You've killed a Goblin (lvl 2 Scout).

You've earned 50 xp! What a mighty hero you are.

GG? Good game? Brutal.

The notification popped up, and I immediately shunted it away, making the mental note to hold shit like that until combat was over.

I spun the spear around to get the pointy bit towards the goblins, then looked at what I imagined had to be my most dangerous opponent, the boss goblin. But he just had his sword out while waiting for the underlings to do the work. Typical boss.

The next goblin up had a sword out, a crudely made thing that had a very roughly serrated edge and a fine coating of rust.

He swung wildly.

I jumped back, but his blade still managed to cut some of the fur off my midsection. I lifted the spear straight up as the goblin pulled his sword back for a mighty thrust, and just as he was about to strike, I brought the spear straight down, striking the goblin's big head. I hit with enough force that the point went right through the guy, all the way into the frozen ground.

He made a disgusting gurgling noise, a green black ichor pouring out of his mouth.

A quick tug let me know the spear wasn't leaving easily, so I snatched the sword out of his limp hand.

The next goblin was moving towards me in a bizarre fashion, and I was exceedingly confused for a moment until I realized there was another goblin right behind, hiding as well as forcing his buddy into me. A living shield. The shield goblin swung his little sword with vim, vigor, fear, and randomness. I thought about parrying his strikes, but it was easier to just stand back out of the way. As soon as he paused to take a breath, I lunged forward with a thrust, plunging the sword in as hard as I could. It went straight through both goblins.

A notification popped up.

~

DOUBLE KILL! Brutality Bonus! By killing two enemies at

once, you've managed to make one plus one equal three! Congrats on the double XP for the kills!

I GRIMACED and mentally yelled at the notification to get the fuck out of the way so I could see. Then I snatched up a goblin sword and gave it a heft. This one was straight until the end, where it kinked to the left, and had a very clumsily done edge on it. It was more of a club than a sword. All the goblin weapons seemed like they were custom-made. Or, you know, custom-scavenged.

Three goblins remained: two wee ones, and the boss.

In a surprising act of courage, one of the scouts charged at me, sword way back, preparing for a massive swing. He looked like he was posing for a heroic painting.

As if I was playing tennis, I planted my foot and pushed my whole weight into swinging the club-sword. The pointy bit went straight into the goblin's skull. Dude died instantly.

I decided I'd had enough of being reactive, so I charged at the boss goblin. Big mistake. I stepped right into a crater and sank into snow up to my waist.

The boss smiled at me.

"Time to die," he grunted.

The grubby green-skinned assholes came at me from either direction. I could barely move. They were cautious for a moment, creeping at me with their stupid snow shoes keeping them on the surface. Maybe they thought I'd set a clever trap.

I hadn't.

I tried to back out of the snow, but my feet kept slipping on something, glacier droppings at the bottom of the hole I guess. I just couldn't get traction.

With little choice, I just smiled at the boss goblin.

This enraged him. He lunged forward, swinging his big sword right at me.

I leaned all the way back, dropping into the snow just in time to watch the blade sail by.

Kicking my leg out, I connected with the boss goblin's right knee. With a sharp crack, the dude tottered over, crying out in pain.

The other goblin paused, which gave me enough time to get back upright. A quick swing of the sword didn't exactly cut the boss's head off so much as it crushed it Gallagher-watermelon style.

I scooped up the big curved sword with all the rings before turning to face my final foe.

We locked eyes for a moment, unsure who would make the first move.

The little asshole turned and burned, running away from me.

I took a chance, and hurled the big sword at the retreating goblin.

The sword looked pretty fucking awesome tumbling end over end through the air. I held my breath, hoping it was going to just carve through the coward.

Not so much.

The sword hit, I was on target in one respect, but the impact was more pommel than blade. There was a very loud thunk, and the goblin face-planted into the snow.

I crawled out of the deep snow, then ran along until I caught up with the struggling goblin. For a moment, I wondered if killing the thing was the right move. Clearly, it was a sentient creature, possessing its own language, and—

DAMMIT!

The little fucker stabbed my foot with an obsidian dagger.

I gritted my teeth and grabbed the boss sword. With a wide and wild swing, I lopped the asshole's head clean off, and watched the oversized head twirl through the air until it landed and disappeared in the snow. A miniature geyser of gore erupted out of the shorn neck.

Done with the carnage, I sat down.

Then I threw up.

11

I sat in the snow, feeling the pain radiating out from my injuries, and I let the world wash over me. I also took the time to go through the notifications I'd received during the battle.

~

GG! You've killed a Goblin (lvl 1 Scout).

You've earned 50 xp! What a mighty hero you are.

~

GG! You've killed a Goblin (lvl 1 Scout).

You've earned 100 xp! (Base 50 x 2 double kill bonus) What a mighty hero you are.

~

GG! You've killed a Goblin (lvl 1 Scout).

You've earned 100 xp! (Base 50 x 2 double kill bonus) What a mighty hero you are.

~

GG! *You've killed a Goblin (lvl 1 Scout).*

You've earned 50 xp! What a mighty hero you are.

~

GG! *You've killed a Goblin (lvl 3 Scout Leader).*

You've earned 150 xp! What a mighty hero you are.

~

GG! *You've killed a Goblin (lvl 1 Scout).*

You've earned 50 xp! What a mighty hero you are.

~

KILL ALERTS. Could be very useful in the future when I wanted to know for sure if I'd managed to kill something.

~

COOL BEANS, *you've learned the skill* **Swords***. Now you can swing sharp objects and likely not hurt yourself. Soon, maybe you can hurt others. +5% damage. +5% skill.*

~

COOL BEANS, *you've learned the skill* **Spears***. Now you can swing* *a sharp stick and likely not hurt yourself. Soon, maybe you can hurt others. +5% damage. +5% skill.*

~

HEY-HO, let's go! You've discovered an ability: ***THE SWORD OF MY ENEMY IS MY SWORD.*** *You've found that, in a pinch, EVERY weapon will do. +1% dmg for each new weapon used in a combat.*

~

NICE.

Weird, but nice.

Then I did the nasty. Which, in this world, meant pawing over dead bodies until I had made sure I had everything of value and the corpses had nothing left worth taking. In this case, it also meant I encountered something odd. While looking over the corpses, I noticed a weird glow about the goblins' ears. So, uh, I cut one of them off.

~

YOU HAVE FOUND one (1) Goblin's Ear. You have the feeling this might be useful for a potion.

~

VERY INTRIGUED, I promptly cut all their ears off, and put them in a pile. I was very tempted to cut open the bodies and see if there was anything glowing inside, but I'd engaged in enough butchery for the time being.

Most of the loot was useless, broken goblin armor or rusty daggers. But some of the swords looked okay, one of the spears was straight, and each goblin had a pouch. Three of the pouches held coins. One had a bunch of frozen worms, one had a few rocks, one had some jewelry and coins, and the last one had a bunch of dead rats. I dumped out the rats, put the goblin ears into the rat pouch, then tied all seven pouches to my belt. Even the worms. Might need them for fishing.

Each goblin also had a small ring, most of them around a rusty chain or leather strap, one on his toe, another in his ear, each one with a series of runic letters on it, written in Goblin, and denoting the identity of the Goblin in question.

I took a moment to actually examine the boss sword, casting my spell on it and everything. I think it was kind of impressive. I had nothing to judge it against, sure, but it seemed cool.

~

Goblin Boss Chopper

Item Type: Trash

Item Class: One-handed sword

Material: Iron

Damage: 8-12 (slashing)

Durability: 3/10

Weight: 3.2 lbs.

Requirements: none

Description: The symbol of authority for a Goblin in command, the Boss Chopper is a large (for a Goblin) one-handed sword with a swooping blade, sharp on one side. Holes are made in the blade to decrease weight and increase speed, something ameliorated by the addition of rings won in duels or battles.

IN EXAMINING THE SWORD, I noticed there were words carved or stamped into the blade around each hole that had a ring through it. And, thanks to my perfect knowledge of the Goblin language, I realized that I was looking at the names of those the Scout Leader had defeated in combat.

There was also the obsidian dagger I'd pulled out of my foot.

Goblin Sacrificial Dagger

Item Type: Common

Item Class: One-handed dagger

Material: Obsidian

Damage: 21-25 (Slashing)

Durability: 8/25

Weight: 1 lb.

Requirements: none

Description: An unbelievably sharp blade used for ceremonial sacrifices to Goblin Gods, Spirits, Shades, Chiefs, Bosses, or Chefs.

I WAS IMPRESSED how much I learned about the Goblins just by identifying their equipment. I slipped the smaller swords into the backpack, and even though the handle stuck out the back, I forced the Boss Chopper in there as well.

12

I sent up a silent thanks to Mister Paul for his glorious boon while I let my wounds heal up. Sure, it hurt like a motherfucker to have all the healing happen so fast, but getting stabbed in the leg and having no mark whatsoever ten minutes later? Priceless.

Now whole, I decided I needed to see whatever the Goblin boss had been so interested in, so I crawled up to the edge of the ridge and peeked over. That's where I received my first view of civilization in this new world.

It was underwhelming.

Twelve, maybe thirteen buildings. They were low and made of dark stone, with heavy snow on steep pitched roofs. Some had smaller outbuildings, perhaps for animals, or maybe workshops. Either a guard tower or a watchtower — I don't really know the difference — sat at one edge of the village. The whole place was unassuming, but did have one thing going for it: the road that went straight through the middle of the town from one side of the mountain range to the other. It made it the perfect spot for a town, really. A place to collect some tolls, fix a few wagons, feed a few teamsters. And if you ignored the whole perpetual winter, no wood, no way to grow food, no way to be outside sort of thing, you might actually want to stay there.

I knew I didn't have much sunlight left in the day, but I decided to watch the village from a different angle for a little longer. I wanted to get a read on the situation, see if it was full of goblins or, you know, people. Hell, I wasn't even sure people other than me existed here.

I saw some horses, big black steeds with patterned barding. They blended in with the rest of the bleak darkness that was the village center. Near them, figures in dark armor held blades out to a group of men gathered in a circle. At the outskirts, figures in black held back the other villagers.

I let out a long, irritated sigh. This was not an ideal first brush with civilization. I'd been hoping for an inn where I could peel potatoes and earn my keep until I had enough money to find a fucking lake and fish. Instead, I looked down on what seemed to be a massacre in the making.

My first instinct was to steer clear of the village. Let things take their course and, you know, find a different town to set up in. Or I could just wait it out, go into the town post-massacre. That could give me the chance for some free loot.

Just then flurry of movement caught my eye. A young kid dropped out of a hut's back window. He made a run for it, and did pretty well. He got to the steep part of the rise that led almost straight to me before four of the figures in black came darting around and grabbed him. They pulled the kid back to the building and slammed him up against it.

I looked down at the village and thought about my previous life, the world I left behind. The messes I made, the hearts I broke, the lives I destroyed. So much of that was because I ran away instead of confronting my problems and actually dealing with them. Maybe it was time to switch things up.

Seems like an intelligent decision, thought the man with low intelligence.

I would stick my neck out and get involved. And anyway, I hate bullies and unfair fights (unless they're unfair in my favor).

Four against one?

Definitely unfair.

I got up and started running down the hill. Midway down, I lost footing and started tumbling, both goblin spears snapping into pieces as my back hit the snow.

This wasn't going to be the grandest of entrances.

With a slice of luck, and perhaps showing what a good idea putting points into that stat was, I managed to get my feet underneath me and started running again.

I reached the flat, maybe fifteen feet from the house. One of the figures in black had a naked blade out, swinging towards the unlucky lad. I pumped my feet and barreled straight into the swordsman, giving the asshole a tackle my linebacker coach would have thumped me on the butt in praise for, a blindside hit on an unready opponent.

My new friend and I flew through the air for the barest of moments before smashing through the flimsy wood wall of the hut. We crashed to the ground on the other side, landing directly in the fire pit in the center of the room. Sparks flew everywhere as I rolled over the figure, whose clothes had started to burn.

A notification popped up, but I immediately shunted it to the side, and made the mental note to keep the notifications to a minimum for the time being.

The dude didn't move. He just sort of lay there, burning.

I didn't want my primary possession — my furs — to

start burning, so after a quick glance about the really sad and tragic basically empty hut, I jumped through the window.

Outside, there was a heartbeat to get a read on the situation. The figures in black were wearing cloth uniforms over their armor, which was also black. It looked like a mixture of scale mail and chainmail, with some of the more delicate bits having the scale over the chain. Their helmets were basic, with a nose guard coming straight down. Black boots with black leather trousers — not the best of looks, and a poor choice given the weather.

I shot my identification spell their direction.

Human

Lvl 4 Swordsman

So there were humans on Vuldranni. That was nice. But these ones seemed intent on my demise. Two of the remaining three held the kid against a wall, while the third stood closer to the hole in the wall, trying to figure out where their buddy had just disappeared to.

Hint: he'd found the hottest spot in the town.

The kid, meanwhile, had blood gushing out of his nose.

All four looked at me as soon as I straightened up after crawling out the window. Then, one of the men in black screamed.

I snapped my arm out and popped him right in the kisser, quick and hard. He spun a little and started falling towards me.

The other two let go of the kid.

I pulled the helmet off the falling man and used that to smash in the face of one of the guys. Then I threw it at the other.

It didn't hit him, but it flummoxed him enough that he hadn't quite gotten his sword out. I knew I had to keep him from his sword, because unlike the goblins, I was pretty sure this guy actually knew how to use his blade. I could be in a world of hurt.

So, I bear-hugged the man, tight as I could, pulling his feet off the ground.

His breath was fetid, and his teeth were appalling. He groaned as I squeezed, and did his best to head butt me. But he had no real leverage with his neck. I pulled in as I took in a great big lungful of air. Something popped, and I felt his ribcage give. He had no air in him, and bloody froth came from his lips.

I dropped him to the ground, giving his face a swift kick.

But by that point, the man I'd punched had a dagger out and pointed at me.

The man started to talk, and after a second, I got a pop up:

Smashing! You've learned a new language, ***Common Imperial****.*

"What is this?" the man in black asked the panicky kid.

"Why the fuck you asking—" I started to say.

The man in black shrieked at me, his dagger leading the way.

With a slight twist of my torso, it got stuck in my furs, and not my stomach.

This left him pretty much wide open.

I'd done karate as a kid, tae kwon do as a teen, and kung fu as a young man. But it was the few years running as a one percenter that really taught me to fight. Brawling had become my main hobby in the past few years, followed closely behind by running guns and drugs throughout the Western United States. The single stab from this asshole showed me that these guys were relying on fear to get the job done. They didn't have real fight in them.

I grabbed his arm and pulled as hard as I could while I turned my body. The asshole flew over me, sailing through the air before slamming onto the ground. Bonus: he left his dagger behind. I tested the blade in my hand as I surveyed the scene around me.

One man was burning in the fire. One was crushed. One was knocked out from a helmet to his face, and one was probably knocked out from the throw over the shoulder. I could hear running and the jingle-jangle of metal gear coming from the other side of the house, so help was likely on the way.

I took a deep breath, thinking about Vuldranni — the savagery and the presented realities on display — and I knew what had to do. I cut the throats of all the men around me, and read over their death notifications.

Meanwhile, the kid was still up against the wall.

"Get the fuck in the house, asshole," I growled at the kid. "And stay to the darkness. Might be, they forget you were the reason they came back here."

The kid didn't move.

"Fuck, dude," I said. I grabbed him and shoved him through the new opening into his house.

"Hide," I snapped.

I felt around in the snow, looking for one of the swords I knew the assholes dropped. Then I heard a twang, and felt a pop on my back. No pain though.

I looked over my shoulder.

About ten yards away, I saw a new figure in black.

A woman.

Her black armor was shiny leather, and she had a bow. And a lot of arrows. One was, in fact, currently nocked. She pulled the string back quickly and fired, almost one smooth motion.

It thwacked into my chest, and sort of quivered there.

Again, no pain.

I looked down at it, confused, but quickly realized her arrows weren't making it through my furs.

It made me laugh.

She went white in the face, about as white as my furs.

Then she ran. Screaming about a monster.

I ran after her, coming around the corner at speed. I looked at the center of the village and came to a skidding, sliding halt. I barely managed to keep my footing.

The villagers were on one side of the open area, and a few of the black armored assholes were opposite them. It seemed that my interdiction had, at least, caused the release of the men of the village. Everyone was now in one big unhappy group.

The female archer seemed more secure now that she was back with her group.

Every last one of them looked my way. Four archers, bows armed and ready, and three men with swords. One of the men with swords had some plate armor and a very snazzy helmet with a human skull covering his face.

Ooh, threatening.

Skull Helm said said something to the men around him.

~

SMASHING! *You've learned a new language,* ***Mahrduhmese****.*

~

THIS WAS DEFINITELY the best way to learn languages.

"Fire!" Skull Helm shouted.

Four arrows streaked my way. I threw my arm over my face, just in case.

Thwock! Thwock! Thwock! Thwock!

Like Debbie LeGrande told me, I definitely think I felt two pokes, but no pain.

I stood back up and screamed in defiance.

The archers, plus two of the swordsmen looked fearful. They certainly weren't used to people fighting back, and it seemed that coming across something that didn't mind being shot with arrows was demoralizing.

"Cowards!" roared Skull Helm.

He pulled a massive sword from his side and charged, blade held high, screaming all the way.

In my previous life, I'd held my own in more than one knife fight. But my only experience with swords was the goblin-killing I'd just done.

As Skull Helm closed the distance, I stood still, not knowing what to do.

Closer.

Three yards.

Fuck it, I thought, *not like I can die. Not really. Not yet, anyway*.

I laughed and threw my sword at him. It made him

falter, but didn't do any real damage. Then I charged him, getting in too close for his big sword, and slammed my shoulder into his midsection. That drove him to the ground.

He slammed the pommel of the sword on my back repeatedly. It hurt like a mother.

A dagger on his belt dug into my side, and I knew it was the best chance I had for a weapon. We rolled on the ground, moving one way, then back. Finally he dropped his sword, realizing his steel gauntlets were more useful than the big blade. With a clever move, he wound up on top of me, got his big hands around my neck, and started to squeeze.

I reached up and slid my hands beneath his stupid helm. I could feel his actual face. A beard, a nose, and then, what I was looking for: his eyes. I dug my thumbs in as hard as I could, and felt the pliant orbs give way.

The man screamed and released my throat, trying to get away from me. But my thumbs had a good hold in his sockets, and I wasn't letting go. We stood together, me pulling him up by his head, him screaming, his blood pouring down my hands, and definitely getting all over my furs.

With a twist of my torso, I swept his legs, and let his face meet my knee on the way down. He fumbled, clearly having trouble seeing. I grabbed his sword from the ground and swung the great big blade around with all my might.

It would have been an awesome end to the fight if I'd managed to hit his neck first, but my aim was a bit off. The sword skipped off his pauldron, and went into his neck with less force than it needed. Sure, it got, you know, halfway through and was definitely a fatal blow. But not, like, instantaneously fatal.

Skull Helm shuddered and blood rushed out of his neck. A low moaning sound came out of his ruined face.

I had to swing a second and third time before the head tipped to the side, hanging on by one grim tendon. Or ligament. Bit hazy on the difference.

There were definitely a few gasps behind me. I heard someone get on a horse.

I turned and threw the sword as hard as I could, the blade going end over end, steel flashing in the fading sunlight. Finally it worked, sinking deep into the face of the archer trying to get on the horse.

Far more brutal than I intended or expected. There was a lot of blood and certainly more than one fluid I couldn't accurately identify.

I was ready to get stuck in with the rest of the meanies in black when the villagers finally got some nerve back. They swarmed, beating the remaining figures in black.

There was a moment of stillness as the armored assailants took their last breaths.

I gave a little wave.

"Howdy," I said.

13

The entire town stared at me, despite my suave and debonair wave. Then the kid popped out of the house, and started running to a woman. His mom, I'm guessing.

"Olief!" the woman cried out, running across the village square and grabbing the kid with both her hands. She dropped to her knees and cried with relief. "I feared you dead!"

"He saved me," Olief replied, pointing at me.

All eyes back to me. And again, because apparently it was the only thing I knew how to do in this situation, I waved.

An older man with a neatly trimmed salt-and-pepper beard took a step forward. "Are you," he started, then looked at the rest of villagers for courage or reassurance, "human?"

"Oh. Yeah," I said, pulling the arrows from the fur and tossing them to the ground before removing the face mask and pulling back the hood. "Just, you know, got a bit carried away with the cold-weather gear."

As soon as people realized I was just a regular dude

under the furs, things relaxed. Some came over to clap me on the back and thank me. I was kind of digging on the praise and whatnot, but it was short-lived. In no time the whole town was arguing about whether they should leave, stay, hide, or what.

Before I could ask for some clarification, the old man who spoke to me put his arms high in the air. "Enough!" he shouted. "Night will be upon us soon. Take the horses to the barn."

The man continued to bark orders, and the townspeople hopped to. Olief and his mother came to me, and took me by the hand over to the largest building. Inside was a wide open space with a large central fireplace. There were tables all around, almost like a meeting room, but clearly more set for food and drink. Doors were along one wall with a massive bar opposite. The fireplace didn't seem to have much in the way of wood, so I assumed it was burning the poop of the herbivores in the barn.

Soon, I was sitting on a bench with a steaming bowl of something in between soup and stew in front of me.

I didn't care what the food was — I just wanted it in my stomach. The boy and his mother watched me in silence, and gave me a second bowl when I finished the first.

"Drink?" I asked.

Olief looked to his mother, and she nodded. He ran off.

After a moment, he returned with a mug of something that smelled gloriously like beer.

"Thank you kindly," I said, and took a long pull on the mug. It wasn't good, but I've had worse.

I leaned back, and let some of the notifications wash back into view.

*HUZZAH! Against all odds, you have reached **Level 2**! You receive 6 attribute points to distribute in the next 36 hours or you lose them. Dare to believe you can survive, and achieve greatness. Or don't.*

*HUZZAH! Against all odds, you have reached **Level 3**! You receive 6 attribute points to distribute in the next 36 hours or you lose them. Dare to believe you can survive, and achieve greatness. Or don't.*

TWO LEVELS from killing some goblins and dudes in black? Not bad.

*COOL BEANS, you've uncovered the innate skill **Unarmed Combat (lvl 9)**. You can strike with the fist or the foot, a tool without a tool. -13% stamina drain. +13% damage.*

*THERE YOU GO, leveling up the skill **Swords** to lvl 2. Aren't you just a blade-swinging fool? +1% dmg, +1% skill.*

THE SNARK in the messages was a bit much. I wondered if it came from Mister Paul, or if there was another entity behind the scenes writing all this out. Also, innate skill was a thing.

So maybe some of my previous life managed to transfer over to this one. Hopefully just the useful stuff.

I knew the clock was already counting down on point distribution. But as I polished off the second bowl, I saw the boss-type man from outside staring at me, so I made a mental note to distribute them soon. I wanted to talk to the guy first. .

"Who are you?" he asked.

"Montana," I said, extending my hand. "You?"

He looked at my hand for a minute, then back to my face. "Hroar Grisson."

"Oh, hey," I said. "Nice to meet you."

"You have a strange name," he quickly replied.

"Well, fuck you very much," I snapped.

He frowned. "I did not mean for you take offense—"

"Nice way to go about that."

"Rather, I should have said that I have yet to meet someone named in that manner."

"Oh. Right. I wasn't super clear on the naming conventions in, uh, Vuldranni before I came here."

"Where might you have been prior to Vuldranni?"

"Uh, would you believe me if I said there's a whole other world out there—"

"As far as I am aware, there are an endless number of worlds out there."

"Oh."

I was stunned at first, but it made sense. This was a completely different universe, as far as I could tell. Maybe in this universe, traveling between worlds was as normal as sorority girls drinking pumpkin spice lattes. "Yeah, so, I mean, I came from another world."

"Into the mountains?" Hroar asked.

"Yeah, a peak up there."

Hroar nodded, thinking. He lifted his hand and caught the barmaid's eye.

While he looked away, I did the mental casting and shot *identify* at the man to see what I might find out.

A little text popped up above Hroar's head.

Hroar Grisson

Human

Lvl 6 Innkeeper

GRISSON TURNED BACK to me and smiled. The woman slid two mugs of ale in front of us.

"I take it," Grisson said, "you know little of our world."

"Not yet," I replied, licking the ale off my mustache. "I'm pretty clueless."

He nodded, and took a deep breath.

"You have saved us from something quite bad. Because of this, I will offer you advice. Do not admit you are not of this world. There are those who will hate you for it, and there are those who will hunt you for it. The queen of those men you faced today, she will pay a bounty for any such as you. Enough that any man may live in one of her cities in comfort for life."

"Well, seems to be my poor luck."

"Perhaps you need more points in luck."

"Yeah," I said, taken aback. "Does, like, everyone have character sheets and stats and stuff?"

"Of course."

"That's crazy."

"It is the blessing and curse of the Gods."

"Ain't that the way."

"It is the way."

"You were saying something about it being a shitty time to visit, uh, wherever this is?"

"Assuming you know nothing about us or this world—"

"Perfect assumption."

"Thank you. I think. You are currently in Rumib Pass. We are, well, perhaps it is a bit grandiose to think of ourselves as a village. Perhaps calling us an outpost of the Glaton Empire is more reasonable. Those you saved us from today, they came to see if we would like to turn our backs on the emperor and join the queen."

"There was a goblin dude who asked if I was with the queen. I said no, and he tried to kill me."

"Goblins? Here?"

"Watching, up above."

"So they had no intention of allowing us to join them. Goblins. Did you kill them?"

"Yeah."

"Good. They are sneaky, conniving, savage, stupid, and unrelentingly evil. Kill them. All. They murder for sport. They eat any meat, and will run off with any baby they can grab, for it is the chief delicacy in their foul culture. In small groups, they are irritating. But in large groups, it is as if they compete to see who can be the most savage and disgusting. And if there were some here, it means the queen is truly dark, for she has willingly engaged their services. And she does not trust her soldiers."

He took a long pull of his ale.

"The queen — she's not, like, with the Empire, is she?" I asked.

"No. She is from Mahrduhm. Our neighbor. We have

held a peace with them for as long as I remember. But they have fallen under the sway of a dark queen, one who arose from the shadows and has taken over the country. From what I have heard — traders like to talk while they drink — she has been busy pushing out her borders every which way but towards Glaton, which means it is only a matter of time before she declares war on us. Perhaps that time has already come."

"So what does that mean for Rumib Pass?"

"Tis a good question, one I cannot yet answer. When her soldiers do not return to their army, I am confident the army will be prodded to move. They will put this town, my home, to the torch, and all of us to the blade."

I gulped, looking around the homely place. From what I'd seen of it, I wouldn't exactly call Rumib Pass a shit hole, not to Hroar's face at least. But it certainly wasn't worth making a stand over.

"Personally," I said, "and this is just my view of the subject, but I'd probably run."

"Me too," he said. He finished his ale, and slid it down the long table. After a moment, the barmaid collected it.

The rest of the townsfolk had drifted into the room. Most had taken seats along the table, and most were staring at me. I got up and moved towards the back of the room, getting a bit more distance from the fire. The furs were a bit warm for indoor living, and not being the center of attention seemed like a better ingredient to a good time for me.

Finally, an older man with a nasty scar on his face slapped his hands together sharply.

"Let the nonsense commence, Hroar," he said, his voice seeming to appear out of the great grey beard covering his face. "Give us your coward's way out. Shall we start running now?"

I cast *Lifeform identification*, and saw the little blip come up above the man's head.

Human

Lvl 4 barkeep

The lack of a name was annoying, but I guessed I got Hroar's name because I'd already been introduced to him. It was just a nice reminder. Which, you know, would be clutch when meeting people at parties.

"We should leave," a young woman piped up.

"Nonsense," Graybeard replied. "Tis just a group of uppity raiders looking to make rank by delivering us to the queen. She would never be so bold as to attack the Empire."

"If it were not for the stranger," the woman replied, "they would have killed us all. You saw that they were planning to do that."

"And what about this stranger?" Graybeard asked. "Where did he come from? Is he part of the Queen's Army? Is he a demon from beyond?"

People started slapping their hands on the table, and finally Graybeard went quiet.

"Friends," Hroar said, "there is something you should all know. There were goblins with them."

"There is no proof of goblins," Graybeard yelled out. "You wish to have us run because your inn has fallen in favor, and everyone is coming to my tavern instead. Cease your scare tactics—"

With that, the room fell into chaos. Shouts flew back and

forth as all the small town gossip poured out. Any accusation that could be made was made.

I grew tired of their yelling. I wanted to get going, find somewhere safe, somewhere I didn't need to kill anyone or anything for a bit. So I opened my backpack, pulled out the Goblin Boss Chopper, and I swung it in a big arc. The big blade bit deep into the table with a loud *thunk*.

The room fell quiet.

"I took this from the goblin watching your village," I said. "After I killed the other six up there. Makes me think it ain't just raiders poking their noses around here. I'm willing to bet you're gonna have a bunch of angry visitors in the near future. Maybe you want a tavern full of goblins. Do they tip well after they eat your children?"

Hroar pointed in my direction. "Is that enough proof, Ornolf?"

Ornolf stroked his gray beard, glaring at the sword. He shrugged. "Maybe."

The door slammed open, and a man wrapped in black furs walked into the place, snow swirling around him. "There is an army on your doorstep," he said. "Best be leaving afore she gets here."

"Have you seen it?" Hroar asked.

"Ayah. I have. Carries her banner." The man walked to the fire, pulled off his gloves, and gave me a look up and down. He definitely didn't care about anyone else in the place, but given they way everyone watched him, I had a feeling he was an important regular about the town. "Fires stretch long in the distance, and the stench on the wind tells me goblins and ogres are with them at a minimum."

He looked over at the sword in the table.

"Ah. The news of the goblins reached you already."

"The word of a ranger enough for you, Ornolf?" Hroar

asked. “Me and mine, we leave for Arenberg. Ornolf, if you choose to remain, perhaps you finally *will* have the best tavern in town.”

The room went silent.

“Do you mind?” I asked quietly, reaching between two people to pull the blade from the table. “Kinda hoping to sell this.”

I heard the ranger chuckle.

14

Hroar's decision to leave seemed to make the choice easy for the rest of the villagers: no one was staying. Rumib Pass would be clear by daybreak.

The ranger remained by the fire as everyone else disappeared. He looked me over, really studying me.

"Interesting outfit," he said.

"Keeps me warm," I replied.

He nodded. "You the stranger?"

"I guess."

"You kill the queen's men?"

"Mostly, yeah."

"Thank you."

"Uh, sure."

He pulled a large coin from his pocket and flipped it my way. I grabbed it from the air, and immediately looked at it. It was a bronze coin, about two inches wide. One side had a tree, and the other had a bird on it, something like an eagle, but not quite. Thicker, more muscular, different shaped tail.

"What's this?" I asked.

"Coin of my unit," the ranger replied. "This town means something to me, and if you were responsible for saving it, then I owe you."

"You don't—"

"Accept the gift, stranger. When you have need of me, get that coin to any Legionnaire, and they will find me."

"Wow. Thanks."

The Ranger took two steps to land right in front of me. He grabbed my wrist and shook it.

"Vecto Talotius," he said.

"Montana," I replied.

He gave a small smile, and nodded his head. "Safe home."

"You too."

He nodded one more time, and strode towards the door. "Tell Hroar I will see him in Arenberg, that I must leave now to warn the commandant."

"Will do."

He opened the door, and went into the dark and cold.

I looked at the coin one more time, then slipped it in my bag. I pulled up my attributes, and was just about to look at things and make an educated decision about points when the boy I'd saved, Olief, came inside. I dumped everything into strength because it was at the top of the list, and I didn't want to think about it at the moment. Olief set a bunch of armor, pouches, and weapons in front of me.

"What is this?" I asked.

"Loot from the soldiers."

"Oh, thank you," I said.

"The horses are outside. Some of the townsfolk have asked if you will allow the horses to be used to pull wagons."

"The horses are mine?"

"You killed the owners, so they are yours."

"I mean, yeah, sure. People can use them."

The kid smiled, nodded, then ran off.

I took a deep breath, looking over the loot pile. First impulse was to grab the armor Skull Helm wore, but it was pretty well marked as belonging to the Queen's Army. If I was going to stay in the Empire, it'd be a pretty bad idea to wear the enemy's armor around, certainly not if I wanted to avoid conflict. To be fair, there was nothing tying me to the Empire besides my somewhat arbitrary decision to help Olief and Rumib Pass. I could just as easily march down to the Queen's Army and ask to be part of their country. Though, if the Queen had a bounty out on, uh, new visitors, it could be very awkward trying to explain where I came from, if not the Empire.

Plus, the Imperial citizens had given me beer. That's basically like becoming a citizen.

I set the armor to the side, figuring that, at a minimum, I could find a blacksmith and sell it for scrap. The skull helm was badass in a way, but had the totally wrong vibe for me. I wanted dude you didn't pay attention to, not dude wearing a fucking skull and killing people. Into the sell pile inside my increasingly stuffed knapsack.

The dude's sword, though, that was a different matter. It was really nice, much better than the Chopper.

~

Longsword

Item Type: Common

Item Class: One-handed Melee, Two-handed Melee

Material: Steel

Damage: 10-20 (Slashing)
Durability: 20/20
Weight: 4.8 lbs
Requirements: Str 8
Description: A straight-bladed sword having a cruciform hilt with a grip for one- or two-handed use.

THE CHOPPER WENT into the bag, and the longsword onto my belt.

There were six pouches in front of me, and, to save time, I just dumped them all out on the table. Most of the contents were coins, the vast bulk being silver. There were a few gold pieces, small and heavy. The silvers were larger, and the coppers the largest. Also, some of the coppers were semi-circles. Half-coppers I suppose. There was also some jewelry, a number of rings, two simple chains, and a locket. Some of it looked nice, some of it less so. One of the rings was quite bulky, and the top had a hinge to it. It opened to reveal a stylized shield with a bloody bear paw on it. A signet ring, I supposed, for sealing wax letters.

I was about to scoop everything into my own money pouch when I heard a throat clear behind me. Before I turned around, I subtly pulled a leather cuirass over the pile.

Olief's mother was there, holding her hands tightly.

"Hi," I said, not exactly sure what was about to happen, but really hoping it wasn't going to be one of those, let-me-sex-you-up-as-a-reward type situations.

"You saved my son today," she said.

"It's fine—" I started, but she held up her hands.

"Please, I must give you something."

"No offense, but it doesn't look like you've got that much, and I'm doing okay, so—"

"I can still give you a reward for saving my child. It is the way things are done, and the Gods might curse me for not doing as is proper."

So the Gods forced people to give rewards... interesting.

"Please tell no one of this," she said, "for it could mean your end."

I tried to interrupt to find out why, you know, her gift might kill me, but she just kept on going.

"In earlier times, I was an apprentice to a man far to the north, a user of magic. He taught me many things. Many now forbidden." She paused, and her eyes unfocused as if she was looking at something very far away. Or very long ago.

"Okay," I said, nodding at her to continue.

"He was killed before I was able to complete my training, but I learned two spells from him. I have used them sparingly since then, but I will give them to you as repayment. If you want."

"You can give spells?" I asked.

"Do you know nothing of magic?"

"Not a thing."

She looked over her shoulder at the door. "There is little time, but magic is not welcome many places in this land. It is considered evil. Awful. Those who do practice are taken before the emperor and must enter his service or die. You must not allow anyone to see you cast spells."

"Not sure this is much of a reward."

"I regret, I have little else to offer you—"

"It's fine, I didn't mean to— just teach me the spells, please."

"I cannot teach them to you," she said, "there is no time. I must give them to you."

"Is there a difference?"

"When I give them to you, I will no longer know them. The knowledge is given to you."

"Wait—"

"It is a gift for you to take them as well, Montana. You will ease the burden I carry knowing I might slip and be taken away from the life I have. Please."

"Okay. Let's do it," I said.

She exhaled, and flashed a hidden sort of smile, like we were sharing a secret. Which we were, I guess.

"This might hurt," she said. Then, she took my hands and closed her eyes.

I did the same.

My hands started to tingle. Then they felt like they were on fire. I tried to pull back, desperate to stop the pain, but she held on tight. In a flash, it felt like some barrier broke, and the fire spread over my whole body. I took a huge breath in, feeling very alive, yet with the pain echoing out through me.

~

You have been GIVEN the spell HEAL OTHER (costs 100 mana). Through the use of magic you are able to heal another through touch. Heal 50 Hp.

~

You have been GIVEN the spell HUMUS (costs 10 mana). This spell gathers dirt, including organic materials, moisture, and bacterial ingredients within one mile/level of the caster and places the mixture anywhere the caster wishes ,within range. This is humus, the black, enriched soil excellent for growing plants in pots or gardening. Of course, the mage may use it however he wishes, but it is usually for growing things in pots and window boxes. If no such materials are within one mile/level, the spell has no effect.

SHE RELEASED MY HANDS GENTLY, and whispered a small "thank you." Then, she staggered up, moving as if exhausted, and left the inn.

I stood there for a moment, trying to figure out what had just happened. I looked at my hands expecting to see some redness or burn mark. Normal. I felt my body. Also normal. At least as normal as anything had been in this new world of mine. I took a few breaths, did a bit of a stretch. I felt okay.

Heal Other I totally got. *Humus* though? That seemed, well, I won't say completely useless, but somewhere on the level of a fart in a hurricane.

I went back to shoveling everything into my travel pack, then hoisted it on my back. It bulged at the seams. While standing in the warmth of the hall, I pictured it bursting apart while I hiked down the mountain, sending all my ill-gotten valuables tumbling away.

"Stop it," I told myself. "Stop thinking about all the possible bad shit. How about we try being positive for once?"

"Talking to yourself," a voice called out, "usually a sign of losing your mind, right?"

I whipped my eyes around the room, trying to get a bead on who'd snuck up on me.

A woman came out of the shadows. Young, with a wide,

pleasant face. She had a number of small burns on her arms, and a wicked tan, which seemed a bit odd for this perpetually shaded mountain town.

"I was wondering if you might be willing to help us out," she said, her blue eyes meeting mine without wavering.

"More than I already have?" I asked in answer.

"Yes."

I sighed, feeling a quest coming on.

"What's the ask?"

"We must leave this night, and get down to Arenberg before daybreak. You look like you can handle loading a wagon, maybe help an old woman down the mountain."

"Funny, you don't look that old."

She had a half-smile on her face, "Not me, ass. My aunt."

Dovie Keiler has offered you a QUEST!

Help the Town I

The town of Rumib Pass is being threatened, and they must run quickly or be overwhelmed by the impending invading army. Load Dovie's wagon and ensure her aunt makes it out of village safely.

Reward: Increased standing with the town of Rumib Pass and [unknown]

Accept: Yes/No

The reward was a bit crap, considering the town was about to be abandoned. What did it matter what my standing was with a town that didn't exist? But there was also the unknown. Maybe I'd get a boss sword. Or some awesome armor. A bunch of health potions. Or a big sack of nothingness. Maybe it'd be just a hug and a pinch on the cheek from the aunt. I guess that was the danger of the unknown reward. Still, I was planning on heading that direction anyway. What'd I have to lose?

"Sure," I said.

15

Despite the darkness, the night was alive. Villagers darted about — those who had wagons were loading them, and those who didn't were bartering for space in them. The townsfolk were, for the most part, working together.

Dovie lead me around the center of town to her home and workshop.

"You're a blacksmith?" I said, eyeing the massive anvil.

She nodded, and gave a smug little smile.

An empty wagon sat in front of the small home. The front portion of the property had a roof and a fence around a smelter, a forge, and a big ol' anvil. The back was barely a shack. Sitting on the anvil was an older woman. She smiled at me, and I realized I'd been had. She wasn't that old and her biceps were massive.

"This is your aunt?" I asked, not doing a damn thing to hide my incredulousness.

Dovie nodded, her smile getting bigger.

"And *she* needs help getting down the mountain?"

Dovie nodded again.

I shrugged. It was too late for me to do anything else. I'd already agreed to the quest, and I knew backing out would always be worse than going through with it.

"Let's get to packing then," I said.

Nothing they wanted my help with was light. Mainly because they went to pack up their personal belongings in the shack while I was tasked with the entirety of their shop.

They disappeared inside. I stared at the anvil. That was the heaviest item, so I figured it need to go over the front axle, something to help keep the wagon stable. I'd never loaded a wagon before, but I had loaded plenty of trucks, and the technique had to be somewhat similar.

On the plus side, this gave me the opportunity to really put my body to work, to gauge how the numerical value of my strength applied in a real world setting. I chuckled, realizing I'd just called the place the real world for the first time.

The anvil would like be the best first test of my strength. Or, you know, I'd rip something in my back, become paralyzed, and shortly be killed by the oncoming army. And then I'd have to make my way down the mountain again.

I did a bit of stretching, and squatted down for a test lift.

Wrapping my arms around the anvil, I powered it up.

It moved.

The thing felt heavy, but it wasn't, you know impossible. I didn't feel any pain; it just felt like a solid weight I'd lifted. I came to standing.

Then I took a step. Balancing on one leg was a bit much. It looked like I wasn't able to handle tree pose while carrying an anvil, but, you know, I had to have something to work towards. A few more steps, and I set the block of metal in the back of the wagon.

It creaked, and swayed a bit. A lot of pushing, a little

pulling, and a fair amount of swearing, and the anvil was in place and ready to go. Just like loading a truck.

I smiled, looking at what I'd accomplished.

"The metal cannot load itself," came a grating voice from the shack.

Auntie was leaning in the window, looking out at me with a wry smile.

I resisted the urge to flip her the bird.

Instead, I started loading ingots.

Bronze, brass, iron, steel, and more than a few metals I couldn't identify. I tried to use my spell on them, but it fizzled, and I got a little note:

Spell level not high enough to identify target object.

The mana still got taken from my bar though, so important educational opportunity.

There were ingots aplenty at the blacksmith. I needed to get busy and quit fucking around. I layered the bottom of the wagon with the metal, and then moved on to the tools. Hammers on hammers in all shapes and sizes. Mandrels and tongs and pinchers and pliers, oh my! Then on to the horseshoes. Crates and crates full of the fuckers.

The night was cold. A bitter wind swept off the peaks. Snow came down in occasional puffs, sometimes so thick I couldn't see across the village square. Sweat poured down me as I raced to get the wagon packed. I took a moment to breathe, and looked around at the village. Given the moonlight, I didn't even need to use my own dark vision. The village, more or less, looked like it was all packed into wagons, and people were starting to get into a line of sorts. It appeared no one wanted to go alone, so they were going to go as a big group.

Dovie and her aunt passed me, putting two large bundles into the wagon. Then they walked over to Hroar in the center of town. There was a quiet discussion, and some pointing in my direction.

I still needed to get the lightest stuff into the wagon, the large bags of coke and coal. Big burlap sacks of the stuff. I piled them high, and then started lashing everything down with whatever cordage I could find.

"We must make it to Arenberg," the aunt said. "Now."

"We're leaving now?" I asked.

"Now."

I ran a hand through my long hair, and shrugged, watching people bringing animals out of what seemed to be shared stables.

16

Villagers hitched the draft animals to wagons, put blankets over most of them, and then we were off. Since I'd agreed to see Auntie down the mountain safely, I hoisted myself onto the back of the wagon. Immediately Auntie shot me a very dark look.

"Heavy wagon," she said from her perch next to Dovie, who was driving. "You walk."

I smiled, gave a sharp little salute, and then hopped off. Time to walk.

The path from Rumib Pass to Arenberg was a series of switchbacks that seemed to go on forever. One side of the road was always a bit of a cliff, making each turn feel like a death trap. But other than that, you know, totally nice. The wind whipped around everyone, howling and freezing anything it touched. After about an hour the snow started up in earnest, not quite whiteout conditions, but not significantly better. At each turn, though, someone would stand at the edge with a torch, just to make sure no wagons slid off the edge.

I was walking to the rear of Dovie and her aunt, mostly because I was tired of getting the stink-eye from Auntie, but I was also darting back and forth, doing what I could to help out. It's true that escaping an invading army in the middle of the night takes a village. Every time something bad was about to happen, there were people to swarm and assist. Ten people, plus me, gathering on the side to pull a wagon back on track. Me and three other men holding back horses that had gotten too frisky. Switching riders if anyone got too tired. Ferrying blankets between animals to make sure none of the wagon-pullers got too cold or too hot. Hroar even broke out hot cider midway down and made sure everyone had a cup.

As the sky made its way from black to overcast grey, we got to level ground. Thankfully, it was a short distance from level ground to city wall. A wall that was huge. Tall. Thick. All the things a wall should be, I suppose. Because in a world where airplanes weren't the primary mode of getting in and out of a city or country, walls were a pretty big deal. Plus, you know, useful for keeping monsters out.

As soon as Dovie's back wagon wheels hit the flat road, there was a soft ringing noise. Confused, I looked around, but no one else seemed to hear it. I stopped walking and noticed the small light indicating I had a notification begging for my attention.

I let it come.

~

CONGRATULATIONS! you've completed a QUEST!

Help the Town I

The town of Rumib Pass is being threatened, and they must

run quickly or be overwhelmed by the impending invading army. You've loaded the wagon and insured Dovie and her aunt arrived safely at the base of the mountain.

Reward: +500 xp. Your standing with the people formerly of Rumib Pass has gone from DISTRUSTED to LIKED. And, [unknown]

~

CONGRATULATIONS, *you've completed a QUEST!*

Descend from the Peak!

Get down from the peak of the mountain. Preferably with verve and excitement. And alive.

Reward for success: 500 XP!

~

"HEY, STRANGER," Dovie called out.

I shook the notification away, and noticed the wagon had gone a good distance from me. I took a few running steps to catch up.

"Yeah," I said, "what's up?"

"You okay?" she asked.

"Totally."

"Thank you," Dovie said. "You made this possible."

"Sure," I replied with a shrug, always a bit uncomfortable being thanked or praised.

Auntie nudged Dovie, and Dovie sighed.

"Auntie wanted me to give you this," Dovie said. She chucked something at me.

A bag tumbled through the air.

I grabbed it and looked inside.

As a reward, you have been given ten (10) ingots of [???}

"Wait," I said, "what is this?"

"Metal," Dovie called back, snapping the reins and getting the oxen to move a little faster. A pretty clear indicator she was done with me.

I tied the bag onto my increasingly strained belt, and watched the remaining townsfolk pass by. They all looked absolutely wrecked. Exhaustion seemed to radiate from everyone. I felt pretty okay, despite not having slept since, well, yesterday. Maybe this world wasn't going to be so bad.

Hroar came up last, and though his barmaid kept his wagon going, Hroar hopped off and stood in front of me.

"Thank you, Montana," he said. "You have done a great service to the village, though Rumib Pass is no more."

He pulled a heavy sack from behind his back, and pushed it into my hands.

"From the village," he said.

"Dude, not necessary," I tried to push it back, but he was pretty forceful that I should take it.

"It is a small reward, and a shit price for the horses."

I chuckled, and shook my head.

"I appreciate the honesty, Hroar," I said, clasping his wrist.

"Safe home," he replied.

"Safe home."

He released my arm, jogged back to his wagon, and leapt onto the moving cart.

Interesting guy.

I wanted to get into the city before the snow started again, so I hurried along, promising myself I'd look in the sack as soon as I had a room to sleep in.

17

The Arenberg guards, men and women in heavy armor with massive shields and sharp halberds, were no less imposing than the huge gate they protected. They stared up the mountain, seemingly unconcerned with the gaggle of people coming down.

As the refugees, which is technically what the people of Rumib Pass were, got to the gate, more guards came out of the city, and led everyone over to the side where there was an open patch of ground. Some official-looking people with papers and writing boards surveyed the scene. Bureaucrats exist in every world, I suppose. I thought about joining the refugees, and seeing what I could find out about the world from the people processing them, but I decided it was better to sever ties with Rumib Pass. Not that there was anything bad about them. Just, well, I had the feeling they weren't likely to move out of Arenberg, and I had zero desire to get sucked into the coming war. Plus, I needed breakfast. Preferably one with a lot of meat.

Now, you'd think it'd be hard for a man who was a little taller than everyone else, not to mention dressed head to toe in white furs, to slip into the city unnoticed. But luckily for me one of the guards noticed that some of the Rumib horses had the queen's mark branded on them. There was a great kerfuffle, and I took the opportunity to waltz right through.

The main street leading into the city was wide, probably big enough for three wagons to travel side by side. Arenberg's buildings nestled one on top of the other, like the place had been there for quite some time. It had a serious Northern European vibe, which seemed to be in line with the name of the town and its people.

I noticed an interesting shift to the city: closer to the wall, it was built for battle, but as I walked deeper in, the architecture settled down, becoming a bit homier. Friendly almost. The side streets were narrow, and to really force home the claustrophobia, the second and third floors of most buildings extended farther into the street, until there was only about two feet of sky overhead. In some places, the buildings actually touched over the street.

All of it was more than I wanted — I knew I had to get to a smaller town. Somewhere a little more relaxed. Also, maybe without so much snow. Arenberg wasn't as cold as Rumib Pass, not by a long shot, but it was still damn cold. Snow drifts piled in every corner, and just about anywhere there was shade. And I realized I wasn't exactly sure of the seasons, so it could be winter and this cold, or it could be summer and this cold. So I wanted to get somewhere that was a bit more temperate.

Being dawn, Arenberg had just started to come alive. A few carts trundled down the streets, people greeted each other, and smoke twirled out of chimneys. Delicious smells came from bakeries. It was very pleasant. You know, if you discounted everyone staring at me as if I was some sort of monster. Which was understandable — let's just say that

that all signs pointed to current Arenberg fashion tending away from blood-covered white fur. Also, beards were definitely out. I saw a few delicate mustaches, but every other male was clean shaven. I was definitely out of my element.

Rather deep in the city, I saw a heavy wood sign with a flagon of ale tipping over, and a flourish of lettering beneath: The Spilled Mug.

My sort of place.

I pushed the tavern door open and peeked inside.

A burly man shoved a broom around, a bit lackadaisical. Only a few snoring patrons remained.

I focused for a moment, and sent a little identification spell across the room, and got back little in return.

Human

Lvl 11 Barkeep

Level 11 Barkeep. I wondered how he got the tag Barkeep. Was that a class? Were there classes in this game/world?

"Serving breakfast?" I asked.

The man's head snapped around fast. He grimaced.

"Just wrenched me neck," he said, rubbing his neck.

"Hate that," I replied, noting that no one else in the place seemed even a bit bothered by the talking going on around them.

"Yer wantin' food?"

"I am."

"You got coin?"

"I do."

He gestured at his bar with his chin. "Take a seat while I sees what the missus is cookin' up."

After a few minutes, the man came out with a mug of milk and a steaming bowl of something.

"Two coppers," he said.

I pawed through my collection of coinage and found two coppery looking pieces, then plopped them onto the counter.

The barkeep picked them up, looked them over, then stared intensely at one.

"You from Mahrduhm?" the man asked.

"Not in the slightest."

He dropped the coin on the bar, and slid it back to me. "Why you paying in coin of her realm?"

"No good here?"

He looked at them a long time, really trying to come to a decision.

"Does it help that I killed a queen's party to get those?" Which was mostly true. The coins could very well have come from one of the goblins, but what's a little white lie between strangers.

"A bit," he said, rubbing the scruff on his chin. "You give me four coppers, we call it good."

"Exchange rate sucks here," I grumbled, digging through my coins. Frustrated, I dumped all the coins out on the bar. "You want to give me local coins for these?"

His eyes went a bit wide at the mess I'd made. He pawed through the coins, separating them all out, then shook his head.

"Bit o' coin here," he said.

"I know."

"How did you come by it?"

"Killing fools."

He blinked a few times. "Criminal?"

"Not anymore."

He nodded, thinking.

"Guess everyone should get another chance at life. Got a name?"

"Montana."

He reached out his hand, and I grabbed it. "Serge. Serge Albrecht."

"Nice to meet you," I said, "but, uh, have I paid for the, uh—"

"Porridge. And yes."

"Thanks."

"You eat. Let me figure these coins out."

I didn't need to be coerced. I dove into the porridge, which was tasty, thick and rich and filling.

Meanwhile, Serge disappeared under the counter. He fiddled with something for a moment before returning with a pouch. He pushed my assorted coins to one side, and then opened the pouch in front of me.

"Exchange for you," he said, pointing to the pouch.

I opened the bag to examine what he gave me, and it seemed fine.

"Thanks," I said.

"Not counting it?"

"Meh," I said with a shrug, "I have no idea what I'd be looking at, Serge. So I'm just hoping you didn't fuck me on this."

"Fuck you?" he asked and gave me a very confused look.

"Slang from my homeland."

"Where might that be?"

"Detroit."

Same confused look.

"Other side of the mountains," I said, chugging the milk

down just as I realized Mahrduhm was on the other side of the mountains. "Not like the immediate other side of the mountains. Like, you know, a ways past Mahrduhm, and then, you know, that's Detroit. Just, I mean, a long way from here."

He shrugged, and disappeared the coins from the bar.

"Mind if I ask a few questions?" I asked.

"Part and parcel of the barman's trade."

"If I wanted to find a quiet place to live, where might I go?"

"Depends on what you mean by quiet."

"Peaceful. Not a big city."

He raised both bushy eyebrows, and a big smile spread across his gruff face. "Nowhere," he said. "Not in the Empire. Damnation, nowhere I know of outside the Empire, neither. Mahrduhm has the mad queen. Heard nothin' but horror from men coming that way lately. South, you got a great big pile of sand and more monsters'n'you can shake a stick at. East, you got mountains and snow and trees, and if you go far enough, swamp. Northwest, you got the Amber Wastes. Mayhaps you got horse legs tucked up under your fur there — only way you can walk the wastes is being a Centaur. Southeast is the Imperial Ocean, some islands, and a nation of the undead. West, you got the Emerald Sea. I cannot tell you what lies on the other side of that wonder. Now, in the Empire, you got mostly mountains, monsters, and man setting up cities in between. Not much in the way of peace anywhere but a city, and unless you have a lot of coin and noble lineage, you will be fighting your way through any of those cities."

"How big is this Empire?"

"Bigger'n I can figure. You know nothing of this land?"

"Little," I started. I thought of what Hroar said, about

not letting anyone find out I wasn't from this world. Time to lie. "I'm traveling *because* I know nothing. I want to know the world, see the wonders. I've heard of Glaton because it is truly awesome, but—"

He swelled with pride at that, "Damn right. Glaton is the best nation in all of Vuldranni. No more civilized or perfect place to be."

"But there are still monsters?"

"'Tis the nature of the world. You tell me there are no monsters in Detroit?"

"I mean, well, I guess we have our fair share. I just thought Glaton was, uh, better."

"We try. The Legion does much, but the Gods have their games and their reasons for what happens."

I didn't want to wind up talking about the military with the man, I didn't want him to think any more about me being a foreigner than he already was.

"You think I could pass for Glatonese?"

"The Empire holds a multitude of cultures within. I am sure there is some pocket where your look might be, well, normal."

"Furs aren't in fashion, I take it."

"Neither the ones you wear nor the ones you grow, Montana."

"Kinda partial to the ones I'm growin', Serge."

He rubbed his clean shaven face. "No reason to follow a trend if you can start one, eh?"

"Okay, next question: where am I?"

He shook his head, the smile wide and contagious, then pulled a few empty mugs off the shelf. He arranged them in a roughly diamond shape.

"We are here," he said, pointing along the northeastern edge. "Mahrduhm is to the east and northeast of us. I'm guessing you came from here?" he pointed to a spot in the north, and it seemed like a good enough guess for me.

"Pretty much," I said.

"Further south, bordering us here," he pointed to the southeast mug, "is the start of a wide wood. Big tall trees, more lakes and rivers than you can count, and, on the other side, to the east, is swamps. What lies beyond that? No idea. Southwest is the Imperial Ocean, and along it, one of the largest cities of the realm: Reiden. Might think about trying that for peace and no monsters."

"Is that the capital?"

"No, the capital is Glaton. Named after our founder. It is more to the center of the Empire. It is said, at the beginning of our nation, Elissa Glaton raised an army and conquered everything between her and the sea. And thus it has become the Imperial Way, to conquer and grow and spread the best civilization on Vuldranni."

"Doesn't that mean you're constantly at war?"

"Historically, yes. 'Tis but the will of the Emperor to decide our fate in that regard, and most of the Glaton dynasty seem hellbent on claiming as much of Vuldranni as they can. We recently took this," he pointed to an area between where we were and the far west, "and this," a point to the southeast where the rivers and lakes started, "so I would imagine the Legions are but resting before His Imperial Majesty discovers his next target. But I am just a barman, what do I know of politics?"

"Well, bit of a tip: I'm pretty sure that the mad queen is about to hit your city, so—"

"Is this for certain?"

"I just helped a bunch of people escape her from the top of the pass."

"Rumib Pass was abandoned?"

"Yeah. Apparently a large army was coming? Some ranger said he saw the army. It was massive. But I'm just trying to get out to somewhere peaceful."

The bartender pulled a pint for himself, and took a long drink, shaking his head.

"This is dire news. If you wish to miss the fighting, you must head deeper into the Empire. But you will not find a place like you are looking for. I know of none like that. But, were I free to travel, I know there is one place I would visit before I die: the city of Osterstadt, the portal to the Emerald Sea."

"It's nice there?"

"I have only heard the legends of the city, that it is like no where else on Vuldranni."

"I like the sound of the Emerald Sea. Seems, you know, tranquil. Maybe they have good fishing there. How might I get there?"

He laughed. "I like you. A simple man. Best bet for one like you would be to head to the Caravaners' Guild House. Find a trade caravan in search of a guard. There are plenty that run from here to the Capital, and from the Capital you will find one heading up to Osterstadt. Likely, you might make it there by winter. Though, you also might see the Capital and decide you love it, and never leave. Happened to my brother."

"If I get to the Capital, you want me to tell him something?"

"Ask him where's my gold?"

I laughed, and tossed a gold onto the counter. "There's one, at the least."

He snatched the coin off the bounce, and it disappeared on his person faster than I could follow.

"A pleasure, Montana."

"Last question," I said.

"For you, I will answer all the questions you might have."

"I maybe have some, uh, goods to sell—"

"Ah," Serge said with a wink. "I know exactly the place."

18

Serge's buddy was a basically a junk trader. Glorified pawn shop. He sold everything, and was willing to buy everything. He bought the janky goblin swords and their crap armor. He even offered me a whole gold for the Boss Chopper, but I decided I'd keep it. He was happy to buy the Queen's Army Armor, and I was happy to get rid of it. I kept my furs, but put them in a tight pack, and bought some actual clothing, leather pants and a grey wool tunic. I also got a bit of armor:

~

Studded Leather Cuirass

Item Type: Common
Item Class: Light
Material: Leather, Iron
Armor: +12
Durability: Good
Weight: 13 pounds
Requirements: n/a

Description: Made from tough, flexible leather, the armor is reinforced with close-set rivets.

~

AND LOOKED through his shields before settling on a Heater Shield.

~

HEATER SHIELD

Item Type: Common

Item Class: Shield

Material: Ash, Iron

Damage: 10 (Bashing)

Armor: +3

Durability: Good

Weight: 12 lbs.

Requirements: n/a

Description: A smaller shield that can be used either on horseback or foot, the heater shield is in the shape of an iron and provides moderate additional protection from attacks.

~

WHICH I PROMPTLY PUT ON my back. It wasn't anything fancy, just a slab of wood covered with a bit of metal that was painted light blue. Mostly, that is — a lot of paint had flaked off. I got an extra pair of pants, some heavy boots, some underthings, a few shirts, and a poncey sort of hat with a feather. I didn't have the courage to wear it, but I'd wanted one like that since the summer I went to the Renaissance Faire and ate too many turkey legs. I got a wink and a smile when I pulled out the Skull Helm, and laid out the jewelry. Sure, I probably got a bit screwed, but I wound up with a lot of coin for stuff I didn't want in the first place. Happy customer.

My bag felt substantially lighter, and after parting with an additional copper, the man gave me directions to the Caravaners' Guild House. I started moseying in that direction.

The streets were substantially busier now that the sun was out in force. There were people of all different races and, well, species. Humans and gnomes and dwarves and elves and, uh, more elves. Lots of elves. I even saw a massive Minotaur decked out in steel plate armor. He had a sword as tall as me strapped to his back. It would seem all the races got along in the Empire, at least in the city of Arenberg.

The Caravaners' Guild House was a large building near the southern gate of the city, about as close to the wall as it could be. The main building had a large arch in the middle, through which wagons could pass, I supposed. A door flanked either side of the arch. One was very nice, painted a deep red with gold trim and a stained glass window in the middle of it. A small gleaming brass sign said it was for members only. Far more traffic used the door on the opposite side, so I followed along, tailing a rather malodorous gent clearly coming off a multi-day bender.

The door led to a large open room full of humanoids of various stripes. Most of which were seated in long pews, just sort of waiting. Along one wall, there was a huge map of the Empire, with several routes detailed in colorful lines. Opposite the map-wall were a series of stations, much like the DMV. And like the DMV, there were plenty of bored looking individuals manning said stations.

I walked up to the first open one, where a haggard

blonde human who'd certainly seen better days barely acknowledge me.

"Name?" she said, her voice sounding like it came through a pile of pumice.

"Montana," I said.

"Have you worked one of the caravans before?"

"No."

She groaned. "Can you read?"

I nodded.

She narrowed her eyes. "I'm having my doubts."

"I'm one hundred percent literate, and nearly house-broken."

She didn't laugh. Someone behind her did, but nothing from Sourpuss. Instead, the dour lady handed me a form and pointed to a quill and pot of ink.

"Fill this out."

Using a quill was a challenge, and I managed to get a number of bizarre ink blots all over the paper, but in the end, I think my handwriting was somewhere in the neighborhood of legible. Which, you know, kind of a win. The form was basic: name, strength, skill level with swords, with shields, willingness to travel, have you been in the Legion. I considered lying, what with my skills being trash, but what'd that get me?

Finished, I slid the form back over to the lady. She was lazily reading a small pamphlet. She looked up at me, then at the form. There was, for a heartbeat, the slightest eyebrow raise, as if I'd managed to impress her ever so slightly by writing letters.

She held out her arm, and a small black symbol appeared on the inside of her wrist. Then she did a little bit of waggling of her fingers, and finally looked at me. Like really, really looked at me. Then, at that moment, her eyebrow went up.

"Impressive," she said. "Do you have a route preference, or any job anywhere?"

I looked over at the map, then back at her.

"Look lady," I said, "I'm just trying to get to Osterstadt, so, whatever it is that gets me there."

She made a few marks on the paper. "Take a seat."

I sat down where I could look at the map. I had little to go on for scale, so just relied on Serge's assertion that the Empire was huge. It seemed to be broken into a ridiculous number of, well, states. Or countries. Little dotted lines and self-aggrandizing names littered all areas of the map. There were red lines running from certain cities, and I assumed those were roads. Or just caravan paths. One went straight west before it hooked a sharp left and went south to the capital. There was little to no topographical information on the map, so I had no idea of the terrain I'd be looking to cover. But it really seemed like I'd be able to make it without any trouble. That I didn't actually need a caravan to do the deed. Maybe I could just waltz out of this joint and mosey down the street.

Probably not the best idea, but theoretically possible.

I watched as other humanoids in the waiting area were called into a side room. Most never returned. Those that did looked irritated.

Somewhere about the time my stomach started rumbling, I heard my name called.

"Montana?" came a tentative voice, sounding like they weren't sure how to pronounce it.

I stood up and looked around.

A young lady motioned me over, and told me to follow her. I did as told. She was exactly the type of girl who'd gotten me in trouble my whole life over. Tiny and curvy. A pert nose and intense eyes. The only saving grace was that her tiny was, like, really tiny. Three feet tall tiny. So, not exactly an anatomical match for my new sometimes-I-have-to-duck-under-the-doorjam size. I clamped down on my inner ego and steeled my innards. I wasn't in Vuldranni for women. I was here for myself. Thankfully, the girl was just guiding me. She took me to another large room. This one had far fewer people inside it, and just a few old desks spread out. The girl pointed out a desk in the far corner, the darkest portion of the room where just the edge of a lantern's glow reached.

"Thanks," I said, but the girl had already gone. I walked over to the indicated desk, and sat down. The uncomfortable chair creaked under my bulk, and I made sure to remain very, very still.

An older man with pointy ears, fine features, and very hard eyes sat across the table. He had a pipe sitting on the desk, one that looked like it hadn't been lit in some time. The piece of paper I'd filled out was in front of him. He looked at the paper, then me.

"You ever fight?" the man asked.

"Yeah," I replied.

"Win more than you lose?"

"Type of fighting I did, losers didn't get to walk away."

"You steal? You a bandit?"

"Never," I said. I thought about the laundry list of jobs I'd had. Roughneck in the Dakota oil fields, deckhand on a seismic ship, trucker in Texas, roustabout with a circus, and the list goes on. But the bulk of my work experience came from my time with the motorcycle club. Sure, there I ran drugs and guns, bounced and bartended, loan sharking and debt collection, but never stealing of any kind. "The kind of work I did was, well, be a guard for the wrong people I guess."

The guy leaned back in his chair, and looked me over. Intense like. Almost as if I could feel his eyes pierce through me.

"You have shit for skills," he said. "And you have no levels. But you are strong. Look big. Mean."

"Yay?"

A hint of a smile. "You are smart enough to read. To write. Can you count?"

"At least to ten," I said, waggling my fingers at him.

He wasn't amused.

"I can do math," I said, "just not complex stuff, like multivariate questions. Algebra though? Geometry? Fine."

"You can add, subtract?"

"Yeah. And handle bookkeeping if needed."

He nodded, but looked a mite confused. "If you can do all this, why be a guard?"

"Is there something else?"

"A man who can read and do maths is in demand."

"I'm new here."

"Clearly," he said. "The standard rate for a guild guard is 5 silver a week."

"Sounds fine."

"You are not a guild guard. You are a random man who has gone through the most basic of screenings. Given what I have seen of you, I doubt you can even swing a sword properly. I will offer you a chance to come onto my caravan as a guard, but I will pay you two silvers a week until you are at an apprentice level with at least one weapon. Preferably a blade. Do you have a blade?"

"Sure."

"Then the deal is amenable?"

I didn't really want to tell him that I wasn't super concerned about money. At least not yet. I had some gold, enough that I could figure out how to earn more once I got to Osterstadt.

"Yeah. Totally. One question—"

"I would you have more than one question."

"One to start. Apprentice, what rank is that?"

He stared at me for a long time. "For skills, you will be an apprentice when you achieve level 25 in any particular skill."

"Okay, sure. No problem. Second question — you know, since you want me to ask more — how long is this journey we are taking?"

"If we are lucky, if we avoid all the horrors along the route, and we have nothing but perfect weather, we will hopefully be in Osterstadt in eight weeks."

"And if we're not lucky?"

"We never arrive."

"Awesome."

A bemused smile spread across his face, and he extended his hand. "Welcome to my caravan, Montana."

"Thanks, Boss."

We shook.

The man did a little writing of his own on some papers, pulled a stamp out of his pocket, and stamped the papers before filing them in a number of different envelopes. Then he stood.

I followed as he led me through to the other side of the building, the members' side.

It was substantially nicer on the members' side.

A large dining room with a massive hearth overfilled with burning logs dominated the space, but there was also a lounge, a den, and a place where snooty men played some sort of game with balls.

"Cleeve Dye," the boss said.

"Sorry?" I asked, confused.

"My name."

"Ah, Montana."

"I know."

"Right, you got that, uh, my information."

He gave me a look, that universal look that said he thought I was an idiot, yet found me amusing.

19

We left the member's area and stepped outside into the open space around the building. Wagons of all types and sizes were lined up in rows, and plenty of different animals were pawing at the ground, eating various foods, all getting ready to pull. Men and women with weapons and armor sat around on wagons, while animal handlers checked harnesses, and, well, some other people loaded and lashed goods.

Cleeve weaved us through various teams until we got to a group of four wagons. It was something that would be considered small when compared to the rest of the groups in the yard. They were bigger wagons though, and there were absolutely massive horses attached. I counted five people with weapons and four drivers.

Cleeve raised a hand. Everyone turned to pay attention.

"I have an additional hand for us," Cleeve said. "This is Montana. We will be training him to be a guard, but, for the moment, he is here to help in whatever way we need."

I swallowed the frown I felt forming. I was pretty sure I signed on to be at least a guard in training. But, you know, what was I going to do? So I employed my signature move in this world: a weak wave.

Barely a response from the guards — just grim faces and a slight sneer from one of them. They looked very hard, and their armor was well-worn. There were two men and three women, a mix of races and species. They seemed to give me just enough of a cursory glance to know I wasn't a threat, and then returned to their stations.

The drivers, on the other hand, approached me with smiles on their faces. A short man with a massive beard came first, his meaty hand out. "Hademar," he said. If I had to guess, I'd call him a dwarf. He was stocky, but to a degree that I'd never seen in humans. Maybe four and a half feet tall, but also somewhere in the region of four and a half feet wide. His boots were massive. Everything about the man was massive, save his height.

I shook his hand, feeling nothing but callouses.

"Welcome to the Empire," he said, slapping his hand against my thigh, bringing me back to my football days.

"That obvious?" I asked.

He winked.

Next up was a young woman with dirty blonde hair in tight braids that went most of the way down her back. Human. I think.

"Bruna."

She was gruff and had gnarly scars on her arms.

We locked our wrists together, and I had the uneasy feeling she was testing my strength.

Third up was a wiry-looking guy. Younger, clean shaven, but with old blue eyes that looked out on the world as if they'd seen it all already.

"Lee," he said, and he shook hands with me. Pointedly

shook hands. "Oddly enough, I'm not originally from the Empire either."

I raised an eyebrow.

"Detroit," I said.

"Minneapolis."

A huge smile spread across my face.

"We'll talk," he said.

The last driver rolled over, a gruff sort with a huge drooping black mustache.

"Cole," he said, grabbing my wrist and giving it a single pump.

I started to say I was excited, but then everyone went back to work, and I was left to myself.

"Lots for them to do," Cleeve said from behind me. "There will be time to talk on the road, but walk with me a moment."

"When do we leave?" I asked as we started strolling.

"As soon as Darius returns from the feed store," Cleeve replied, giving a lazy wave to one of the other caravan leaders.

"There's one more?"

"Darius handles the animals. Well, helps handle the animals. He also provides a little extra incentive to not bother us. He looks a bit fearsome."

"But isn't?"

"A gentle giant, let's say."

We got to the edge of the open area, and he leaned against the fence.

"I'm taking a bit of a chance on you," he started, "and I think you could be a good person—"

"I'd like to think so," I said.

His mouth snapped shut and his eyes hardened, making it exceedingly clear he did not appreciate interruptions.

"Sorry," I said.

"I need to see your sword," he said, pointing to the sheath on my hip. "Take off the belt. Do not unsheathe it — just give it to me."

I did as he requested, handing over the longsword. He looked at it carefully, rubbing his fingers over the pommel and the guard, then sliding the blade free of the scabbard a few inches to peek at the metal.

"I am taking this weapon from you," he said.

"Wait—"

"It is for your good and mine. This is not just any sword, is it?"

"I have no idea about it, really."

"Are you telling me you just happened upon this blade? Perhaps tripped over it while gallivanting about in the flowers?"

"The guy who had this tried to kill me. And I got a bit lucky, and well, he wound up leaving it to me. In a way."

"You can say you killed him."

"I killed him."

Cleeve nodded. "This is a sword given to officers of the Mahrduhm army when they have won the favor of the queen. It is said she is able to keep track of those who have them, that she knows when the blade is unsheathed. The swords cannot be bought in that realm. They are a visible mark of her favor, and they carry great weight in that culture. With tensions rising, it will only make things difficult for you, and likely us, if people have the impression that you have the queen's favor. Those people will judge you with hostility, and, therefore, will judge me and my trade. I cannot let you jeopardize my caravan because of a sword you know nothing about."

"Dude, no problem. I'm happy to give it up. Seriously, I

have no connection to the sword. It's just a weapon. You know, my only weapon."

He gave a slight smile. "I will provide you with weapons as long as you give this up to me."

"Dude, you get me out of this city before the war comes, well, then I'm your huckleberry."

"War?"

"The Queen's Army, the one I took that blade from, they're right up there," I said, pointing towards the pass. I could just sort of make out where it was, as the clouds moved away from the mountains for a moment, revealing a deep azure sky.

"You are sure of this? She took the pass?"

"Rumib Pass? She didn't take it; the townsfolk gave it to her. And I'm sure because that's where I just came from after tussling with Goblins and some Mahrduhm soldiers. There was a ranger who said he saw the army, and it was huge. I helped the townsfolk get down here last night, and now that I've seen the sights of Arenberg, I'm ready to get out and head west. I've heard about cities under siege, and—"

"Do you know if she is bringing her entire army?"

"That I don't know. I know the ranger said it was big and carried her banner. And that, I mean, I killed a man who carried the sword that says the Queen favors him."

He looked me over, as if he was trying to figure out whether or not to believe what I'd told him. Then he nodded once.

"If what you say is true, I have at least one last errand to run before we can go."

"You've got some way to make money on this?"

"Ah, there is always money to be made in war. It all depends on what you are willing to do when you know the war is starting."

"You think I might invest?"

He frowned. "If you have enough coin to invest, why are you taking a low-level position on my caravan?"

"Happy accident? I just happen to have some gold, and I mean, as long as we're being honest, my main goal is to get west. I'd prefer not to spend all my savings doing that, so, going across with you, earning money and earning skills, that's a much better deal. But I've got 30 gold I can invest."

His eyes went a little wide, but he quickly hid any emotion, and stopped to think about his potential deal. "I can always use a little more gold, and the horses can probably pull a tad more weight. I cannot guarantee a return."

"I know how investing works," I said, and passed over the coin.

He looked it over, and did a quick count. "At least this isn't the queen's coin."

"That'd be annoying, huh?"

20

There wasn't a ton left to do to get the wagons ready. I hefted a few barrels here, tied some knots there. But eventually we were all left sitting there, waiting in the sunshine.

Somewhere in the neighborhood of a half hour later, Cleeve came back, moving very quickly, followed by a giant minotaur. It was unnerving to see a creature from fairy tales, with the head of a bull and the body of a human, in real life. Or whatever this new life was. The dude was huge. Shimmering black fur covered his body, and he had a brilliant gold ring between his nostrils. Each shoulder was the size of a basketball, and he had to stand at least eight feet tall. His pecs strained against a thin shirt, and his horns were massive, pointy and a little terrifying. The minotaur had a chest over one shoulder and a massive sack of something in his other hand.

Cleeve carried a heavy bag of his own, though he was having a bit more trouble with his bag then the minotaur.

"Move out," Cleeve yelled, "on the double."

It seemed like something was wrong. Of course, that was usually my reasoning for any time I had to leave quicker than normal.

Everyone snapped into action, as if this was just normal. The wagons were already moving before I could ask anyone what I should do.

The minotaur hopped onto the third wagon, with Lee, and snapped the reins. So, clearly the driver. Cleeve had mounted a horse and was already riding along with three of the guards, also on horseback. That left one guard on the first wagon, one on the second, and the minotaur and Lee of the third. Who was supposed to be the guard was still up for debate, though I suppose the minotaur could be doing double duty as guard and driver. I grabbed the last wagon as it passed, and hauled myself up to the seat right next to Cole, getting nothing more from the man than a taciturn grunt.

Let's just get this out of the way first: wagons aren't comfortable. They're bumpy and they jostle and toss you all around, and it's loud as hell. And horses fart constantly. And horse farts stink.

Still, riding out on a wagon train was kind of awesome at the same time. It wasn't quite noon, so the sun was just on the morning side of the sky. The air was cold and crisp and fresh, and we were moving. We passed through the city wall, and, again, I was impressed at the edifice of stone. It was like marching out into a different world.

Farmland spread out before me, as far as I could see. People worked the fields with horses, oxen, and all sorts of old mechanical machines I'd never seen before. The road below us was stone, wide enough for two wagons to pass comfortably. The Empire followed the English rules of the road, so we drove on the left.

It was quaint, almost relaxing. But even though the long days were starting to wear on me, I felt my job was to be a guard, which meant I needed to be alert. I shook my head, tried to get the sleepiness to evaporate, and really looked around at my immediate surroundings.

We remained the last wagon in the train. Two horsemen rode a ways behind us on nimble little horses, and two horsemen rode up front, ahead of the first wagon. The wagons were big, certainly larger than I was expecting. About six feet wide, large enough that I could sit a bit distant from Cole. The bottom was three or so feet from the ground, and the top soared to twelve feet. Each was about twenty feet long. Large hoops went up and around the bed of the wagon, with a heavy canvas cover stretched across. Oregon Trail-style, but bigger and beefier. Same for the horses. Big draft horses who towered over me when I stood next to them, with backs so broad I could sleep on one comfortably. All chestnut colored, they had long white socks and almost an overabundance of muscle. Despite the wagons being loaded to the gills, the horses didn't seem to have much trouble hauling. The goods we were carrying were all covered by boring beige cloth, tied here or there so all I could tell there was a box here or a barrel there.

"What are they growing?" I asked Cole, pointing to the farm we were passing.

"Crops," he said, not even bothering to look.

"Do you know what kind?"

He glared at me long enough it got uncomfortable, and then went back to driving the wagon.

I sighed, resigning myself to an interminable and boring ride. Which lasted just long enough for me to remember that my only weapon was a shield. There was no way I'd be able to do anything if there was an attack besides shield

Cole, something I didn't particularly want to do. Clearly, the bossman expected me to rest during the day. At least this one day. I leaned against the backrest, and crossed my arms, then my ankles, and just enjoyed watching the scenery bump on by. Eventually, I found something like sleep.

21

My wake-up call came in the form of a sharp pain in the ribs.

I opened my eyes. The sun was close to the horizon, right in front of us, and the sky was transitioning to twilight. Our wagons had stopped and formed a loose square. Cole jabbed me in the ribs again.

"I'm up," I said, smacking his hand away.

"Down," Cole snapped.

I swore under my breath, but jumped to the ground. I did a little stretching, feeling very tight after the pseudo-sleep on the road, and observed the group.

The drivers gathered up the horses, hobbled them, and, following the directions of the minotaur, started evening care. One of the guards who'd been riding was tending a fire. He had something in a pot as soon as the fire was hot enough.

Apparently, during our day's journey, we'd traveled beyond the bounds of the farmland, and it looked like we were in something approaching wilderness. It was just grass and trees as far as I could see, though the road was still perfectly maintained. We had stopped for the night in a copse of trees, a spot where our wagons would be difficult to see from any real distance. I had the feeling Cleeve wanted the keep the wagons from as many prying eyes as he could. He had guards on for a reason.

Cleeve walked up to me with a massive axe in his hand. He shoved it into mine.

"Follow," he said.

I checked the axe.

Battle Axe

Item Type: Common

Item Class: Two-handed Melee

Material: Iron

Damage: 18-36 (Slashing)

Durability: 20/20

Weight: 9 lbs

Requirements: Str 12

Description: A double-bladed axe meant for cleaving.

The weapon had twin blades, each about a foot long and a haft about six feet long. The whole thing was metal, no wood. The end of the haft was wrapped in leather, providing an obvious grip, and there was a sphere of metal at the end, my guess, to provide some balance for the huge axehead. I hefted the axe and followed.

Cleeve led me outside the wagon square and to the other side of the road.

"The axe," Cleeve said. "A tool for chopping. Best for unarmored opponents."

He had a length of wood in his hand.

"Attack me," he said.

I shrugged, and gave the axe a big ol' swing.

He parried the chop and smashed his stick into my arm.

I hissed. It fucking hurt.

"Again," he snapped.

We fought, and he taught. Mostly through beating his stick against my person. I never got close to hitting him, though I did manage to take a massive chunk from an irascible tree that refused to get out of my way.

Cleeve was breathing hard, and held up a hand. I leaned against the axe and I waved. I mean, he was an older dude — I couldn't exactly expect him to keep up with me. We stopped sparring, and he taught me a few forms, ways of swinging and stances to fall into so that I could develop the muscle memory I'd need to survive an ambush or a surprise fight. Then, he showed me what to do if I over-extended after a big swing, how to control the weight and speed, and how to stop the axe to make quick counterattacks.

Sweat was pouring off me when a chime rang out. Cleeve gave me an extra smack.

"Food," he said. He walked away without saying anything else.

I stood there, breathing hard for a second, but as soon as I was able to take a few deep breaths, I felt fine. Like I could do this all night if I could just have a moment's rest every now and again. I noticed a little blinking light in the corner of my vision.

Cool Beans, you've learned the skill **Axes**. *Not just for trees, axes can also chop down men and monsters. +5% damage. +5% skill.*

~

There you go, leveling up the skill **Axes**. *Not just for trees, axes can also chop down men and monsters. +2% damage. +2% skill.*

~

Back over the road and through the wagons, there was a nice fire going with a few improvised seats around it. The guard who'd tended the fire and made the stew handed me a bowlful, along with a piece of hard bread.

The stew was good. Filling. Peppery. And the bread, when used to soak up some of the stew, was tasty in its own incredibly chewy way. Most everyone went back for seconds, but after watching the Minotaur scrape the pot into his bowl, I just leaned against the wheel and enjoyed the almost full feeling.

"New guy. Montana. First watch," Cleeve called out. "Donner, second, Teela, last."

Donner, a guard with a massive scar running down his face, through his eye and disappearing into his armor, nodded.

Teela was smaller, but seemingly more rough and tumble. She gave a snappy little salute.

Everyone seemed to know what to do. They all got to their feet, handed their bowls back to the cook-guard, and then went about tidying things up and pulling bedrolls and pillows from hiding spots on the wagons. Everyone seemed to have their own little sleeping spot already picked out, and the span of time from finishing dinner to general snoring was ridiculously quick. No one slept under the stars except the minotaur, who went and leaned against a tree among the horses.

Cleeve was having a terse chat with Lee, and I walked over near them, leaving enough room, I thought, to be polite.

"Why are you looking?" Cleeve asked.

"I wanted to give you the axe back."

"Need it for guard duty, don't you? Return it in the morning."

"Yeah, that makes sense."

I felt like an idiot. I walked over to the opposite side of the wagons, and I stood there with the axe. I paced around the camp a few times. The fire in the middle burned low. I made sure not to look at the fire too often, something I picked up from a book. In the Scouts, we never bothered to set watches at night. I mean, I had no idea what I was guarding against. There could be squids in these woods for all I knew.

The night dragged on, and nothing came down the road. The bats stopped flitting through the sky and the insects all seemed to settle down. It was just me and the gentle snoring coming from a number of different caravan members.

The moons came up, one after another, looking big and beautiful, and I took more than a few moments to just drink them in. The night sky in this new world of mine was stunning. Zero light pollution means there was an endless display of stars and galaxies twinkling across the black.

I was bored, and not at all tired, so I started going through the axe motions again. Swing, restore. Swing, restore. Jab with the butt of the haft. I started doing twirls and flourishes. Then I realized I looked like a total tool, and this couldn't have any positive bearing on actual fighting.

So I did push ups.

And pull ups, until a branch broke.

Stretches, lunges, squats, an entire body-weight exercise. Jumping jacks. It was getting a little cool, so I pulled out my fur coat and slipped it over the leather armor.

Still on watch.

I kept moving, working out when I thought of another exercise. Doing the bits of yoga I could remember, anything to keep my mind from starting to wander. I knew, if I let it, my brain would start running through my life on earth. The decisions I made and the path that brought me to Vuldranni.

Finally, I started working on throwing the giant axe. Sure, not at all what the weapon was meant for, but that didn't mean it couldn't be successfully accomplished. Definitely super awkward at first, especially considering the unwieldy size of the weapon. Still, I started to get a feel for it, how to release, how to throw and get the blade to hit. How to put power behind the throw and keep it on target.

And then, out of nowhere:

Cool Beans, you've learned the skill ***Large-weapon Throwing.*** *Take that massive weapon and throw it away! +5% accuracy, +5% damage*

I couldn't help smiling. This weird game world thing I was stuck in had a ridiculous library of skills. It made me wonder how many there might be in total. Maybe there was an infinite amount. I mean, I'd gotten a level in falling.

I regaled in my new skill for a moment, and then went back to work. I was determined to get a few more skill levels before my replacement woke up and took over. I hefted the big axe up and whipped it over my head. It flew through the air, end over end, and I could practically hear it, *whoosh-whoosh-whoosh*, until it hit a tree with a satisfying *thunk*. On and on, I threw the axe until I was getting a solid hit every time.

Thunk.

Thunk.

Thunk.

My muscles and lungs were burning. I'd managed to really drain my stamina bar. I took a moment to lean on the axe and look around. The sky far to the east had gotten a little lighter, and birds started chirping. It was morning. I'd stayed up all fucking night, chucking an axe.

I twirled the axe in the air, feeling like I'd managed to get pretty good at it during the hours of darkness. Which made me think about the day-length in Vuldranni. Was it 24 hours? Was the night 12 hours long? Was an hour the same length of time? So far, it'd seemed roughly equal, I mean, at least close as I could tell without any timepieces. Whatever. Questions to ask someone later. At that moment, I figured there wasn't a long wait until actual morning, so why bother waking anyone else up for watch. I'd just ride it out.

Finally, I heard stirrings from within the camp. There was a quiet curse, and Teela, the woman, who'd had third watch came running out of the circle, buckling her armor up. She skidded to a stop when she saw me leaning against my axe.

I watched her face move through a few variations of confusion before settling back to normal.

"Morning," I said.

"Morning," She replied, resettling her armor and tightening a few straps. "Stayed up all night?"

"I did."

"Why?"

"No one came to relieve me."

A big smile spread across her face. "Follow, fool," she said, and walked over to the lead wagon. Up by the driver's position was a large sand timer.

She flipped it over.

"One turn equals one watch," she said. "Timer's up, you wake the next person."

"Yeah," I said, feeling very much like an idiot, "that makes a lot of sense."

"How would the sleeper know what time to wake?" she asked.

"Yeah, I guess you don't have alarms here."

She raised an eyebrow, and pointed over to the wagons.

"You can nap if you want. I'll finish out the watch."

22

Breakfast was bread, dried fruit, and mystery dried meat washed down with weak mead. Cleeve noticed that I didn't seem too tired, and he decided I'd best serve the Caravan by taking two watches overnight.

The guards, myself included, sparred. We basically did a good ol' practice session while the drivers got the horses hooked up and ready to go. Once we got a solid sweat built up, we did weapons and armor care, sharpening blades, oiling armor, all that doldrum-y stuff they don't tell you about in fantasy novels. Once we finished, I noticed the drivers were sitting in their wagons, and the wagons were in a line, ready to move out.

The minotaur went along the caravan, inspecting the lines connecting the wagons and horses, and looking over the horses one more time. And then we took off, rolling down the road, where I got to sit next to Cole and have the most fascinating conversations. By which I mean I'd ask a question, get a single word response, and sometimes a mighty glare if I dared to ask a second.

And that's pretty much how things seemed to roll. We

drove most of the day, turned off the road somewhere close to sunset, and circled the wagons. Well, squared them at least. Kind of tough to make a circle with just four points. Then I trained with Cleeve, ate some stew, did two watches during the night, threw axes, did pushups, worked up to being a bad ass.

When we passed other caravans, maybe once or twice a day, there was a sort of professional courtesy wave between drivers. Mutual respect and disregard. We'd pass farmers more often, usually a single wagon doping along, sometimes driving right down the center of the road. Then Cleeve or one of the other guards on horseback would have to ride up and get the wagon to move to the side. Occasional bands of armed men on horseback would ride by, always sitting up tall in their saddles, letting their flags whip in the wind. Twice, we passed small bands of the Imperial Legion, marching in time with long polearms and heavy shields. They were serious groups, and we'd often slip off to the side of the road to let them pass. I swear, once we passed a group of adventurers. Disparate races, outfitted with a ton of weapons and armor, only five of them. It was the only thing I could think of that made even an iota of sense.

This went on for a week and a half. My skills slowly improved, first with the axe, and then in the war hammer and the spear. Cleeve still used wooden rods, smacking the shit out of me on a regular basis. But the notifications kept popping. My skill in the arts of war was leveling up. I got closer to touching Cleeve, but it was very clear he was significantly further up the skill tree than me. Also, I'd managed to get nowhere leveling. Killing the goblins and Mahrduhm soldiers on day two of Vuldranni life had done significantly more for me overall than my week plus of being a caravan guard. It forced me to wonder if there'd be any sort of leveling purely through skill development. Were normal people kept low-leveled because of this?

The leveling bothered me, but nowhere near as much as the one thing that truly sucked about this world: no one ever talked to me. I expected the guards and drivers to keep separate, but once we were on the road, there was perpetual mixing. At least socially. Everyone talked to everyone. Except me.

I sort of got it — I was the new guy, and a super-green new guy at that. They were waiting to get the measure of me. But if I was being totally honest with myself, I was doing the same with them.

Darius and Lee were very good friends, which made sense, considering they shared a wagon. But it was a delightful picture seeing the two next to each other, with such a massive disparity in size. They spoke quietly together, and since I knew Lee was new to the world, I started to wonder if the minotaur, Darius, was as well.

Cleeve spent a long time looking at maps, reading books, and writing things in a little notebook. Any talking he did was more or less business oriented. Watching the guards, there was a hint they were all ex-military, as they still saluted on occasion. I wondered if they'd all been part of the Legion. If they'd all been in the same company even.

We passed two small towns, stopping briefly to restock our food and water, but spent our nights under the stars in the middle of nowhere. It almost made me feel like a Boy Scout again, the campfires and sleeping outside.

23

On a frost-tinged morning at a crossroads, I finally saw the full might of the Imperial Legion. It sounded like the road itself was rumbling, as a cloud of dust rose from the south. Mounted soldiers came first, taking up the entirety of the road. They didn't have on full plate, but I assumed that was because they were in traveling mode. Hundreds of heavy calvary rode on massive destriers, looking hard and grim. Then, hundreds more light cavalry. A ton of wagons, laden with supplies of all sorts. And then thousands of foot soldiers. Hundreds more archers. The command group was somewhere in the middle, a bunch of very smart looking men in uniforms in a single extra-large wagon that took up most of the road. There were military units I couldn't really identify, men and women, races of all kinds, massive creatures I would have pegged as monsters, and even a host of machines of war, like siege weapons and ballistas.

As soon as it was clear the Legion was approaching, we'd pulled off to the side and gotten down from the wagons. I stood there with my mouth agape. It was incredible to see the fighting force the Empire was able to put in place.

"First time seeing the Legion?" Lee asked softly.

"Yeah," I replied, not taking my eyes off the mass of humanity. And other races. I realized the term really no longer applied in Vuldranni. There were plenty of dwarves, elves, and man-beast hybrids in the ranks. Yet the bulk was still human.

"I've been meaning to talk to you," Lee said.

"Same," I replied.

"Never really a great time, really. Life is busy on the road."

"And there's the training."

"That too."

"Are there a lot like us?"

"From Earth?"

"Some," Lee said. "Darius is."

"I suspected as much. Just the way you two talk and stuff."

"He's the only one I've met, so, I mean, the only one I can totally confirm."

"Earth?"

"Oakland."

"No shit?"

He nodded. "Cleeve hired us on the same day. He thought Darius would be good as a guard, but, well, Darius isn't exactly—"

"Cleeve mentioned something about that."

"Yeah. Turns out, though, he's amazing with animals. Was a vet in, you know—"

"Previous life."

"Yeah. And I was hired to cook the books."

"Accounting?"

"Yep. Surprising amount of math involved in the caravan trade."

"What's Cleeve's story?"

"His to tell."

"I suppose that's fair."

"It's also due to me knowing little about the man. I've only been on from Bergamo to Arenberg."

"Where's Bergamo?"

"South."

"Like, south south? Like big bad desert south?"

"I spawned in near there. Thought I wanted to see it. Saw it. That was enough."

"Why's that?"

"I was in a city there, mind you—"

"Bergamo?"

"Yep, and even that was more dangerous than I could've imagined. It's still the Empire, but the Erg is full of monsters. Stuff I never believed could exist. Like, breaks the laws of physics existence."

"Could you give me an example?"

"You ever read *Dune*?"

"Yeah, a long time ago."

"Like that. But there's a clear line, grass meeting sand, very weird, but literal. One side green grass and trees, the other, sand. Now, some sand blows over or whatever, but it doesn't really accumulate. But those worms will come right up to that line, fighting each other and trying to snag anything moving on the other side. It's a pointless place. A place of death and nonsense."

"Sounds like Florida."

Lee laughed. "Not far off."

The last of the camp followers trundled by. Those

offering services to the soldiers didn't move with as much discipline, but they made up for it in speed.

Finally, we all saddled up or got on our wagons, and continued west. The Legion had come from the south, made a turn and headed east, and I figured they were going to supplement the Arenberg defenses. Which is totally just something I overheard from the guards and realized was probably the case.

Cole, as per his usual jovial self, looked out at the road with disinterest and displeasure.

"Pretty cool, huh?" I asked Cole.

He looked at me, raised his eyebrow just a hair, then looked back out over the landscape.

We were back to routine.

24

From the crossroads on, the road became less and less cohesive. There were definitely sections where it appeared someone had made off with the cut stone, leaving hard packed dirt behind. We were out of the of the forests again, and into something closer to rolling hills. Lots of grass, trees here and there, and a lot of rivers. Most were small, with simple stone bridges across them. But one was large enough that we needed to ford it, driving rather deep into the water. Thankfully, being the end of the summer, the rivers weren't swollen with water, so it was more an interesting exercise than anything actually dangerous.

It was peaceful there, very tranquil. Guarding the caravan was turning out to be remarkably easy. And in those grasslands, it was easy to see things from a tremendous distance, so even if there were bandits or monsters looking to ambush us, it wasn't exactly likely to happen.

We hadn't passed many travelers in a while. There were some farmers, wagons trundling along. Mostly though, it was hunters, who were always willing to trade meats and pelts. Cleeve (or Lee) had clearly planned for this, and had plenty of small items ready to go. Bundles of arrows, bags of arrowheads, bow strings, even a new bow for a particularly delicious sturgeon. It was nice to have fresh meat for a change.

Weeks three and four were in these river lands. Mountains stood tall far to the north, and behind us in the east. The road, however, headed ever westward. Occasionally, we'd see forts and castles in the distance, some looking powerful and strong, some looking like they'd fall over if you sneezed nearby. Cole was masterful in ignoring my repeated questions about what those castles were or what they may be guarding.

I continued to practice nightly, most often directly with Cleeve, but occasionally with one of the other guards. Cleeve would always be there, though, instructing me against the other guard. At first, it was hard to get anyone to help, but as soon as they realized they were allowed to actually hit me, a host of very excited volunteers signed up overnight. The pain was a bit much, but considering how quickly I healed, it didn't really bother me. Besides, any time I was actually sparring, my skills jumped up much quicker, and I could feel my muscles finally understanding what I wanted them to do. They knew how to move a sword to catch a thrust, they knew how to recover when I'd overextended with a war hammer, and they knew how to stop the axe to countercut on a dime. After a month of pretty much constant work, I got a notification.

~

Congratulations! Due to hard work, you've gained ***+2 STR!***

CONGRATULATIONS! Due to hard work, you've gained ***+3 CON!***

CONGRATULATIONS! Due to hard work, you've gained ***+2 DEX!***

I FELT STRONGER and leaner than I ever had in my life. My muscles were huge, veins popping out everywhere. My body fat had to be in the single digits. My hair was still growing, long and luscious, and my beard was full and seemingly perfect. I looked like I belonged on the cover of a viking romance. It felt good.

Bumping about the wagon in the middle of the day, watching over rippling grass fields, I decided to look over my character sheet.

MONTANA - LVL 3 Nothing

Traits

Race: Fallen

Height: 6'2"

Weight: 220 lbs

Eye Color: Hazel

Hair Color: Blonde

Renown: 0 - No one even knows you exist.

Statistics

HP: 139

STAM: 428

MP: 212

Armor: +12 (Studded Leather)

Active Effects: None

~

Attributes

Strength: 34

Agility: 15

Dexterity: 17

Constitution: 23

Wisdom: 13

Intelligence: 13

Charisma: 17

Luck: 27

~

Unassigned points: 0

~

Skills

Riding - improvised (LVL 1): You can now ride improvised devices. +5% to handling.

Falling (LVL 1): You can flail through the air with the best of them. Watch for the sudden stop at the end.

Animal Handling (LVL 5): You can calm down a domesticated animal, keep a mount from getting spooked, intuit an animal's intentions, or, if you're really lucky, tame a wild best.

Investigate (LVL 1): Now when you don't know, try and figure it out! +5% to find the hidden, +5% passive perception.

Harvesting (LVL 5): You can pick plants, you can grab fruit, you can cut neat things out of creatures you slaughter. That'll save the world, right? At Level 5, you are able to harvest common elements with no penalties. +10% successful gathering chance

Swords (Lvl 2): You can swing sharp objects and likely not hurt yourself. +6% damage. +6% skill.

Spears (Lvl 1) Remember, the pointy end goes towards the enemy. +5% damage. +5% skill.

Unarmed Combat (Lvl 9): You can strike with the fist or the foot, and must register your hands as lethal weapons. -13% stamina drain. +13% damage.

Axes (Lvl 8): You can chop down limbs of trees or men. Or monsters. +19% damage, +12% skill

Large Weapon Throwing (Lvl 9): Take that massive weapon and throw it away! +13% accuracy, +13% damage

Warhammers (Lvl 5): Everything IS a nail. +9% damage, -9% stamina drain

Light Armor (Lvl 3): A little bit of leather goes a long way. +7% dmg reduction, -7% movement penalty

~

Abilities

The Sword of My Enemy is My Sword: You've found that, in a pinch, every weapon will do. +1% dmg for each new weapon used in a combat.

~

Feats

None

Boons

Powerful Build (Mister Paul) - You are bigger than you look. For all strength roles, you are counted as one size category larger than you actually are.

Regeneration (Mister Paul) - Outside of combat, your body will repair rather quickly. Given enough time, it's possible you will heal from nearly any wound.

Gift of Gab (Mister Paul) - Should you encounter a language you do not understand, as long as you hear at least three words of it, you will understand it, and speak it, perfectly.

Indicium

None

RELATIONSHIPS

Rumib Pass (destroyed) - Liked

LANGUAGES

Goblin

Imperial Common

Mahrduhmese

Spells

Lifeform Identification (Lvl 1) (costs 1 mana) Identify uncommon or lower lifeforms.

Basic Object Identification (Lvl 1) (costs 1 mana) Identify any non-magical common or lower item.

Heal Other [lvl 1] (costs 100 mana). Through the use of magic you are able to heal another through touch. Heal 50 Hp.

Humus [lvl 1] (costs 10 mana). This spell gathers dirt and organic materials, moisture, and bacterial ingredients within one mile/level of the caster and places the mixture anywhere the caster wishes within range. This is humus, the black, enriched soil excellent for growing plants in pots or gardening. Of course, the mage may use it however he wishes, but it is usually for growing things in pots and window boxes. If no such materials are within one mile/level, the spell has no effect.

NOT BAD. I was moving up in the world, to an extent, and I could definitely see how my nightly sessions were helping me. Despite that, my best skill was, oddly, throwing large weapons. Something I don't think Cleeve, or anyone else on the caravan, had any idea that I did. I wasn't exactly sure how useful it'd be in real combat, seeing as it'd mean relinquishing my main weapon, but, well, it might be a good finishing move.

I asked Cole about his character sheet, and about leveling and how this all worked. If there had been any, like philosophical exploration of why there were leveling systems in place. But, the moment I opened my mouth, Cole glared at me until I shut it again. I'd have better luck talking to horses.

But, looking at the sheet did make me realize I wasn't doing what I could, well, as a gamer, to really maximize my build. Any minute of any day could be spent grinding in some form or another. So I started identifying each and every life form I passed. It was mostly trees and shrubs, but there were plenty of birds too, and some occasional rodents. I tested the range of the spell, trying to get a bead on life-forms that were farther and farther from the wagon. I discovered it could go about a hundred yards. After that, nothing. Also, I needed to keep my attention focused on the object for about an entire second, which doesn't seem like a lot of time until you try to focus on a bird a hundred yards a way while riding a bumpy wagon.

At night, I added some more spell-work to my routine, identifying everything in walking range, then casting humus over and over again, leaving small clumps of fertile earth everywhere. And whenever I found a hurt insect, or anything really, I healed it. *Heal other* as a spell can be very versatile because it seems to heal anything living that isn't me. Including plants. Every place we camped became a little healthy oasis, and I felt good leaving every morning, knowing that, at the least, I'd made a small place better.

25

We left the river lands and climbed up a long set of hills. The land became thick with trees, big deciduous things, and there were lots of little critters about the place, scurrying about and chittering at us from their upper bough safety.

Coming around a bend in a thick part of the forest, we found the wagons in front of us had stopped. So we stopped.

I saw something across the road, so I pulled the axe out of the wagon. I walked up on the side of the wagons until I heard muffled voices. Cleeve and Nikolai, the head guard, sat on horseback, talking to each other.

"... obviously an ambush," Cleeve said. "Question is, what kind."

Nikolai looked around, "Shoddy. They have given us too much time."

"New at this?"

"Perhaps. Tree is fresh cut."

They looked around the area for a bit.

"They will need the wagons and the horses," Nikolai

said. "We are far enough from Saumiers they will not be able to traverse the distance with our goods on foot."

I got a view of the barrier. A thick tree had been felled across the road, its trunk nearly ten feet wide.

Nikolai was still mulling things over when dangerous-looking men and women came out of the forest and the branches of the fallen oak. Most had bows, some had daggers and short swords. There was one ginormous dude — just a straight brute — who had a hunk of wood attached to a handle, kind of like a massive war mallet or something.

I did some quick counting. This was bad. Our adversaries outnumbered us almost two one.

The horses whinnied, nervous.

The bandits, an assumption at the time that later proved true, were all dressed in dark brown leathers with hoods over their heads. Most had masked faces. Their leader sauntered along the tree and dropped to a seated position.

"Looks to be our lucky day," he said in a genteel voice. "Plenty of goods in this haul to make even the most jaded king of thieves smile for a moment."

"King of thieves, is it?" Cleeve asked. "And here I thought you were but a common highwayman."

"You are in the presence of royalty," the self-styled king said with a slight bow and flourish.

"Be still my heart," Cleeve replied, giving his face a fan of the hand. "Am I blushing?"

"No, sir," Nikolai answered quickly.

"Just a little," offered up one of the other guards.

"Ah," the king of thieves said, "if you are so taken by me, perhaps we can have a little lunch after you give all your goods to us. Just hand them over without violence."

"Oh," Cleeve said, sliding his blade free from his scabbard, "I wish I could."

"But you can. 'Tis easy if you try."

"Just as easy as letting us through without taking anything that doesn't belong to you."

The king mimed weighing the offers in his hands. One clearly won out. "No, I am afraid we need what you have got, good merchant. Are you sure you want to die for it?"

"Are you?"

There was a moment of feigned calm as we reached the edge of battle. I tried to figure out my first move.

Cleeve moved faster than I could comprehend, pushing forward out of his saddle with his sword lunging towards the king of thieves. The king barely got his own blade up in the way, and there was a great clang as the two swords met.

I realized the brute was charging me, his hammer above his head, ready to knock my head off.

As fast as I could, I pulled the axe up, swung it around my back, and launched it at the brute.

The brute's eyes opened wide as the battle axe spun end over end until it slammed into his nose, lodging deep in the man's gory remains. It hit with enough force to stop the man's charge, and send him to the ground.

His mallet, on the other hand, continued forward, sliding on the ground until it hit my foot. I kicked it up, and hefted the thing. Massively unwieldy and unbalanced. I sent a tingle of magic down my arm.

~

WarMallet

Item Type: Trash

Item Class: Two-handed Melee

Material: Wood

Damage: 20-30 (Bludgeoning)

Durability: 7/9

Weight: 18 lbs

Requirements: Str 18

Description: A hunk of wood on a handle. One step above a club.

THE FIGHT HAD TURNED into a maelstrom in the short time between throwing my axe and picking up the war mallet. I tried to see what the other guards were doing, but things were moving too quickly. Plus, there were definitely a lot of people who were looking to kill me. I needed to pay attention to myself.

An arrow smacked into me. It hurt like a motherfucker, and made me angry. I ran at the woman who shot me. She fumbled with her bow, trying to get another arrow on the string, but gave up, dropping the bow and snatching the dagger off her belt just as I brought the hammer around into her midsection.

The hunk of wood slammed against the woman, and with a sharp crack, it sounded like all her ribs broke at once. She dropped the ground. I brought the hammer down, and her torso flattened. Blood bubbles formed around her mouth, and she stopped breathing. She was done.

And I'd done it to her.

For a heartbeat, there was this feeling inside me, that I'd committed this great act of violence, and I could never be the same. What had I don—

Nah.

I'd done worse before. And given Vuldranni seemed to be predicated on savagery and violence, I'd likely do worse in the future. I'd just hoped that, with a second chance, maybe I could put some of those skills to use being a savior. Finally be the good guy.

Three bandits converged on me from the woods: A man with a black mask and a club, a woman with a sword, and a man with a mace.

I took a broad stance, then feigned throwing the hammer.

They all flanked, and I took their momentary distraction to attack. I had basically nothing in the way of defense — my stupid tiny heater shield was back in the last wagon — so I knew I had to keep the pressure up.

I swung towards Maceman. He brought his weapon up to block, holding it with both hands, but he misjudged the sheer size of the hammer's head. Even though he got his handle against mine, the hammer had enough reach to slam into his face, basically caving it in.

Maceman collapsed, a vague moan coming out through bloody bubbles in the mess that used to be his face.

His collapse, however, meant I was overextended and open to my two opponents.

I felt a burning in my midsection, and looked down to see a sword sticking into my gullet. Immediately, I dropped the hammer and grabbed the blade.

Before I could make the first pull, a club soared towards my face. I reared back, ignoring the pain spreading across my midsection. The club missed my head by mere fractions of an inch. I felt my mustache whiskers blowing in its wind.

The swordsman tried to pull her blade back, but I held on and gave her a smile. Instead, I snatched her tunic and ripped her to me, and slammed my head against her face, feeling her nose crush against my forehead.

The pain shocked her enough that she released her grip on the hilt.

I gritted, tore the sword out, and brought it up just in time to block the club coming back in a return swing. It thunked to the side.

A quick step forward to get out of the way of Clubber, and I brought my shoulder into Swordswoman just as she unsheathed a dagger, driving her back. She stumbled over some roots and the limp legs of Maceman, and fell backwards to the ground. I drove my sword at her, but at the last second, clubber blocked my move.

I growled, angry that my kill had been stolen.

A step back, and I was in position. My midsection howled with pain, but I did my best to ignore it. I knew the wound was serious, and it took everything in me not to slide my hand down and probe the damage.

Clubber and I squared off, while the swordswoman, now sword-less, crab crawled away.

When it comes to close-quarters melee, the club has a few distinct disadvantages compared to a sword. For example, lunges don't do much. You need to swing to get any real damage. Preferably a big swing. And, each parry of a sword risks losing chunks of your weapon.

My opponent seemed to realize this, and was on the defensive, circling me around.

I caught a flick of his eyes to the side, and I knew something bad was about to happen. I pulled my delicate bit (my head), inward and brought my more beatable bits (my shoulders) up, and the speeding mace connected with my upper arm instead of my skull. It hurt like blazes as the blade-like flanges struck deep into my deltoid. My left arm was useless as anything but hamburger as the swordswoman, now Macewoman, ripped it free.

A guttural and barbaric "Yawp," escaped from my throat. Burning rage washed over me, hot one minute, and frighteningly cold the next. All I wanted was to kill the assholes hurting me and trying to hurt my friends. I didn't care if I made it out alive as long as they didn't.

Clubber swung.

I accepted I was going to be hit, and lunged forward with my blade straight.

My sword went through his throat as his club slammed across my face.

I spun, blood spraying out of my mouth, then tumbled to the ground.

The woman was already above me, mace high above her head, ready to crush my skull into bits.

As my death neared, everything slowed down for a moment. My brain, never my staunchest ally in the past, seemed to click on, and started running through the scant strategies I had left. Only one thing stood out.

Magic.

I shot my arm out and pointed at the woman's head. My fingers twisted, and I forced the mana through my hand, I cast *humus.*

Dirt flew out of the ground and gathered tightly around her head. Roughly a cube of beautiful, black, fertile earth coalesced about her face.

She shrieked, and started coughing. Which just caused more dirt to go into her lungs. She swung the mace, but nothing was behind it, strength wise, and she had no aim because she couldn't see. Which meant she had no idea that I'd already rolled out of the way.

The mace smacked into the ground.

The woman pawed at the dirt, coughing desperately.

I had enough time to grab the sword out of her comrade and slice through her throat.

Then I made sure the other two were finished.

I leaned against a tree, and finally let the pain actually wash over me. I was probably going to die. I felt my stomach. Big hole. Very ruined. Lots of nasty fluids commingling in ways I knew they shouldn't. I spit out some blood and what seemed like a tooth. I ran my tongue around my mouth to confirm I was missing a tooth and came to realize I was missing several. And had a few only partially there.

"Thuper," I lisped.

26

As I sat there, I realized I couldn't hear much. Groans, sure, but the clash of steel on steel had stopped. I stumbled out of the woods, and saw our fight with the bandits had ended.

Cleeve looked fine, not even a hair out of place. The King of Thieves, however, was very much dead. His head had been separated from his body.

Lee peeked out of his wagon, Darius hiding right next to him.

The rest of the caravan looked pretty good, and even though I thought I'd been close to death, by the time I limped over to Cleeve, my teeth had, more or less, reformed.

"You fought well," he said.

"Good teacher," I replied.

"Let Cole see to you," Cleeve said. "He'll patch you up."

Cole was at our wagon. He'd opened up a small hatch, making a work station of sorts. There were some medical tools in place, as well as various first-aid errata required for treating wounds. I also spotted a few small bottles filled with a glittering red liquid. Other guards were downing them, but by the time I got there, Teela quaffed the last one.

Cole was busy with one of the other guards, wrapping a bandage around the woman's arm where he'd just pulled an arrow free. The already-treated guards busied themselves lining up the bandits' bodies and stripping them of everything. Clothing, armor, weapons, pouches, all of it got set in front of the first wagon.

I leaned against the wagon, waiting for Cole to finish with the others.

He motioned to me.

"Armor," he said.

My shoulder worked well enough that I could pull my ruined leather cuirass over my head and drop it to the ground. My shirt was soaked in blood. Like, I could wring blood out of it. Cole grimaced as he saw the damage to the armor and the shirt. He helped me get the shirt off and then tossed it to the side — there was no saving it. Then he reached over for what I assumed would have been a health potion, but only found empty bottles.

He growled.

Instead, he grabbed a waterskin and aimed a stream of water at my torso, washing off the blood as he searched for wounds. Eventually, he'd washed off my whole abdomen. He poked at a pink scar on my stomach. Then he looked over my shoulder, which was just smooth skin taut over a bulging deltoid.

Cole prodded at me for a moment or two. I could tell he wanted to ask me how I'd healed so fast. But asking such a question would require more than the single word a day he allotted to me.

"Guess I'm good," I said.

He rubbed his thumb against my abs, as if he was trying

to clean a smudge off them. Then shook his head when he realized that the pink scar had even faded.

I looked at the other guards and drivers, and it didn't seem like many managed to make it out without injuries of some kind. Some, like Teela, had gotten health potions, but others were clearly hurting. I thought about my spell. But using it would make my ability to do magic very apparent. I would have to go to the Imperial government and would likely be pushed into service, whatever that meant. It didn't look like anyone was permanently damaged, so I just let it go.

There was a definitive method to how the loot was divided. First, all the coins were put together. Half went to Cleeve, and the rest was doled out equally. Then, the objects. Cleeve got first pick, then the rest of us by seniority. There were a few choices pieces, mostly those belonging to the king of thieves. I noticed everyone bypassed the unblemished chainmail, so that once it was my turn, it was basically the only thing of value remaining. Clearly, they'd seen I had no armor at the moment.

I picked up the chain, and gave it a once over.

~

Chainmail Shirt

Item Type: Common

Item Class: Heavy

Material: Iron

Armor: +24

Durability: Good

Weight: 45 pounds

Requirements: n/a

Description: Made from interlocking iron rings in a 4 in 1 pattern, chainmail is excellent at protecting from slashing attacks, fair at protecting from piercing attacks, and not great at protecting from bludgeoning.

COUPLED with a padded shirt from the dead brute, I had a decent set of armor again. Definitely snugger than my leather, but it offered significantly more protection. The chain went down to my thighs, and then all the way down my arms. Practically speaking, there was a lot of other armor I needed, but now I was particularly looking for a pair of gauntlets.

Everything not chosen by the caravan was taken by Lee and inventoried before getting tucked into his wagon. Ultimately, everything could either be sold or bartered. I had a feeling I knew where the trade goods we had for the hunters had come from.

I retrieved my axe, still quite covered in gore from the fight, and wiped it off on the grass. I slid the axe into the side of the wagon, in reach of my seat. Just as I pulled myself up, I noticed Darius was having a very serious discussion with Cleeve. Also, there was still a giant tree across the road with forest encroached on either side. We'd need to move the tree before continuing our journey.

The guards had grabbed block and tackle from under one of the wagons and started to get a pulley system set up so we could drag the tree out of our way enough for the caravan to squeak by.

Reluctantly, I hopped back down, pulled the axe back out, and headed over to the tree.

Before I got there, Cleeve shouted from on top of the first wagon.

"Oi!"

Everyone stopped.

"We have a minor problem we need to solve before we move further," Cleeve said.

"Besides the tree?" piped up one of the guards.

"I can make you chop the tree into pulp. What I can't do is make you pull the wagon. We've got two draft horses down, plus all four guard horses down."

Everyone looked over to see the horses behind Darius. Most were limping. Blood trailed down their hides, a particularly poignant sight with chestnut draft horses. Darius was rubbing noses gently.

I felt a twinge of happiness that none of our horses had been killed in the battle — there's just something about animals dying that made me so angry and sad. Still, I saw the problem: we had a wagon full of stuff and no way to pull it.

"Drivers," Cleeve called out, "unload as much as you can from the first wagon, and add it to yours. I know we'll overload, but it's mostly flat until Saumiers, and we only need to make it there. Everyone else, on the tree."

While my curiosity lingered on the horses, I forced my focus on working on the tree. For the first time, the other guards gave me some attention. There was some joshing and talking, and even a few personal questions asked. Also, I finally learned the rest of their names.

There was Makkal Hamidov, with dark skin, big eyes, and one of the biggest smiles I'd ever seen. He was clean-shaven, which seemed to be the general look for the Empire.

Virginia Licinius was small but muscular with perfect black hair, a pert nose, and heavy armor. A small sword rested on one hip, and a larger sword hung on her back. She was really good with knots.

After getting all the pulleys set, we went about chopping all the branches, roots, and anything else that might prevent the tree from rolling. As a group, we grabbed the line, and started pulling. The trunk slowly moved off the road, and soon there was enough room for a wagon to squeeze by. The road wasn't completely cleared, but it was enough for us. It felt great to accomplish something together.

27

We turned our attention back to the wagons. The lead wagon was still very much full. The drivers were standing around arguing about which wagons could take more weight, and which horses weren't exhausted. Basically, they'd made exactly zero headway while we cleared the tree. Cleeve looked nearly ashen — this was something of a nightmare for him. Darius physically held up two horses while Cole tended their wounds.

I looked over at the harness, an idea forming. Then I pulled up my attributes just to be sure.

Attributes

Strength: 34

Agility: 15

Dexterity: 17

Constitution: 23

Wisdom: 13

Intelligence: 13
Charisma: 17
Luck: 27

UNASSIGNED POINTS: 0

34 SEEMED HIGH. But how high? I'd never really put it to the test, beyond pulling up an anvil. Plus, I was supremely curious how Mister Paul's Powerful Build boon applied to me, and the world. This was a chance to see where my limits were. And I kind of wanted to know.

I set my axe in my wagon and walked over to the empty harness. How could I get the leather straps made for horses match up with a lowly human? I tried settling the big collar around my neck, and I leaned into it.

The weight was immense. At first. But once I got my legs down and really pushed, the wheels creaked, and the wagon moved.

I heard shouts all around me, and everyone stared. I didn't care. I had something to do, something to test myself against, and that was everything I wanted at the moment.

It took virtually everything I had to pull the wagon, which was great, because it meant there was nothing left for my brain. Finally, there was quiet in my head. I didn't think about home, I didn't think about people I missed, people I'd wronged, people I'd loved. I just pulled a big fucking wagon.

My stamina bar dropped precipitously, but I kept going. This was my challenge. My legs burned. My heart screamed at me. Blood pumped around my body, and it felt like I was on fire. I gulped air in like I was drowning, but I kept going. I could barely see where I was going. There must've been people who helped guide me along, because I made some turns.

And then, there was someone standing in front of me, gently pushing me back.

"Time to stop," came a soft voice.

I nodded, dropping to my knees, taking in breaths in ragged gulps. True exhaustion washed over me. I thought, maybe, I might just keel over and die. I did the keeling part, and a wave of darkness crashed over me.

28

I woke up to someone poking me.

Cleeve stood above me with a sharpened stick.

"You need to eat," he said.

I mumbled something in return, and he lashed out, snapping the stick against my shoulder.

"UP," he barked.

My body started acting before I did. I shook off the cobwebs, stood up, and stumble-walked from the road where I'd fallen to the fire where Cleeve guided me into a seated position on a stump. Teela pushed a bowl of stew in to my hands.

I drank it down.

Immediately, my bowl was refilled.

The second helping took a moment or two more. As soon as it was done, I felt a real warmth in my stomach, and things didn't seem so bad. I handed the bowl back and stretched, letting out some sort of godawful roar as I pulled my screaming muscles apart. My body just wanted to remain still and small, and I knew that was the worst possible thing I could do after strenuous exercise.

The whole caravan stared at me.

With a little wave, I awkwardly slipped out of the circle of firelight, over to the outside of the wagons, where I grabbed my axe and started my guard duty.

The sun had slipped below the horizon, but it wasn't quite dark. It was that magical twilight sort of time where the sky was a brilliant, almost iridescent, purple, and the stars were only starting to twinkle far to the east. Back in the river lands, I'd spent this time watching the murmurations of birds, but here, the trees blocked most everything. If there even were starlings above these forests.

I did a bit of stretching, rolling my shoulders, jumping up and down. I knew I'd be in pain tomorrow, regardless of my regenerative ability.

There were footsteps coming from around the wagon. I turned to watch Cleeve come around and lean against the wagon in front of me.

"Few questions come up about you," he said, pulling out a pipe from a pouch.

I leaned on the axe, and smiled back. "You're welcome to ask," I said, "I'll answer what I can."

"You want to tell me who you actually are?"

"I have."

He pushed something into the bowl of the pipe, used a small piece of metal to somehow light the pipe, and puffed a moment before blowing a cloud of blue smoke into the sky.

"Kid," he said, "the oddities in this world are beyond counting, and I have seen well more than my fair share. But this marks the first time to see a man fight like you did, take wounds dire enough to destroy armor and leave you covered in blood, and then pull a fully loaded wagon that normally needs two draft horses for over half a day."

"I guess I'm special."

"But what are you?"

"Just a human."

"Human," he muttered, but there was much left unsaid there. He clearly knew I was hiding something.

"Look man," I countered, "I'm just a dude trying to find a better life here in the Empire, okay?"

"Are you now," he said flatly.

"I am."

"And you come from?"

"Like, over the mountains."

"Which mountains."

"The ones above Arenberg."

"Oh, the Wind Spires."

"Exactly."

"There is no mountain range called the Wind Spires."

"Well, we called them the Wind Spires."

"No, you did not," Cleeve said with authority. "Here, between the two of us speaking as free-thinking sentients, let us be honest, let us tell no lies."

I took a deep breath and met his eyes.

"No lies?"

"None."

"I come from another world," I said. I started to add *like Lee*, but I didn't want to out the man.

Cleeve nodded. "You are wise to keep that quiet. There are many who would see your kind exposed and exploited."

"Not you?"

"Not me."

"So there's the truth. I'm from Detroit. Earth."

"And now you are here."

"Now I'm here, trying to figure this bizarre world out."

"I have heard there are some differences."

"Tons. You know how there are character sheets here?"

"Yes," he said with a slight nod, blowing smoke rings into the sky.

"Does everyone?"

"Far as I know."

"Isn't that, I mean, weird to you?"

"'Tis how it has been from time immemorial."

"No one asks why?"

"I am sure there are many who ask why. Philosophers ask all sorts of stupid questions. Why does it matter why? For men like us, or at least like me, there is no time to ponder the why of the world. This is the way of it. Find the best way to work within the system of the universe. Or, spend your time asking the universe why. For me, it only matters what I do with it. What *we* do with it. Time spent pondering is time spent not doing. And I would rather do than think."

"I guess, I mean, can I ask about your character sheet? Is that, like, secret? Rude? I don't know. But I do know I have these boons. I think that's the reason I was able to pull that wagon. And why I can heal. And speak all sorts of languages. And maybe do other things. I mean, what skills do you have? And, like, what the hell are Indicium?"

"You do have many questions." Cleeve pulled off his jacket and bared his left arm. He closed his eyes, and a mark appeared across his shoulder: a bird of prey encircled by a wreath and a word. It disappeared before I could actually read it. "That it is an Indicium. This one means I was a member of the Imperial Legion. As far as character sheet, I am not sure there is a way to show you. Not unless you are wizard, and know the specific spell revealing those details. But, should you be a caster of magic, we have a whole new problem to deal with."

"Yeah." I smiled. "About that."

"Are you—"

"Why is magic outlawed?"

"Beyond the emperor decreeing it such?"

"Yes."

"In the early days of the Empire, there were problems with certain magic users. Three hundred years ago, the Empire was nearly overrun by a group of wizards who wanted to rule Vuldranni."

"So, it's like, totally illegal?"

"No. Those with the talent for magic and the will to engage with the mystic arts are simply required to be part of the Imperium. There are not as many as you might think. The will to use magic is much greater than those with the ability to do so. Some choose to fight with the Legion. Most are dispersed unto the countryside and work with farmers to ensure the Empire eats. And some—"

"Heal?"

"Healing magic is much more rare. More common is for a cleric to provide the means. Or an alchemist. Cole is one such alchemist. He makes potions for us, and for trade. He was once a healer."

"Why'd he stop?"

"That is a question you must get him to answer."

"Yeah, good luck with that."

Cleeve smiled, and blew another smoke ring out. "Yes, that might be a story that disappears with the man. But magicians, those are the men and women responsible for more nightmares in this world than anything else. This is why the Empire puts limits upon them, to make sure they are working for the good of the Empire instead of the end of the Empire."

I scratched my cheek, and then ran my hand down my

beard, giving it a tug and getting a few snarls out of it. I needed some oil.

"Can you tell me how to earn experience points?" I asked.

"Quests. Above all, quests will give you the most XP. They give the most points and offer the greatest chance for other benefits. Most believe the path to greatness lies in killing, for you do receive points for each creature you slaughter, but that is ultimately a fool's errand. The common folk, they often do not rise far in levels, only receiving what points they may through leveling skills or the few career-specific quests they encounter. But if you sit in a tavern any night, you will hear them complaining that if they just had skill with a blade, they too would be challenging kings and emperors."

"Where do quests come from?"

"Philosophically?"

"I'm looking more for the practical, but I'd take the philosophical I guess."

"The answer to both questions is the gods. They give the quests, they run the world. But if you keep your eyes and ears open, you will see quests appear. And, from what legend says, if a god decides to stand behind you, you will find quests just appearing everywhere."

"Is there, like, a job board in towns or something?"

"Sometimes."

"Will those be quests?"

"Sometimes. More often, they are just jobs."

"What about skills? You mentioned something about leveling up by leveling up skills."

"I did," Cleeve said. "While this holds true for most skills, there are some that are different. You receive a measure of experience points when you reach each new level in the hierarchy of skills. Level one: green. Level 10: novice. At that point you get some XP."

"How many levels are in the, what, hierarchy?"

"Eight."

"Naturally. I've noticed eight seems to pop up a lot here."

"'Tis true. Green is one through nine; Novice, 10 through 24; Apprentice, 25 to 49; Journeyman, 50 to 79; Professional, 80 to 94; Specialist, 95 to 99; Master, 100 to 199; and ultimately Grandmaster, which is 200 and above."

"Grandmaster is the top?""

"As far as I know. Finding a Grandmaster is rare. Exceedingly so. I have encountered but one."

"What is the highest you know of?"

"There is a baker in the capital, has been making bread for nearing two hundred years, and he has a level of 202 in baking. Day in, day out, he's making bread. These days, for the emperor and his family, save one day a week when he sells it in the market. Magical stuff. Legend tells of a swordswoman across the ocean and under realm who is nearing 300 in swords. Has never lost a duel, never lost a battle. But that 'tis but in legend. Perhaps when she reaches 300, we will see if the gods have another level for us. At present, it tops at at Grandmaster. And, at each new level, you receive more XP than before. So, despite never killing anyone, the baker is quite high-level."

My brain was starting to feel heavy with all the information Cleeve was dumping in it, so I decided it was time to change the topic. Besides, I was starting to get really tired, and I was worried about staying up for guard duty.

"Totally different topic, but have you seen the Emerald Sea before?" I asked.

"Once. I have thought often of returning. It is truly a

wonder. As long as we are here under the badge of honesty, 'tis one reason I am selling my medallion there."

"Medallion?" I asked.

He pointed to a small metal shield riveted on the side of his wagon. "Certifies I am part of the Caravaners' Guild. Gives me access to cities, countries. Even some of the most dangerous cities on the planet are still willing to receive Guild caravans."

"You can go anywhere?"

"Usually. Times of war might make things more problematic. But mostly, everyone leaves the guild alone. Otherwise the guild might leave them alone. Despite almighty power, one cannot march an army on an empty stomach. At some point, you will need a caravan. And without the Guild, you will likely not find one."

"But you can sell the medallions?"

"In a manner. Legally they remain property of the Guild. Should you wish to sell yours, you must go through the Guild. They hold an auction, and the Guild will pay you all but five percent of the auction price. Allows the Guild to keep control of their ranks."

"Seems complicated."

"Bureaucracy often is. And the Empire is nothing if not a massive bureaucracy."

"There's a lot about this world I just don't understand," I said.

"If you have questions, ask," he replied. "I cannot guarantee I have the answers, but I will try."

"Why are you being so nice to me all of a sudden?" I asked.

"You think you can pull the wagon again tomorrow?" he asked with a wink.

I rolled my shoulders and jumped on the balls of my

feet, trying to feel what my legs were willing to offer on the morrow. I wouldn't say I felt good, but there was some give.

"Probably," I said.

"You realize you are saving us with this, right?" he asked.

"Just doing what needs doing," I said.

He smiled a little, rueful. "We appreciate it. I appreciate it. Now get some sleep. You don't have to guard tonight."

Cleeve took a long pull from his pipe, and settled against the wagon. I nodded, and found my bedroll already laid out under a wagon. I was asleep as soon as I laid down, without even realizing how tired I'd become.

29

Morning arrived with a real surprise and kick in the teeth. It felt like the sun was in my eyes just moments after they were closed. Even the act of raising my hand to block the sun sent burning pain all around. My muscles were angry, and they were letting me know. I could barely move.

In both jest and kindness, someone had placed food next to me… in a feedbag.

Everyone else was awake, breaking down camp and going through the morning routine before travel, which meant I'd been allowed to sleep in. Which, you know, was nice. Considering.

I ate the dried meats and fruits and stood. Going slow. Very slow. I did some soft stretching, clenching my teeth together to swallow the screams of pain. It was interesting, because my HP was full, but the pain was still there. All new and fascinating stuff to figure out in this game world. So many things didn't make sense based on what I expected from reality.

I knew I needed to stop thinking about things in Earth

terms. I had to look at my new world, see how it played as a game, see how things lined up. It was a challenge, but if this really was a game, I had to keep up the grind. And I needed to see if there was some way I could tweak the system in my favor.

Lee sat atop his wagon, jingling the harness in my direction.

"Giddy up, buttercup," he said with a giant smile across his face.

I winked as I slipped into the harness.

"Neigh, motherfucker," I replied.

We weren't quite ready to go; camp supplies were still being loaded into other wagons. I leaned against the harness, letting it hold me up, feeling the tug on my shoulders.

"I gotta ask," Lee started, "how do you do it?"

"Do what?"

"Pull this thing."

"Just have the right strength score, I guess."

"How high is it?"

"Uh, hold on," I pulled my attributes up, and, as I did, I got some notifications.

Congratulations! Due to hard work, you've gained ***+9 STR!***

Congratulations! Due to hard work, you've gained ***+12 CON!***

I frowned a bit. Something seemed off with the numbers. I

guessed there was a chance the gods who built the game never factored in a human pulling a loaded wagon all day, but it just seemed, well, high.

~

Attributes

Strength: 43
Agility: 15
Dexterity: 17
Constitution: 35
Wisdom: 13
Intelligence: 13
Charisma: 17
Luck: 27

~

Unassigned points: 0

~

"Well, now my strength is, uh, 43," I said.

"Sweet Mary," Lee replied softly.

I was about to tell him about my boon, but I figured, maybe telling him about the strength was enough for the moment. I liked the guy, but I hardly knew him. It probably wasn't wise to give away all my secrets.

"What's yours?" I asked.

"Eleven."

"Oh. I'm not sure what's normal."

"Quick tip, hoss," Lee said, "that ain't normal."

"Eleven or 43?"

"I think you know."

I looked up ahead, watching Nikolai and Cleeve have a tense talk while attending their horses.

"What is it?" Lee asked.

"Nothing," I replied.

"You've got a question, I can see it. I just want to know what it is."

"Re-spawning."

"I wouldn't mention that around the locals. Not sure they know."

"So they don't respawn?"

Lee shook his head.

"How many times can you do it?"

"I don't know. I've only met four of our kind. One was heading into the desert, so I'd be willing to bet he'll be the first to know how many respawns we get. One is Darius, and one is you. And one was being executed for some rather heinous crimes."

"How'd you meet him?"

"I took a job in a jail for a short time. Doing their books."

"Sounds, uh, unpleasant."

"It was. Hence why I was eager to come on this caravan into the wilderness. The jails were horror shows. Nothing good about them. But this man was in there, said he could tell by how I mumbled that I was from Earth. That he was from Dallas. That he was someone I would have known. We chatted a few times. He had been in Vuldranni a spell, and he told me that it was a great freedom. To act as a sort of god, because we couldn't die. He felt it was okay to engage in terrible things because there weren't real punishments, in his eyes."

"He didn't mind the pain of getting killed?"

"I'm not sure. I might have mentioned something to the

jailer prior to leaving. So perhaps after being drawn and quartered, he might have a different view on things, but he said beheading wasn't so bad. Went by the name Sithus. Nasty man. Hope I don't encounter him again."

"You think you might?"

"I'd imagine, should he find out what I said to the jailer, I might."

"Okay. Well, Sithus is on the shit list. Got it."

"Have you died?" Lee asked.

"Yeah. It was awful."

"I have yet to have the displeasure."

Cleeve gave a big holler, and I did a jaunty little wave before starting the pull. I strained against the harness, swearing the wagon felt heavier than the previous day. But, after a moment of exertion, it started to roll. And then it was on.

Head down, watching my own feet, step after step. Going forward, inexorably forward, hoping we'd stop.

It wasn't easy. Shortly into the pull, the pain started. But the pain was less than the day before. There was more oomph behind each step, and I could pull the wagon a little faster.

My stamina bar still dropped pretty steadily. But once it hit zero, even though my body screamed at me and my health began to dip, I didn't want to stop. I couldn't. Quitting here, not going far above and beyond what was expected or needed, that seemed like a perfect recipe to get sent home. If I even could get sent home. Maybe it was a recipe for having a crap life here. Which wasn't an option. I had a second chance, and I was going to make something of myself. I was going to have a fucking good life as a good guy.

I kindled that fear, fanning those flames into a burning rage, daring the world to take this from me. Even though the leather straps felt like they were sawing through my shoulders, I pulled. Even though my legs felt like they were made of lead, I picked them up and pushed against the world. Hour after hour, I pulled that fucking wagon.

At some point, my body accepted the situation. It had two choices: adapt and overcome, or die. And my brain found a way to take me somewhere else. I thought about Detroit. About motorcycles and the wind in my hair. About my brothers in arms. About our fights and our parties. Our lives and our deaths.

How I was so fucking alone in this new land, and what the fuck was I going to do when I got to Osterstadt? See the Emerald Sea and find a beach shack so I could be a lonely hermit and fish? Maybe I was fated to make the same mistakes here as I did on Earth. It would be easy to fall back on violence against innocents to make my way through the world. Not that I'd been that bad back home. I didn't like, go around mugging people.

But I did make money by making sure people paid their debts, which sometimes required a little, um, incentivizing. And sometimes I delivered drugs. Sometimes I dealt drugs. And yes, I made a ton of money selling drugs to the elderly. The Club's single best money-maker was this place called Latte Bloomers, a cafe inside a retirement community. It was just the way I knew how to make money after all my legitimate means dried up.

And, because there was no way around it, because I had no means of controlling my brain, my thoughts went to her. Our perfect little life. Our dreams. We'd played games like this one together. I wondered what she'd think of living in one. How she'd want to play this new world.

No.

I shook myself out of it and got back some measure of

control. I pulled harder. I completely disregarded my body in an attempt to drown out my memories and thoughts. I stumbled forward, just pulling and pulling. My hitpoint bar dipped lower and then up, then down and up and down and up. My regeneration seemed to balance out the damage my completely depleted stamina was doing. Bit of a loophole — I wasn't technically in combat, so my regeneration seemed to handle keeping me alive. It hurt like a motherfucker, but I wasn't dying. And the more pain that came, the less I could think. I decided I'd stay in this pain-limbo indefinitely.

30

Darkness swept over and we came to a halt.

I dropped to my knees, my muscles quivering. I swallowed hard, doing my damnedest to keep from throwing up. I'd definitely pushed myself harder than the previous day, and by the end of it, my regeneration hadn't been able to fully keep up with the HP drain. In a technical sense, I was damn close to death. But I'd gone as long as we needed — I'd pulled the wagon all the way tonight. I knelt there, my body shaking, wondering if I'd be able to do it again tomorrow.

A hand rested on my shoulder.

"You think you can do a bit more?" Cleeve asked quietly.

I looked up at him, wanting to punch the man. To be completely honest, I was telling my arm to move, to punch him right in the fucking face, but my body wasn't able to follow through with it. I just stared at him instead.

"How much?" I finally managed to croak out.

Cleeve helped me to my feet, and he pointed. The sun had set in front of us, providing a beautiful spray of colors behind distant mountains. But there was a gentle point of light at the bottom of a gentle grade, somewhere in the neighborhood of half a mile away. "That is our destination," he said.

"Osterstadt," I said, relief flooding my voice.

Cleeve just laughed out loud, a deep barking laugh, and shook his head. "No, Montana, not even close. That is Saumiers. The end of civilization. At least, it is the end until we get to Osterstadt."

"Wait—"

"No roads after Saumiers."

"I want to ask why. I'm just—"

"Tired," Cleeve replied for me.

"It is newer land for the Empire. The only road to Osterstadt runs straight from the capital. There are no lords yet. Land is there for the taking. Opportunity exists there like no other, provided you are willing to tame the wilderness."

"But Saumiers—"

"Was, in the not-too-distant past, the last city of the Empire. Well, perhaps city is too generous. Village with walls is more accurate. We need to get there, transfer some goods, and heal some horses."

"Transfer goods?"

"Not something you need worry about," Cleeve replied, giving my shoulder a squeeze. He turned and addressed the rest of the caravan. "Able hands, assist Montana. We make Saumiers *TONIGHT!*" he shouted.

Cleeve pulled himself into the harness, and started pulling. The wagon didn't move. Not wanting the man to look weak, I wearily stood, and started pulling again. Everyone else, save the three drivers, swarmed the wagon. We made our final push.

31

The last bit of the haul through the gate was done by yours truly. I'm not exactly sure why the group wanted to let me finish, but they did. The presence of the guild badge made entrance into Saumiers simple. As soon as the guards saw the badge, they whipped the giant door open. It revealed a positively provincial little town that ticked every last box I had in my head for "medieval Europe." Cobblestone roads, thatched roofs, wattle and daub housing. There was quite a bit of common green space within the walls, and sheep lazily grazed on the grass.

The rest of it is a little fuzzy. I remember the guards directing us towards a particular inn and hauling the wagon to a large open space next to it. I didn't bother to do anything to help the caravan; I just stumbled out of the harness and into the inn. I gave someone some coin, and was led to a room where I promptly crashed into a bed and passed the fa-huck out.

32

I woke to moonlight, or moonslight I guess, considering there were four moons up in the sky, streaming through the window and across my face. With the moons high in the sky, I figured it had to be quite a while until dawn. I moved slowly, trying to get up without a ton of hurt.

It didn't happen.

The pain was intense, and I had to fight to get upright. It felt like I was ripping my muscles completely apart. Which, to be fair, was kinda what was happening. I'd almost killed myself through over-exertion. Had it not been for the incredibly generous boon from Mister Paul, I would have died. It should have been an impossible task.

Instead, I pulled it off.

Hah.

Pulled.

I never wanted to pull anything ever again, but I had a terrible feeling that wasn't going to be possible.

I looked around the room while I sat on the bed and let the pain surge through my body. It was a small room, with a single bed taking up most of one wall. A heavy writing desk sat under the window and a tall dresser rested against the wall opposite the bed. On top of the dresser, I saw big pitcher of water sitting in a large bowl.

There was barely any floorspace, but I managed to adapt a stretching routine I remembered from my time doing jiu jitsu. The pain lessened. I started to feel limber again, less constrained by my body. A body that was, as I looked at it, vastly different than when I'd first come into the world. Or how it had ever been on Earth. I used to be strong and had muscle, but it was under a heavy layer of fat. Here though, I had a metric fuck-ton of muscle rippling over my entire body. Way more than I'd ever had in my previous life. I looked like the guy who kicked sand in Conan's face. Who knew what we'd been eating on the road — I had a feeling I didn't actually want to know — but the end result was definitely a stripping of the body fat I'd started with. I was jacked A to the fucking F. I wished I had a mirror, or even better, a body building competition to enter. But, the gamer in me was yelling. I was making a hyper-focused strength build, and I needed to get my agility and dexterity attributes on the same level. Otherwise I'd wind up being some muscle bound idiot unable to wipe his own ass.

I took some water from the pitcher and splashed it on my face. Then I slicked my long hair back. I said a quiet thank you to Mister P — he'd done a good job on the hair. I'd yet to see my face, but I loved the beard. In the old life, I didn't have the genetics to grow much of a beard.

Then, I slipped out the door and walked down the hall. Plenty of grunting was coming form one of the rooms, so I started tiptoeing. I didn't want to ruin anyone's after-hours activities.

33

The staircase led down to the tavern space, where a fire still burned, providing just enough light to see around the room. Small tables made of rough-hewn wood were scattered about, surrounded by simple chairs. Broad beams ran across the ceiling, and a thick bar held the entire north wall.

A heavyset man stood behind the bar, cleaning a mug with a rag. He looked up sharply as I hit the last step, which creaked.

"Morning," he said cheerily. A smile took over his ruddy face.

"Is it?" I replied, really starting to miss having a watch. It was such a small thing, but never really knowing the time bothered me.

"Somewhere closer to sunrise than sunset."

"Did you sleep?"

"Not yet."

"Oh. I—"

"Come on over — let me get you something to eat."

"No, that's—"

"Comes with the room."

I shrugged, realizing the man wasn't going to let me go. I weaved through the tables, noticing one drunkard clumped in a dark corner and a duo opposite him who were, well, busy.

At least I wasn't the last patron.

He pointed to a stool, I sat, and he slid a large plate in front of me. A whole chicken. Then, he produced a side plate heavy with fried potatoes.

"Drink?" he asked.

"I know it's weird, but milk?"

"Butt milk?" he asked, but before I could respond, he cracked up at his own joke. "Coming up."

A second later, I had a massive mug of milk next to my wooden plate.

"Now," the innkeep said, "the name is Owen Stillingfleet. You?"

"Montana," I replied.

"That is it? Just one name?"

"That's it. Is it odd?"

"'Tis. For the Empire at least."

"I don't know that much about the Empire. Just, you know, that I'd like to be here."

He winked. "Glad to have you."

"Thanks. Could you, like, give me the heads up on the Empire? Maybe tell me a little about the place?"

"I am an innkeep. I can tell you something about anything if you buy my food and drink. But perhaps you could tell *me* something afore I tell you something."

"Sure."

"Did you really pull that wagon out there in my field by yourself for two days?"

"Just a day and a half."

He reached out and grabbed my shoulder, giving it a bit of squeeze. "I might actually believe that."

"Believe what you'd like," I said, ripping off a chicken leg, and taking a big bite.

"Now what is it you would like to know?"

"This was the border of the Empire, right?"

He nodded.

"What happened? Who did you go to war against to get, like, whatever is next to you?"

"There be plenty who will say the land here still belongs to no one, despite the emperor. I hear you are all headed over to Osterstadt, yes?"

"Yeah, is that a ways from here? Still trying to pick up the geography."

"Osterstadt was its own nation. Own state or what have you. The city has excellent exports, so a fair amount of coin to toss about and keep control. But about five years, I think, or less — I lose track of the seasons up here — Osterstadt became unable to handle its monster problem. They believed they were going to be overrun, and so they reached out to the emperor for help. The emperor, of course, wanted more empire, so he asked Osterstadt to bend the knee. When they did, the emperor did what the emperor does — protected what is his. He sent the Legion and they thumped the monsters and drove them back into the Emerald Sea from whence they came.

So, even though Osterstadt made no claims on these lands, none else had either. So the emperor felt it was his, and made known that everything from this small town of Saumiers to the shores of the Emerald Sea were his. Mark my word, the emperor will be trying to take the Emerald Sea next."

I laughed and popped a potato into my mouth. They were delicious, and I told Owen as much.

"The missus will be happy," he replied with a smile. "Her recipe."

"How long has the Empire been—"

"Here? My great-grandfather fought this city as a Legionnaire. He spilled blood on this spot. They took the city, and they conquered its people. After the war, when he retired, he returned and bought this tavern." Owen pointed over my shoulder to a sword and shield mounted above the fireplace. "As a whole, the Empire has been around a thousand years. Sometimes growing. Sometimes shrinking. The Gods alone know who will be a good leader, and who will guide us to ruin. But still, the Empire remains."

He snatched a mug from below the bar, pulled on a spigot to get a frothy mug of ale, then took a long drink. He sucked the foam from his mustache, and leaned back against the wall.

"You," he said, gesturing with the mug and spilling just the slightest drop, "might want to do a better job hiding who you really are."

"How do you mean?"

"The Empire, as a general rule, is most fond of, well, the Empire. Now I know you are with Cleeve Dye. I know the man. Actually know him, not just of him, and I wager if he trusts you, you are a good sort. But you are either of the Empire or not. So take a second name, and start referring to 'us.' Not 'you.' Especially once you get around those Legion boys and girls. They are quick with the blade and hot blooded, the lot of them. Always eager for a fight and eager to prove their worth to the Empire. If you are not an Imperial citizen, there are many laws you are not protected by."

"Not yet an outlaw, not yet a citizen?"

He gave a rueful smile. "Something along those lines."

"I mean, I guess I was, in a way, born here, so doesn't that make me a citizen? Or, maybe you could just adopt me? Then I'd be a citizen, right?"

Owen blinked a moment, definitely caught off-guard. Then he laughed, a sharp bark and a guffaw.

"Oh," he said, dragging the word out long, "it would be all manner of interesting to have you as part of the family. But I have to decline, sadly. You come into this family, and the missus will have you helping out the family business. Afore long you will find yourself stuck in the ruts of this dump."

"It's no dump."

"Oh, you have yet to see the capital, have you."

"Haven't seen much of anything," I replied. "Basically just the road between here and Arenberg."

"Capital is worth a trip. Most amazing place I ever beheld."

"I'll add it to the bucket list."

He took a sip, and raised an eyebrow at me.

"Saying from back home," I said.

"And here I thought you were a man of the Empire."

"Right. I am. So it's a phrase I made up. A list of things to do before you die. You know, kick the bucket."

He shrugged. "Okay. Not sure that one will do much catching on here. Why would you kick a bucket to begin with?"

"No idea."

"As commonplace as danger and death are in the Empire, probably not good to go around talking about what you want to do afore you die. Probably best to just do it."

"Is it dangerous out?"

"Where?"

"Here. I mean if I wanted to go out for a nighttime stroll—"

"I wouldna."

"You wouldn't, or you wouldn't if you were me?"

"Iffn I were you, I might, but only to knock a few heads in for some rough lads I want to learn a lesson. But lookin' at you, I think you might not know how to pull your punches, and we need all the those lads we got in case something comes down out of the North this winter. But if I were me, and I am, I might go out and be okay because those rough lads and lasses know where the beer is in town, and who would not be getting any if they muck about with me. So, you want to be having a fight, you might go for stroll."

I thought about it, and while I'd never been one to back down from fights in the past, it seemed foolish to go looking for them for no real reason. And I didn't want to be the asshole who murdered a bunch of punks on his first night in town.

"Noted," I said. "Thanks."

Owen gave a lethargic salute with his mug, and then polished off his ale with a last quaff. In an incredibly swift and smooth motion, he went from drinking to hurling the mug right over my shoulder across the room. There was a hollow *thunk* from the darkened corner.

"Ouch!" came a cry.

"Get your lazy arse down the stairs and into your bed you worthless sack of troll dung!" Owen shouted.

I watched, bemused, as the young man extricated himself from a young lady. The man went through door, while the lady went upstairs.

"Evenin'," Owen said sweetly to the girl as she passed.

She blushed in response, and ran a little faster up the stairs.

"Sorry 'bout that," Owen said. "But I thought it time I get to sleep."

"Was that—"

"My worthless spawn? Yes. My son is betrothed to that lovely girl. We are waiting for the solstice afore they get married, but, as her family has a farm a week and a half north of here, she chooses to live and work in the inn. Learn the profession she will have. And she is fantastic. Best serving girl we have. My son, on the other accursed hand, is worthless. Cannot cook. Burns the simplest of foods. Cannot chat or serve drinks. Says it is beneath him. Says he is allergic to horses and hay. So he cannot be around the barn. He thinks to join the Legion. Thinks life there is glory and medals. Shiny swords and shimmering armor, not willing to listen to an old man tell him that this here, this is the easy life. Little does the little lad know. Anyhow, to bed, good sirrah. Sleep well."

It was perfectly clear he was shooing me from the dining area and back to my room. I thanked him again for the food, and retreated upstairs.

34

I hopped into the bed and tried to sleep. Mostly, I just stared at the low wood ceiling, so I finally went through the notifications I'd been ignoring:

~

GG! You've killed a Human (lvl 5 Bandit Berserker).
You've earned 250 xp! What a mighty hero you are.

~

GG! You've killed a Human (lvl 4 Bandit).
You've earned 200 xp! What a mighty hero you are.

~

GG! You've killed a Dwarf (lvl 3 Bandit).
You've earned 150 xp! What a mighty hero you are.

~

***GG!** You've killed an Elf (lvl 6 Bandit Archer).*

You've earned 325 xp! What a mighty hero you are.

~

*Oooh, your skill in **Large Weapon Throwing** has gone up to lvl 10. Fancy a game of catch? +3% dmg, +5% skill.*

~

*Oh my gosh, shut the front door, you reached level 10 in the skill **Large Weapon Throwing**! You are now a Novice Large Weapon Thrower! For that, you get 1000 xp!*

~

*Huzzah! Against all odds, you have reached **Level 4**! You receive 6 attribute points to distribute in the next 36 hours or you lose them. Dare to believe you can survive, and achieve greatness. Or don't.*

~

Crap, I thought, and hurriedly looked at my character sheet. The six unassigned points were still there. When had I gone up in level? It must have been after pulling the wagon for the first afternoon. Whatever the case, I still had the points for the moment, so I quickly tossed two points into Dexterity, two into Agility, and two into Charisma.

~

*Congratulations! Due to hard work, you've gained **+12 STR**!*

*Congratulations! Due to hard work, you've gained **+18 CON**!*

*Wowza, a trait! Despite pain, despite depleted stamina, despite riding on the cusp of death, you did not give in. You did not waver. You have gained the trait, **IRON WILL**. Stamina no longer applies to you. What a beast you are.*

Not a bad haul. Apparently nearly killing yourself all day long is a pretty good way to pump up some attributes. Still, I felt like I wasn't doing quite enough to really make sure I was going to be able to take full advantage of the game I was living in.

I pulled up my character sheet to look at things and try to make a plan of sorts.

Montana - Lvl 4 Nothing

Traits

Race: Fallen

Height: 6'3"

Weight: 280 lbs

Eye Color: Hazel

Hair Color: Blonde

Renown: 0 - No one even knows you exist.

Statistics

HP: 239

STAM: n/a

MP: 232

Armor: +24 (Chain Mail)

Active Effects: None

~

Attributes

Strength: 55

Agility: 17

Dexterity: 19

Constitution: 53

Wisdom: 13

Intelligence: 13

Charisma: 19

Luck: 27

~

Unassigned points: 0

~

Skills

Riding - improvised (LVL 1): You can now ride improvised devices. +5% to handling.

Falling (LVL 1): You can flail through the air with the best of them. Watch for the sudden stop at the end.

Animal Handling (LVL 5): You can calm down a domesticated animal, keep a mount from getting spooked, intuit an animal's intentions, or, if you're really lucky, tame a wild best.

Investigate (LVL 1): Now when you don't know, try and figure it out! +5% to find the hidden, +5% passive perception

Harvesting (LVL 5): You can pick plants, you can grab fruit, you can cut neat things out of creatures you slaughter. That'll save the world, right? At Level 5, you are able to harvest common elements with no penalties. +10% successful gathering chance

Swords (Lvl 3): You can swing sharp objects and likely not hurt yourself. +7% damage. +7% skill.

Spears (Lvl 4) Remember, the pointy end goes towards the enemy. +8% damage. +8% skill.

Unarmed Combat (Lvl 9): You can strike with the fist or the foot, and must register your hands as lethal weapons. -13% stamina drain. +13% damage.

Axes (Lvl 8): You can chop down limbs of trees or men. Or monsters. +12% damage, +12% skill

Large Weapon Throwing (Lvl 10): Take that massive weapon and throw it away! +13% accuracy, +13% damage

War Hammers (Lvl 5): Everything IS a nail. +9% damage, -9% stamina drain

Light Armor (Lvl 3): A little bit of leather goes a long way. +7% dmg reduction, -7% movement penalty

~

Abilities

The Sword of My Enemy is My Sword: You've found that, in a pinch, every weapon will do. +1% dmg for each new weapon used in a combat.

Iron Will: Stamina no longer applies to you. What a beast you are.

~

FEATS

None

Boons

Powerful Build (Mister Paul) - You are bigger than you look. For all strength roles, you are counted as one size category larger than you actually are.

Regeneration (Mister Paul) - Outside of combat, your body will repair rather quickly. Given enough time, it's possible you will heal from nearly any wound.

Gift of Gab (Mister Paul) - Should you encounter a language you do not understand, as long as you hear at least three words of it, you will understand it, and speak it, perfectly.

Indicium

None

RELATIONSHIPS

Rumib Pass (destroyed) - Liked

LANGUAGES

Goblin

Imperial Common

Mahrduhmese

Spells

Lifeform Identification (Lvl 1) (costs 1 mana) Identify uncommon or lower lifeforms.

Basic Object Identification (Lvl 1) (costs 1 mana) Identify any non-magical common or lower item.

Heal Other [lvl 1] (costs 100 mana). Through the use of magic you are able to heal another through touch. Heal 50 Hp.

Humus [lvl 1] (costs 10 mana). This spell gathers dirt and organic materials, moisture, and bacterial ingredients within one mile/level of the caster and places the mixture anywhere the caster wishes within range. This is humus, the black, enriched soil excellent for growing plants in pots or gardening. Of course, the mage may use it however he wishes, but it is usually for growing things in pots and window boxes. If no such materials are within one mile/level, the spell has no effect.

I GUESS I LOOKED GOOD. I mean, I hadn't seen a single other character sheet, but based on gaming I'd done in the past, I felt pretty reasonable about it. My strength was starting to get away from me, which could be good, could be bad. Regardless, I needed to work on agility and dexterity, or I'd be in trouble. Technically, I needed to work on a bunch of stuff. I was still green in every single skill I had, and I needed to get those up. Especially if I was ever planning on going up against something more than a low-level bandit. And my best skill involved throwing my primary weapon away. I doubted even I'd be able to carry enough battle axes, war hammers, or great swords to make it through an entire fight throwing them.

With time to kill — I couldn't sleep — I knew the best thing I could do was start grinding a skill. I pulled a knife out of my pouch, and was about to work on small weapon throwing when I rethought that particular gem of an idea. It'd be a spectacularly dick move to ruin Owen's walls just because I wanted to get better at knife throwing.

Instead, I looked over the room, trying to think of something I could practice without damaging anything. Or disturbing anyone else. I got out of bed and looked at the desk. Seemed sturdy. I stood flat footed, and jumped up on to the desk. Not super hard, but there was a real challenge do it, making sure I didn't catch a toe and defenestrate myself.

Jump after jump, my quads were starting to burn a bit. Then it happened.

*Cool Beans, you've learned the skill **Jump**. You can leap, skip, perhaps even hop. Perhaps with enough practice, you'll be able to leap tall buildings with a single bound. But let's not hold our breath. +1% to distance, +1% to height.*

Boom. New skill.

By the time the sun rose over the hills to the east and shone down on the village, I'd done enough jumping. I'd managed to get it all the way to level 6, and though I couldn't quite make it to the top of the dresser, I was getting closer. And, I was feeling the cabin fever. I wanted to do something outside. I practically bounded down the stairs into the tavern. Cleeve sat at the bar talking to Owen. Some of the guards and drivers were scattered around, eating their breakfasts. Everyone had a warm smile for me. I gave my awkward wave.

Cleeve looked up and motioned for me to join him. As I walked over, Owen whispered something before sliding away and out a door behind the bar.

"You got something, boss?" I asked.

"I do," he replied. "Before anything else, did you really mean to pay for everyone's rooms last night?"

I blinked a few times and frowned, thinking. "Maybe?"

"You gave him a gold. Rooms here are a silver. I was going to cover the cost, but—"

"No, that's fine, I meant to," I lied. What's money anyway, right?

"Very generous. A fair amount needs to get done in town today. Most of it rote boring stuff that a man of your skills is not exactly suited for."

"No wagon pulling?" I asked with a slight smile.

"No, not for the moment. We are done with wagons for a spell."

I must have looked very confused because Cleeve just laughed at me.

"From here to Osterstadt, there's no roads," he said. "But there is a lake."

"There's a lake. Is—"

"Sometimes I forget that you have no idea of the geography here. Saumiers borders a rather large lake."

"So, boats?"

"You leave that to me, Montana. For today, I need you to work with Nikolai."

"Training?"

"No."

"Then wha—"

"Just ask Nikolai. He has the details, not I."

"Got it, boss," I said, turning to look for Nikolai.

"Oh, and Montana," Cleeve suddenly asked, "did you really ask Owen to adopt you?"

I shrugged. "Seemed like a potentially good idea."

Cleeve shook his head and turned back to his breakfast.

There was a whistle, and suddenly Nikolai was standing next to the exit of the inn.

"We are off, rook," he said, turning and leaving the place before I could respond.

35

The morning air was crisp, fresh, and amazing. I took in deep lungfuls, feeling invigorated by the whole world around me. Hoarfrost hung on the edges of leaves in the shade. It smelled like fall.

Nikolai was already over by the wagons, glaring at me for doing such ridiculous things like smelling the world. Darius was already out with the horses, brushing them, checking their wounds, that sort of thing. Nikolai pulled his armor out of the wagon and checked it over, pulling some of the straps and making sure everything was ready to go. Then, he pulled it on. I hopped in to help with some of the harder to reach buckles. He had a pretty impressive set: banded iron cuirass, big metal pauldrons, a chunky metal collar thingy—

"Can you, I guess, tell me the name of the armor bits you've got?" I asked.

He blinked at me a few times, and then sighed.

"Helm," he said, pointing to his head. He had a full face cover with a large T cut out of the front for eyes and nose and mouth. "Gorget." The chunky metal thing around his neck. It went down both his chest and back and covered some of his clavicles. "Cuirass." The banded metal bit covering his torso. "Pauldron." His shoulders. "Vambrace." Forearms. "Gauntlets." Gloves.

He took a deep breath. "You want all the bits I don't have on?"

"Sure."

"Greaves cover the lower leg. Cuisse covers the thigh. Sabaton goes on the foot. Sometimes you'll have a Poleyn to cover the knee. The Besagew covers the armpit. Rerebrace covers upper arms. Couter covers over the elbow. Faults go to hips. Plackart is extra belly cover. And there is more. Lots more. Little bits and bobs of metal to keep you safe from the smallest little poke, and all pointless if you do not know what the fuck you are doing. All of that, the bits and bobs, is what comes with a full set of plate given to a noble puke so they can ride down peons and goblins and return home in one piece covered in glory. No one I know has full plate, because it is fucking expensive. You should concern yourself with this," he held up a shirt of chainmail that looked to cover torso and arms. "Hauberk. Probably all you get for a spell."

"Are there pants?"

He looked a me for a moment, then dug into the storage portion of the wagon. He pushed a bunch of stuff around, and then pulled a pair of chain mail pants out and held them up.

"Chausses," he said. "Put 'em on."

"Thanks, Nikolai."

"Yeah. Sure. I suppose today is about learning."

"Yay?"

He shoved the mail onto me. "Time is wasting."

Chain Mail Hauberk

Item Type: Common

Item Class: Medium Armor

Material: Iron

Armor: +16

Durability: 80/100

Weight: 44 lbs

Requirements: Str 10

Description: Interlocking iron rings designed to stop slashes, stabs, and comfortable sleep, chain mail has been a staple armor since shortly after the invention of swords.

I PULLED the armor on while he strapped belts and scabbards about his body. He gave me my large axe and a small sword.

SHORTSWORD

Item Type: Common

Item Class: One-handed Melee

Material: Steel

Damage: 7-12 (Slashing)

Durability: 14/20

Weight: 2.8 lbs

Requirements: Dex 8

Description: A straight-bladed sword having a cruciform hilt with a grip for one-handed use.

I GAVE the sword a few practice swings, just getting a feel for it.

"Put that in the scabbard already and stop looking like a fucking twit twirling about," Nikolai snapped.

Suitably chagrined, I slid the blade in the scabbard.

Nikolai did a quick check of my armor, pulling things, shifting it, looking me over.

"Can I ask what we're doing?"

"No," Nikolai replied.

He waved to Darius, who nodded in return, and then Nikolai started off down the street. I followed, trying to quell the terrible feeling rising. I'd spent too much of my previous life following blindly, and it'd turned my life into a dumpster fire. And I didn't want another dumpster fire, not when I had the chance to actually live. But was I just falling back into my old patterns? Was I just fated to be the same idiot in this life as the last?

36

We headed through the gates of the city, out towards the wilderness. As we climbed the slight hill just north of town, I got a good look at the world around Saumiers. To the west was a huge lake, extending off into the distance, taking over a good portion of the horizon. High cliffs surrounded the lake, a dry and ominous opposition to the blue below. It was astounding how green and fertile the world around me was, and how dry and dead the world was around the lake. To the north I saw more large mountains — a rather ubiquitous sight in Vuldranni. Or at least in this part of it. Lots of glaciers glittered in the distance as well. Excitement welled in me as I thought of exploring this new land of mine.

We were on something like a path, like maybe it had once been a path, but had been mostly neglected, left to fend for itself against nature's incursions. It was more than a game trail, because in a few spots steps had been cut into the hillside, but there was a lot of overgrowth to push through. We passed by a bench, and my curiosity flared. The path had obviously been cleared for a reason, with a destination in mind. Why had it been forsaken? What might be there now?

Birds were everywhere around us, squirrels darted here and there, and a hundred animals I couldn't identify made noises as they went about their day, not seeming to care that we were interrupting them. It was a greater explosion of nature than I'd ever experienced, despite my Boy Scout years. This was a much more primal world than Earth, not necessarily younger, but filled with more life and, well, just filled with more. Everywhere I looked. Everywhere I listened.

We continued to climb, the town disappearing behind the dense forests, only to reappear in our vision every now and again. Steep drop-offs were commonplace, and I was keenly aware that a single poorly-placed step would get me splattered on the rocks below.

I don't know how long we climbed, but after a while, I just started to relax into the hike. I enjoyed the sunshine on my face. The wind in my hair. The deep smell of pine.

Until up ahead, I heard a thunderous roaring sound. Nervous, I slid the axe off my back and let it rest in my hands. We came around a bend, and discovered a staggeringly tall waterfall pouring into a surprisingly small pond. A small but very deep pond, it would seem. There was just enough hard rock to take the pounding of the waterfall and form a bit of a pool before disappearing down a hole. I could see no river leading away. Waves of mist blossomed out and enveloped the area in undulating waves.

Nikolai stopped at the edge of the pond, knelt, and filled a waterskin.

He drank deep, then tied the bag back to his belt.

Nikolai turned to me, his face hard. Impassive.

"Montana," he said.

"That's me," I replied, still not exactly used to the name, kinda wishing I'd picked something different. It just sounded so, well, like a beast of burden.

"It is time I told you what we are doing."

"Okay."

"We are here because it is time to talk about who you are and who we are."

"Dude, I can barely hear you," I replied, basically shouting at him. "Is this a hazing thing?"

"Only in part," he said, his voice somehow coming straight to my ear like he was right next to me. "Much like Montana is not a real name, Cleeve Dye is not a real name."

"Wait, is he a—"

He held up a hand, and cut me off, saying, "Your questions will be answered. First, though, I need to get a measure of who you are. You see, I need to know who and what you are before I kill you. Or let you live."

"Wait—"

"You may attack if you feel that necessary," he said, gesturing with his longsword at my axe. A longsword that I hadn't even noticed him drawing from his scabbard. The dude was fast. Scary fast.

Immediately, I tossed the weapon to the ground. Not only did I know he outclassed me, I didn't want to fight him. "Dude, I don't, I'm just trying to figure things out. It's all a bit of a shock."

"You concern me," he said. "Your strength is unusual. Minotaurs are known for their strength. Darius can move the wagons around unladen, but he is out of breath after twenty yards. And yet, you—"

"Hey," I said, hands up to make sure he knew I wasn't threatening him, "I was just as surprised as you."

"I do not think so. We know you come from another

world. The same world as Lee and Darius. And yet, they are not like you. I have spoken with them about their world at length, and about you. Dye as well. They are higher level than you. Yet, you are so much stronger than them. Than anyone. You are faster and fight with, well, not grace that is sure, but brutal efficiency then. That will not serve you long-term. Should you survive today, we will need to break you of that habit. You are an enigma. Immense power and yet stupid. You traipse about as a newborn, desperate for a family, for guidance, yet able to knock down a barn. Is this an act? I wonder."

"I'm completely new here—"

"As was Darius. According to the man, we were among the first faces he encountered here. Though we did not know immediately he was from your world, when he was level one, he had nothing like what you do. And, he did not blunder about as you do. He was actually able to blend in to the Imperial society, to a degree."

"So I'm new and stupid. Is that a crime?"

His blade swept up to my throat as I blinked. I never even saw the blur of movement; it was just there.

"Are you a demon?" he asked.

"No," I replied, being very careful not to move in the slightest.

"A devil?"

"Not even sure those are different."

"An abyssal fiend?"

"No idea what that is."

"What is your true form?"

"This?"

"You told Dye you were a criminal. Are you still?"

"No."

"What kind of criminal were you?"

"Bad? Enforcer? Debt Collector?"

"You hurt people?"

"I did."

"For money? Pleasure—"

"It was the only thing I could do that paid, man," I snapped, grabbing his blade and pushing it to the side. He let it move, but kept his hard eyes glued to mine. "And at the end, it was the only job I could get because I'd fucked my life up. The only person I never screwed over gave me the portal to this world because he knew I was about to be killed. And it just so happened I was in the mood to not die, so I didn't pay attention to what I was doing — I just tried to escape as quickly as I could. I have no idea about the Empire. I didn't hear anything about it until I got to it. I don't know where I am or what the rules are here. I have no idea of your history, your geography, the people, the culture, the monsters, I don't even know what language I'm speaking right fucking now. I'm just walking around like, I mean, yeah, a fucking toddler, hoping I don't die before I figure out what the fuck is going on, okay?"

Nikolai frowned. Then he flicked his sword down into the ground, sticking it perfectly in a small tuft of grass, the hilt wavering ever so slightly.

He put his hands together, closed his eyes, and his breathing slowed down. A slight glow came around him, and he reached out to grab either side of my head.

I saw purple. Different shades. Different shapes. It was all internal though, like my brain was exploding and moving around at the same time. My insides felt weird, like someone was poking and prodding at my spleen or something.

And then, it stopped. Everything immediately went back to normal.

Nikolai had removed his hands from my head and taken a step back, Then he looked me up and down, confused. Finally, he took a breath, and shook his head.

"Things are not as they seem with us," Nikolai said after a lengthy awkward pause. "With Dye."

"I know, it's a fake name."

"You know nothing—"

"Hey, was that magic?"

"Shut the fuck up," Nikolai barked. "I will give you a moment for questions, but that moment is not now. You will give me answers when I ask, and if I do not like your response or you attempt to lie, I will kill you. Everyone else believes we are on a quest right now, and I will merely say you died fighting goblins, trolls, or snipes."

He waited for me to say something, but I had the feeling he was testing me, see if I would pipe up again. I just stood there. Waiting. Which, frankly, was difficult. I'd never been able to hold my tongue when I needed to. I'd blurt out anything that came to my stupid mind. Say the wrong thing, be a pain in the ass while trying to be funny or cool. But this time, being quiet just seemed right.

The waterfall seemed to get quieter and the mist seemed to grow. Either this place or I was crazy. I didn't like my odds.

"Cleeve Dye is nobility. From a noble family with a long line of service to the Empire, spotless with honor. Thirty-five years in the Legion. Countless battles won. Medals from his head to his heels and a personal friend of the Emperor. Dye has the chance to be among the top of the land. To elevate his family to a level it has never been. He has promised to offer a place for the men and women who have served him where they might raise their families in safety, with the promise of a good and wholesome society. In order to make this future happen, he has given up his entire life, and tied it to that caravan out there. We need to get it to Osterstadt before the first snows fall."

Nikolai stopped to let this sink in. I just nodded.

"I cannot tell you why, but Dye has an attachment to you. He is curious and he likes you. I do not. I tried to have you removed from the caravan. Dye overruled me. I expected you to fight with the bandits, not against them. You fought bravely. Not well, mind you, but with courage. Your resolve to pull the wagon seemed a foolish stunt destined to end your life. And yet, you managed to stay alive and get us out of that jam. I hate to say I was impressed. I have looked inside you, taken the measure of your character as much as I could. You have immense potential with ridiculous strength. But I cannot help but wonder. If you were but an adventurer, why not remain for the coming war with Mahrduhm? War is the great path to experience and levels. You would be rewarded with both riches and fame staying there, welcomed with open arms into either army. Yet you fled. You leave me with questions and no answers."

Nikolai walked around me, looking me up and down. The mist was incredibly thick. I could barely see Nikolai after a moment. And when I blinked, he disappeared entirely.

"I have never actually met a Level Four Nothing," Nikolai said, right next to my ear.

I spun, trying to track him, but the man disappeared into the mist. Everything disappeared into the mist. Everywhere I looked, mist. I couldn't even see my feet.

"Tell me who you are, Montana, tell me and make me believe that killing you is the wrong idea. Or die."

"Even if you kill me," I said, "I will only come back stronger. "

"There are ways to bless a man with the final death,"

Nikolai said, stepping out of the mist, his longsword in his hand. A dark shimmer ran down the blade, and a spark shot off the end. He had a grim sparkle in his eyes, as if he was almost excited about something.

He swung his blade, and instinct took over for me. I wasn't ready to leave this life.

I snatched my sword from the scabbard, and got it up to block his blade, just in time. A sharp clang rang out as the swords met, and a chip of metal flew out, slicing along my cheek.

Hot blood leaked down into my mouth.

Nikolai pushed my blade away, and took a step back.

"Who are you, Montana?" Nikolai asked once again.

"I don't know."

"You agree with your classification of Nothing?"

"I do!"

His blade move so fast, even though I brought my sword up, his edge was right against my neck.

"Look, man," I shouted, my desire to live pushing my voice up an octave, "it's fucking accurate, okay? I was a nothing in my old life. I just, I mean, I did what I had to do in order to not die, I guess. I wasn't good at anything. I stole things. I killed a few drug dealers, stole their cash and their stash. I gave loans out and beat people when they couldn't pay 'em back. I drank beer on weekdays, dealt drugs to junkies, and I don't know. I didn't have parents, so I grew up in a foster system designed to fucking fail. But then for one glorious year, all I did was pound stakes into the ground, set up circus tents, sweep floors, groom horses, and was part of something like a family for the first fucking time in my life. But then, like countless times before, I followed a girl and wound up in a horrible fucking mess I wouldn't wish on any fucking person."

The mist started to dissipate, the falls returning to their original volume, and, in a moment, sunshine streamed down around us again.

Nikolai had something like a smile on his face. He had such hard features that even a grin came off more like a grimace.

"This way," he said, and pushed past me to start heading back down the trail. "Don't forget to grab your axe."

37

It took all of my willpower not to scream at Nikolai. I wanted to curse at the man because I'd been scared as fuck I was going to lose my shot at life, and he seemed to think that everything was fine and dandy after he basically said he was going to kill me. Of course, he was moving so fast, I didn't really have the chance to do anything like that.

I assumed we'd go straight back to Saumiers, but after a short traipse along the trail, Nikolai took a sharp turn, and we headed uphill. I was definitely jogging. I was tempted to pick up the pace, but I figured that might be dickish and prone to getting myself lost. Nothing like trying to take over the lead when I had no idea where I was going.

I lost track of the time again, something that seemed to be increasingly problematic. I wondered, once more, if there was a means of portable timekeeping in this world.

Finally, we came up to a rise, the trees thinning out just a bit. Nikolai slowed down and stopped right before we'd have crested the ridge.

He knelt, and motioned for me to do the same.

"Montana," he said, "it is time for you to begin training to be in this world."

"Okay—"

"First lesson: Talk less. Right now, you know nothing. You are nothing. Understand?"

I nodded.

"Based on your perplexed look," he said, "you are much more confused than normal. Which makes me think you have yet to learn to pay attention to the notifications you receive."

"I, uh—" I started to say, but Nikolai's hand blurred, and there was an audible crack as he slapped me.

"You will look at the notifications as you get them."

"It blocks my view," I whined. "I can't—"

There was a very deep and disappointed sigh from the man, like he just realized how stupid his pupil really was, and how much trouble any education might be.

"You are so new here, so unknowing. It is hard to believe. Let me start with the basics. You know how to read, yes?"

"Yeah."

"So you are not getting pictorial notices, this is good. We are now one step above toddlers."

"They get pictures?"

"Some. Pictures, feelings, intuitions, verbal even. The Gods know not everyone is able to read, so they make the system work. Do not ask how, it is not—"

"I wasn't—"

He slapped me again. I shut up.

"Reading is best. You have more control than other methods, and more information. But it requires you to be active. It requires you to think and make actual choices to get that information. Bring up your notifications. I know you have some."

He was right — there were a few in the corner. I willed them forward.

"Before you read them," he snapped, noticing my eyes were already unfocusing, "work on them to make them less invasive."

"Like, transparent?"

"Whatever works best for you. Place them where you will, how you will, just so long as you read them, absorb them, pay attention to the messages from the fucking GODS. They will stay in the places you put them. Find what works, and stick with it."

I thought about it for a moment, and the windows of text got a little clearer. Now I could see through them. I had trouble reading them, though, so I fiddled with the text coloring and the brightness, messed with the font a bit, then I started moving them around and—

"I did not realize how long you would need to do this," Nikolai said. "Perhaps find a good enough setting for now, and then when we are sitting around doing nothing, instead in the middle of the wilderness where any wandering monster might stumble upon us and chew us up into tiny tasty pieces, you can finalize and make it as pretty as you want to, pumpkin."

Pumpkin?

"Done?" he snapped.

I did a quick move of things, just so I could see the notifications in the edges of my vision, arranging everything so it was a little more like a traditional FPS UX. I felt like I was ready to go, and I saw what Nikolai wanted me to see.

You have been invited to join ***Nikolai's Party!*** *Do you accept? Yes/No*

I selected *Yes*.

Immediately, a small set of colored bars appeared above mine, matching my own: Nikolai's hitpoints, manapoints, and stamina. Red, Blue, and Green.

There is a party quest, you have automatically accepted the quest.

There is a party quest, you have automatically accepted the quest.

"We have quests?" I asked.

"There you go, getting on board," Nikolai replied. "We are here on a quest and a clean up. And I told you we were on a quest."

"To kill goblins."

"That was just a ruse. Come."

He crawled up the ridge and peeked over.

I followed and saw a small grey castle sitting in a slight depression. It was up against the hillside beyond, and looked pretty wrecked. One of its three towers had mostly collapsed and scattered bits of the southern wall across the area, leaving it with roughly two and a quarter spires. The portcullis was down, where it should be, but the gate was missing. Not a scrap of wood remained.

"Unique fixer upper opportunity," I whispered.

"Pay attention," he snapped back under his breath.

I wasn't exactly sure what I was supposed to be paying attention to, but after a moment, I saw movement. A humanoid walked across a window.

"What is this—" I started to ask, but Nikolai clamped his hand over my mouth, and pulled me down below the ridgeline.

"What have I said about speaking?" he hissed.

"Don't do it," I replied.

"We are here to rescue some missing townsfolk inside, and punish those who've been harassing and worrying Saumiers. They outnumber us. They likely out-level you. Your education begins today."

He crawled back to the ridgeline and peeked over. When I attempted, he used his foot to keep me from moving.

A moment or two passed, and I rolled over to look up at the sky, watching the clouds, clouds which got ominously dark over towards the west.

"Toddler," Nikolai said, "listen."

I ground my teeth together, but looked back to him.

"A storm will hit soon. My guess, it will be heavy rain. As soon as that comes down, we go over and around. I have a feeling there is a better way in along the side. Near the fallen tower."

"Who, or, I mean, what are we going to find in there?"

"Same as before. Bandits mostly. There is a chance of nastier enemies, but I did not have the time to do the reconnaissance I would like."

We watched and waited.

And waited.

The rain started to fall, and the clouds blotted out the sun. The castle glowed as torches and fires were lit inside. It made the place appear oddly comfy.

"Follow," Nikolai said. "Crouch down. Be stealthy."

As I opened my mouth, he held up a finger.

My jaw snapped shut.

He crouched-walked from tree to tree. I did as he did. Trying to put my feet where he put his and doing my best to match him. Still, I managed to make a lot more noise than him. It was frustrating to step in the same exact spot, but somehow snap a fucking twig. A damn twig I swear wasn't fucking there.

The rain saved me, its noise doing a stellar job covering up my mistakes. It soaked me through to the skin, and I could see my breath steaming out, but I didn't feel the cold that much.

The ground around the castle had been cleared a long time ago, but in the intervening years the trees and shrubs made a comeback, and there was just a bit of cover to sneak under.

Nikolai straight up belly-crawled to the wall.

I, too, crawled. Which brought about a number of issues. First, the chainmail picked up every bit of vegetation I slithered over. Second, the battle axe dug into my thighs, to the point where I thought I was going to wind up hamstringing myself before I got to the wall.

The stones of the wall were rough, old, and not well hewn. Clearly something that had been done by hand, though. They were stuck together with crumbling mortar — it really seemed like the right poke would topple the whole thing. I wondered if climbing was going to be a good option. Or a bad option. Good, easy handholds. Bad, the stones might just come out as soon as you put weight on them.

Nikolai looked up, then along the wall. He pointed to me, then pointed up. He pointed to himself, and then along the wall. Towards the mountainside.

I nodded.

"Do not wait for me," Nikolai whispered. "We do not know where they are keeping their victims. You must attack when you have the opportunity."

He didn't wait for any sort of affirmation from me. He just turned and slinked off along the wall.

38

I tested the rocks in the wall, and they held my weight. More shifting than I wanted, but they didn't fall out of the fucking wall. It was a unique sort of feeling, hoisting myself off the ground without any trouble. In my previous world, I'd rarely been able to do even a single pull-up, and here, I went up with just my arms. Like it was nothing.

At the battlements, I held off for a moment, just hanging on the wall letting the rain pour down over me, trying to listen to the world. Then I peeked over.

Nothing.

I pulled over and made an awkward tumble to the rampart. There might have been a bit of clanging and banging as my battleaxe hit the stonework.

I froze.

No movement anywhere I could see.

Ahead of me was the keep. A door led onto the ramparts. Windows along the side of the building showed there was, at least, light on the inside. So someone was in the building.

I edged along the walkway, shuffling my feet and doing my best to keep my silhouette low and my noise to a minimum. I peeked down at the courtyard, and while it was currently devoid of people, that could change at any minute. I saw several wagons in states of disrepair, looking like they were being taken apart, the wood being repurposed for other things. Like burning. An offal pit sat in the corner, illuminated by a small oil lantern hanging over a workbench nearby. It was disgusting, and I imagined the stench would be nigh-on overpowering were the rain not so heavy. Plenty of tables were down there as well, and it looked like someone had been using them to sort goods they'd taken out of the wagons. Everything indicated a bandit base. And everything indicated all the bandits were currently hiding in the keep, getting out of the rain.

Which left me with the question of strategy and tactics. There was no sign of Nikolai, and he'd done impressively little in sharing his plan of attack. Night wasn't far off, and we were quite a ways from Saumiers. There wasn't going to be anyone running in to save the day if Nikolai and I bit off more than we could chew. All that made me think the best plan would be to hit hard and fast. Shock and awe.

Still, I didn't want to just kick down a door and hope I'd overcome whatever was inside. I needed a little more intel — going in blind could definitely be a death sentence.

I climbed laterally along the wall until I could see in the window. A few minor problems: the bricks making up the keep were a little smaller and less grippy than those of the wall. In order to give me a enough of an advantage, grip wise, I took my boots off. There had been a ton of rain, and it was tough just getting my footholds secure. And, you know, the giant battleaxe on my back just gave me a mild imbalance issue.

Slowly, carefully, I moved across the wall until I was right next to a window. I leaned over just a teensy little bit, just to where my left eye was looking into the keep. The window was hazy — probably hadn't been cleaned in some time — and the glass had a distinct wave to it, making everything inside distorted. The scene wasn't bad, almost homey. A large crackling fire filled the fireplace, and candles had been placed around the room. A long table held a huge roasted carcass of some animal, steam coming out of the various spots where meat had been cut. A number of figures sat around the table, eating, drinking, and laughing.

After a few more moves, I was in front of the door, and back to thinking. Obviously, as Nikolai was so happy to point out, not my strong suit.

I ran through a couple of tactics, including standing on the lintel above the door and then waiting for someone to come out, but decided my best bet was a surprise entrance and a flurry of blows. I'd do my best to whittle down their numerical advantage, and hope Nikolai would hear and come up the stairs from the inside.

Pulling the axe off my back, I spun the haft in my hands, and tested my grip now that it was wet. Not bad. A few swings, and I knew I could hold the weapon. No problems. I shook out my arms, did a bit of light jumping up and down, getting the nerves out and muscles ready. Preparing to dole out death, hoping these were actually bad guys and I wasn't just being used.

39

I leaned back, got my foot up, and Sparta-kicked the door as hard as I could.

The wood splintered, and the door slammed inward, tilting as the top hinge popped off, which cantilevered the door hard enough the bottom hinge popped off. The thick wooden door dropped to the ground with a resounding thud.

Eight heads and sixteen, correction, fifteen, eyes snapped in my direction.

Lightening crackled behind, and thunder crashed as it seemed even the gods themselves were setting me up for one hell of an entrance.

I gave a roar, and threw my axe at the figure sitting at the head of the table.

The axe spun across the room, and slammed into, and partially through his torso. A font of blood erupted from the ruined man, enough that it caused a few cries of disgust. And maybe fear.

I had the sword out, and covered the distance from the door to the table in a heartbeat. I swung wildly, trying to get as much damage done as quickly as possible. I needed people out of commission before I got my ass handed to me by sheer numbers.

A short stocky fellow with a big bushy beard pushed his chair back, fumbling with something on the floor.

I kicked the chair, which flung the man's head against the table with a thunk. Then I jammed my sword straight down into him, through his body, and into the chair.

The blade stuck. I struggled to pull it back, trying to get it free, but whatever reverie had kept the others from leaping to their feet ended with me flailing with a fucking chair.

The other six in the room scrambled to their feet and grabbed for weapons.

I ducked a mace that whizzed right past my head. With no other options, I just picked up the entire chair. And dwarf.

~

You've picked up a **DWARF-CHAIR.**

Dwarf-Chair

Item Type: Improvised-Rare

Item Class: Two-handed Melee

Material: Wood/Dwarf

Damage: 30-45 (Bludgeoning), 3-4 (Sonic)

Durability: 7/11

Weight: 188 lbs

Requirements: Str 24

Description: A dwarf attached to a wooden chair, unable to escape.

~

NOT BAD DAMAGE.

The mace-wielder had left himself open after his wild swing, so I took advantage. The dwarf screamed with pain as I brought the chair down with all my strength. It crashed into mace-man, whose body seemed to double over for a moment before something inside snapped and he folded further. The extra weight of the dwarf definitely assisted in the kill of his former colleague.

I let my chair-dwarf drop, hooked my foot under the mace, and kicked it up. I snatched the handle out of the air, and managed to get the mace around just in time to block an axe blow from the left, while sucking my butt in to miss a sword jab from the right.

A power step and a ducked shoulder, and the slinky swords-elf went tumbling over his chair.

I couldn't finish the elf off because the human next to me, the woman with the axe, had trapped my mace haft with the hook of her axehead. She gave a wicked smile, then pulled hard, trying to disarm me.

But high strength is a motherfucker. I just pulled back, and she stumbled into me. I head butted the girl, feeling her nose crunch disgustingly against my forehead. I smiled — I finally used my head for something. Maybe just a bludgeoning tool, but that's something.

She dropped her axe and wavered on her feet, struggling to stay conscious.

I felt a burning in my stomach, and looked down to see a crossbow bolt sticking out of my midsection. I followed where it'd come from and saw a grinning asshole reloading his crossbow.

Having to use the mace to block an incoming sword thrust from the recovered elf, I picked up and flung the axe towards the crossbow-man. I had less practice left handed, so it didn't hit axehead first, but the weapon tangled him up, and caused his loading to falter.

A quick bit of parrying with the mace, and I got the elf where I wanted. I heard the twang of the bow, and pulled the elf towards me, hoping to use the asshole as a shield. But I fucking got shot again.

I let out a bellow, grabbed on with two hands, and swung the mace as hard as I could, letting my rage pour through the weapon. The elf attempted a block, but it was too weak. I hit his blade with enough force to snap it back and slice deep into his face. It didn't look like a mortal blow, but the wound disoriented him enough that I got another swing all the way around, and slammed the ball of the mace into the man's skull, which kind of exploded like an overripe melon.

Seeing how the mace was embedded, I left it, and snatched the elf's sword instead.

A poor-level longsword.

For the moment, there was stillness as everyone tried to comprehend the situation. Myself included.

They were down four and a half, since the girl with the broken nose hadn't gotten to her feet yet.

At the far end of the room, there was the asshole with the crossbow pulling hard to get it loaded. He was smaller, lithe, and had a very unpleasant face. Anther two bandits were coming on either side of me. One a man with a bushy mustache and two daggers, the other bald, with a sword. There was a conspicuous lack of armor, which, in my opinion at least, was one of the main reasons I'd been able to hold my own so well.

I snuck a look behind me, and saw a minefield of trip hazards. Dead bodies, broken furniture, and dinner detritus.

A quick step to the right, and I snapped the blade out at Baldy.

He parried, the sharp clang of metal on metal reverberating around the room.

Stone walls and sharp noises weren't exactly peaceful combos.

I wondered why they weren't rushing at me. It started to occur to me that they could be stalling.

Mustache came at my side, but with a bit of a twist, I made sure his daggers missed. I tried to get my sword in, but it was too long. I was operating without enough space.

Then I realized their gambit. Mustache dropped his weapons and grabbed my arms just as Baldy lunged in my direction.

I had no option but to trust the too-tight chain mail.

The sword point hit with force, enough that I felt it, but the mail held. Mostly. A few rings popped off, and the blade sunk into my gambeson just a bit, but the final point barely scratched my flesh.

I knew crossbow asshole was going to be shooting in a heartbeat, now that I was theoretically immobilized. But, a little martial arts went a long way, and just as the crossbow twanged, I flipped Mustache over my shoulder.

This time it worked. Mustache caught the bolt in his back right before I slammed him into the stone floor, which caused the crossbow to pop all the way out the front, along with a disgusting spray of his last supper.

Baldy took another lunge at me, clearly aiming for the same spot in my midsection. But I wasn't held back this time, so I grabbed his arm and yanked him off balance, twisting my torso to push him to the ground before I stabbed in through his neck with my longsword.

He gurgled as I stepped over him.

Crossbow frantically tried to load his weapon, but as I walked in his direction, he fumbled more and more until he finally dropped the crossbow. He pulled out a single dagger, holding it in his hand, shaking.

"Who are you?" he asked. "What are you doing here?"

"Avon calling?"

He didn't get the joke.

I snapped my blade up and whacked the dagger out of his hand. It clattered into the wreckage off to my left.

He stood there. Quaking.

I had him dead to rights. I could stab him, filet him, flay him, do whatever. But for some reason, it seemed wrong. So I lowered my sword and gestured at the door to the ramparts.

"Get the fuck out of here before I change my mind," I said.

He took off, and I started towards the the stairs leading down.

I got, maybe, two strides before there was a terrible pain in my back. I did my best to spin and look around, only to see Crossbow staring at me with his nasty face and yellowed teeth. He was hanging on my fucking back!

I grabbed him by his leg and ripped him off me, swinging him around. He screamed as he arced through the air until he crashed against the mantle over the fire, a sharp crack as his ear managed to touch his elbow for a moment.

Then it was quiet, save the crackling of the fire.

I hurt.

Not horribly. A quick check of the HP, and I saw that I had a 'bleeding' debuff, and my health had slowly dropped, but it was still well above half. The bolts came out pretty simply, but the dagger was a bigger problem. I couldn't quite reach it.

After some finagling, I managed to hook the hand guard of the dagger into the decorative curl of a wall sconce and then just dropped to the ground. There was a sucking noise, and then, *pop.* Out came the dagger.

I looked over the disaster of the room, and through it pained me to do so, I slid a sword through the back of the unconscious woman's neck. I didn't want to chance her coming to and killing Nikolai whenever he showed up. Or, you know, sneaking along behind me and stabbing me in the fucking back. Lesson learned. Thank you, Crossbow Asshole.

Another lesson learned — I went through the notifications very quickly, dismissing all the death ones, feeling a little less than great about it all. Granted, according to the game, or the wolds or the gods, whatever, these were all bandits. Bandits who had an evil alignment. So I'd maybe done some good in the world.

My initial impulse was to loot. But, looking around, the bodies in the room didn't seem like they'd account for the entirety of the castle. A quick count of the plates got to 10. I had 8 bodies. At least two missing.

There was a set of double doors at one end of the room, and they opened to reveal a landing. Stairs went up and down from there.

I wasn't keen on either direction, figuring that it was easy to be backstabbed again, if I chose the wrong way.

A cry of pain echoed down the staircase. It looked like my decision had been made for me.

40

As I sprinted up the stairs, I heard someone beg for mercy, and another, gruffer voice say some truly horrific things. The stairs ended at a short landing and a large door, but I didn't stop. I knew something terrible was about to happen inside, so I just barreled straight through the door.

Said door offered the minimum of resistance, and shot inward.

With barely a heartbeat to get my bearings, I scanned the room. It was something along the lines of Lord's chamber, with a large four-poster bed on the far wall and a fireplace nearish. A desk sat underneath a window, a bookshelf spread across one wall, and a number of dressers, chests, and other storage devices made up the rest of the place. A plush rug was on the floor, and a faded tapestry hung behind the bed.

There were women — multiple — tied to the various posts on the bed, and a burly looking green-skinned man at the foot. He was naked, with a bladed whip in one hand. All the women were nude, and one was either unconscious or dead. The others did their best to shy away from their assailant.

He turned to face me as soon as he heard the door slam, confusion swimming over his expression.

Closing the distance to the bed quickly, I planted a foot and threw all my force behind a mighty swing of my axe.

He started to dodge back, but I'd considered that he only had one direction to go, so I'd purposefully aimed just behind the greenskin.

It was a pretty perfect strike, the edge hitting him mid-ribcage and cutting all the way through his torso. There was a slight hitch when axe met spine, but I guess I'd put enough oomph into the swing that the greenskin just didn't have the backbone to stand up to me.

The top portion of his, well, of him slid off to the side in a truly revolting explosive arterial spray, and I managed to last a whole second before emptying my stomach on my wet bare feet. And my beard. Which made me throw up a little more at the vomit covering my face. This wasn't going well.

It was quiet in the room, mostly. The women tied to the bed, the two that were conscious at least, tried to be quiet, but I think they had some, well, issues. Terror being a main one.

I wiped my mouth, trying to get the puke out of my beard. This was not my best look. Finally, I just grabbed a jug of wine off the nightstand and used it to wash my face.

"Uh, I guess I'm here to save you," I said. "Are you from Saumiers?"

The least injured girl looked confused.

"You are not from Saumiers," she said. "I would know."

"I'm visiting, and, like, you know, helping out."

The girls looked to each other — the two that were conscious at least — and seemed to decide going with me was the better of their options. They offered their hands to me, and I tried to untie them. I proved to be not the best with fine motor skills though, so after some fumbling, the blonde one pushed me away and they just undid them on their own.

I took the opportunity to search the room, making sure there wasn't anyone hiding among the furniture or out on the balcony. I pushed open the heavy wooden shutter, and noticed that night had fallen. Also falling: the rain. Still in droves. The very definition of torrential downpour, and it had me wondering exactly how we were going to get back down the mountain.

A moment later, there was a light cough behind me. The three girls had covered themselves with bits of clothing that hadn't been torn to pieces, as well as some larger non-blood stained sheets from the bed. The two who were awake supported the one who was unconscious between them.

"Let me," I said, reaching for the girl.

They shrank back ever so slightly, but I just grabbed her, and fireman-hoisted her over my shoulder.

I carried my axe in the other hand, just in case, and we headed down the stairs and to the dining room. It maybe wasn't the best of choices on my part, considering it held the slaughtered remains of eight people, but it was reasonably safe and had two exits. I laid the girl down near the fire, and looked over the two girls who'd followed me. They were looking just horrified at the state of things.

One was blonde and one was brunette. They had very similar features — not quite twins, but definitely sisters.

"Stay here," I said.

"Where are you going?" Blonde asked.

"How many of them were there?"

"Bandits? I apologize, I did not get a good count."

"Eleven," Brunette interjected. "There are two more somewhere. I believe downstairs. Yunkathu said we were lucky, that he saved us by taking us to his room and not the dungeon."

"How many of you, uh, I mean, like prisoners, how many of you are there?

"Of us? Three."

"So who's down—"

"There are others they have taken," Blonde said. "Yunkathu said—"

I held up a hand, and asked, "Who's Yunkathu?"

"The orc you slew," she replied.

"Oh duh, thank you. You were saying?"

"He said they needed to make a change soon. That the prisoners in the basement were not working hard enough, and they were eating too much. Yunkathu ordered Grug and Dagobert to fix things by morning."

"Shit," I said, "so there's more prisoners and they're probably going to be dead by morning?

"No idea," Brunette replied.

I took a breath and let it out slowly, trying to get my brain in gear.

"Okay," I said, "Two bandits. Downstairs. Grug and?"

"Dagobert."

"And they're downstairs somewhere. Got it. You three wait here. I'll be back in a bit."

"What if they kill you?"

"Then you might need to wait a little longer."

They didn't find that amusing.

"Okay," I said, "keep the door closed. Don't let anyone in and, I guess, wait for the Saumiers guard to come up and rescue you. Or something like that. There is a friend with me, and he's, like, much better at this than me, okay? So we're fine. If someone comes, ask him who our boss is. The answer is Cleeve Dye. Or Cleeve. Or Dye. Any variation on that. If he answers correctly, you let him in. He'll take you back to town. You know, if I die."

I had the feeling they'd keep talking if I waited any longer, and I was worried if I didn't get down stairs, I'd walk in on a massacre. So, I just walked out of the room and closed the door to the stairwell behind me. I waited until I heard them lock the door, and then I started down the steps, wishing I'd been smart enough to put my boots on before heading down. Or even brought them in out of the rain. Lessons learned...

41

The one advantage to going barefoot was being quiet. The stairs went down to the ground level, where there was a large open space. Something along the lines of a throne room or a meeting hall. But, like everything else in the ruined castle, it was falling apart. At the far end, the ceiling was coming in, and rain poured through.

The bandits had transformed the room into a sorting facility. There were large piles of cargo along one wall, and a bunch of bags sat on the biggest table. I assumed coins, or something else equally portable and valuable.

I walked into the middle of the room, axe at the ready, but there was no one around. A huge set of decaying double doors was in the far wall, and I could see the dark courtyard beyond. The archway behind me led to the stairwell and the tower. I only saw one other door in the room, and it was ajar. Not a whole lot, but the door had warped at some point, and it didn't seem possible for it to ever fully close. I walked over and pushed it all the way open, ready for anything.

Nothing.

Just a small hallway with more doors. Two led off to either side, and straight ahead, through an arch, I could see a stairway heading down. Bingo.

Sounds came up from below — two people arguing mixed in with the grunts and groans of physical exertion.

The walls in the stairwell were dark and damp, and by the time I'd gone down two flights, I noticed there was torchlight coming from somewhere below.

At the bottom, I hit a landing that led to a hallway, the door at the other end was open, half-hanging off the hinges. It led into a large room that had a big table in the center, a set of double doors along one wall, a series of jail cells opposite, and a dark arch on the wall across from me.

Two men sat at the table, both leaning back with their feet up, both drinking out of steins. One had green skin and tusks pointing out from his bottom jaw. The other had a trim beard and a big nose. Unlike everyone else I'd encountered in the castle, these two mooks had armor on. It looked like a darker version of my old studded leather stuff. Black armor covered with dark metal studs. No helms or gauntlets though, and as I watched them, I noticed that their armor wasn't tightened as much as it should be. They were definitely in relaxation mode.

The jail cell held mostly women and children, all disheveled and in various states of despair. They all huddled at the back, as far away from the bars as possible, clearly doing their best to keep out of sight and mind of the two thugs at the table.

The grunting and groaning came from the darkened arch across the room. Mixed in was the sound of people hitting rocks with metal, probably digging with pickaxes.

"Tis possible the man does not know what he says he knows," the orc, Grug, said.

"You want to tell him you think he's wrong?" Dagobert replied.

"Oh ho, did I say that? Did I say he was wrong? I just think—"

"Either he is right and we are going in the right direction, or he is wrong and we are going in the wrong direction. No other way. Binary choice, Grug."

"Binary?"

"Just two choices."

Grug seemed to muse over that for a second, then nodded. He took a drink from his stein. Empty. Grug upended it over the floor, and a few drops fell.

"You need more?" Grug asked.

Dagobert held up a finger, drained his own stein, and then tossed it across the table at Grug.

Grug snatched it out of the air. He got to his feet with a groan. He stretched, cracking his neck while trudging over to a cask of ale.

Dagobert slid his feet off the table and got up, all in one move. He moved well, smooth. I started to worry about my chances taking the two of them on. There had to be a way for me to even the odds. Or a way to tip them deeply in my favor.

Dagobert was already across the room, and leaning his head through the dark arch.

"Faster, you feckless dung heaps!" he screamed. "Faster or I start raping your children and you can dig to the tune of your spawn's screams."

Grug chuckled over at the ale cask, carefully pouring the ale as his literal partner in crime made horrific threats.

The rage in me boiled, and I felt the sheer cold of true wrath.

I stood, walked calmly towards Grug, axe held at the

ready. As soon as I was in range, I swung at full strength, slicing across the air.

The axe hit Grug's back with a meaty thwock, and the blade bit deep. It went straight through the orc, hit the barrel, and stuck there.

Grug's legs dropped out from underneath him, but the upper portion of the body sat on the axe. I watched him try to turn around, try to scream, but he had nothing left in his lungs. Or really, of his lungs.

It's entirely possible I'd have gotten away with being sneaky if not for Grug dropping the steins, which caused a stunning ceramic and mead explosion.

"Grug," came Dagobert's admonishment from the other side of the room, right before he turned, "what the fuck did you—" he stopped speaking as he saw me, and scrambled to grab his sword.

I didn't wait for him to arm himself. I ripped the axe out of the barrel, causing Grog's top to join his bottom on the ground. I hauled the axe up, prepping to throw it across the room. The axe, perhaps tired of flight, slammed into a beam, and stuck there.

"Typical," Dagobert said, his sword held almost languidly now. He lazily moved towards me. "Feel free to run if you like. My brethren upstairs would surely appreciate a little leveling. Tell them you are my XP gift to them."

"You know," I replied, feeling along my belt for the sword I was totally sure I'd stuck there, "I tried talking to them, but they all up and died already. Maybe it's something I said."

Dagobert's eyes shot to the doorway behind me.

"I do not believe you," he said. "And I abhor liars. I suppose I will have to kill you myself."

"Lying bothers you, but raping kids is okay?"

"How about we save the semantics for when I pull my sword from your gullet and you would prefer I said blade. Okay?"

He lunged, his sword coming at me unbelievably fast.

But I'd been training with Cleeve, and fast was Cleeve's primary trick in fighting. I jumped back and grabbed a wooden chair.

Dagobert swung hard, and large chunks of my chair were sent flying.

Frantically, I searched the room while holding the chair between us, trying to find some sort of weapon that wasn't the battleaxe hanging from a beam.

We did have something of an audience — those in the jail cells had stood up and taken notice of what was happening. Well, the adults. The women were at the bars, but the children were still hiding amongst the elderly at the back of the cell.

A slice of an idea entered my head.

I made an overly large lunge at Dagobert. He almost laughed slicing it down with his sword, taking most of the support out of the chair, which promptly fell apart in my hands. Then I slid across the table, knocking a bunch of stuff off in the process, but grabbing a heavy metal candle stick.

Dagobert bit, and ran around the table. As he did, I swung the candle stick, hard. Well, making it look like I was swinging it hard. You know, for the fences.

My opponent dodged back, and came right up against the bars of the cell.

Immediately, all the women grabbed Dagobert, their hands snatching at every bit of his clothing and armor. He was completely immobilized.

He struggled against them, uttering curses and shouting

about how he was going to kill everyone who touched him and rape their children.

I didn't particularly want to hear any more of that nonsense, so I just brought my fist around, and slammed it into Dagobert's face.

His cheek caved in, the bones in his face breaking. His body went limp, and he dropped his sword. I snatched the blade quickly, and sliced the man's throat wide open.

Blood poured down the front of Dagobert, and the women let go. The man crumpled to the ground.

"Thank you," I said to the prisoners. They didn't make any eye contact or say anything in response.

I patted the corpse down, and found a keyring. It took a few minutes to unlock the door and get everyone out. No one could move well, and there were a few injuries in the group. Nothing life-threatening, but we definitely weren't going to get back to town quickly. Maybe that didn't matter.

A young woman with dark brown hair and very intense eyes stepped forward, moving between me and the rest of the group.

"Who are you?" she asked.

"I'm not sure this is the best time for introductions," I replied. "There's, I mean — how about we go back to Saumiers and then you can grill me all you want?"

"Grill you?"

"Uh, ask me questions in a violent or intense manner."

"I just asked your name."

"Montana."

"And you say you are from Saumiers?"

"No, I'm not from there. I was, like, passing through, heard that some people might need help, and came up to lend a hand. Heard there was something nasty happening up here."

Intense Eyes looked at me, then at the others. There was a bit of nodding from someone in the back.

"You are here to help?" she asked. "To help us?"

"I think so," I replied, getting very confused with the situation. "Did you need help?"

"Yes, but we are not from Saumiers."

"Eh, won't hold that against you."

"You are not here for the girls from Saumiers?"

"Already got them out."

There was a cry of pain from beyond the dark arch.

"Bertrand!" came a cry from one of the women.

"Hold up," I said. "I'll get Bertrand and whomever else is down there. You just get out of here, ideally to the second floor where the girls from Saumiers are currently holding up. I'll be back up there in a second."

Trusting that the rescuees would do what I said, I ripped the axe free from the beam, strapped it onto my back, and walked over to the dark arch. I stuck my head inside, trying to let my eyes acclimate to the darkness.

I pushed my dark vision to the fore, and soon it was bright as day everywhere, almost painfully so. Still, I grabbed a torch from the wall, holding it my left hand and Dagobert's sword in my right. I knew it could only get tighter as I went deeper, and my axe was just going to wind up a liability.

The spiral stairs wound tight, and, not too far down, I cam across some weak candles. There were six men down at the bottom. They shied away from the torch.

We were in a strange spot, something larger than a hallway and smaller than a room. Decorative carvings wrapped around thick stone pillars. A door had recently been exposed. A giant pile of debris took up most of the space; it looked very much like there had been a wall blocking the door, and these men had just torn it down. Given the wreckage, the wall was several feet thick. Someone really wanted whatever was on the other side of the door to remain undisturbed.

"Good evening gents," I said. "Care to, uh, leave?"

42

I thought the hard part of the questing was over. Now it was time to find loot and escort rescued damsels to their homes before getting a shimmering reward.

I was wrong.

On almost all counts.

The men shouted at me, mostly in surprise. Then they ran right past me and up the stairs, leaving their tools and candles behind. I heard at least one man fall on the steps, but no one stopped.

One person remained behind, looking at the door. Shorter, he had bright red hair and shabby clothing. His shoes were nearly falling apart, and his pants were pretty much nothing but threads.

"Yo," I said, "it's kinda time to go buddy."

"I must open the door," came his monotone reply. "You must come with me."

"Yeah, not sure that's a good idea."

"It is the best idea," he said, and reached for the door.

I didn't make a move because I figured the door would

be locked. That make sense, right? If you build a big fuck-off wall in front of a door, you lock it first.

Nope.

The handle turned like it'd been greased recently, and the door swung open. No noise, no nothing. It was the first fully-functioning door I'd seen in the entire castle.

Naturally, my new buddy walked right on through.

"Dude," I said, following after him since I knew I shouldn't leave somebody behind, "can you do this after I'm no longer responsible for you?"

He didn't answer. He seemed to have no notice that I'd said anything at all. The man kept walking.

I looked back at the stairs, knowing that it was the direction I should go, that I should just let this asshole disappear into the bowels of the dungeon, and yet... So many times I'd left something undone because I lacked courage, lacked the wherewithal to do what needed to be done. A few deep breaths, some rolling of the shoulders, and I knew what I had to do.

I followed the asshole.

I expected to feel something like a great weight, or something sort of magical, a tingle across my skin. There was nothing like that. I just walked through.

The torchlight sent bizarre shaking shadows across the walls. I'm sure I would've gotten freaked out by them, if not for a blueish glow to focus on, coming from right ahead of me.

I walked forward quickly and went through another door, and discovered where the glow came from. Lights, crystals of some sort, glowing by themselves and embedded in the ceiling. It was a big square room with a rug on the floor and some posh chairs along the walls, low tables in between each of them. It looked very much like a lounge. Two doors were along one wall with two doors opposite. The door I came through was the last, making five total entrances into the room.

The ceiling was only about eight or so feet high, so I could reach it easily. I put my hand on a crystal, and it was cool to the touch. I tried to pull it free, but something held it on, and the crystal stayed firmly in place.

The redhead powered on in front of me, getting to another door, opening it, and marching resolutely forth.

"Dude," I tried.

Nothing.

I ran after him.

This door lead into a hallway, still lit with the glowing crystals. Everything down here looked well cared for. Old, sure, but totally operational. There wasn't even any dust on the floor. The contrast to the rest of the castle was stunning.

Red walked down the hall to another fucking door. No pause there either — he just opened the door and walked in.

"Fuckin' a, man," I shouted, half-jogging to catch him. I didn't exactly relish the idea of just strolling into rooms willy-nilly. Something awful had to be down here, and I didn't want to stumble into it and die. Again. One death was enough.

This doorway led into a large rectangular room. Plenty of crystals in the ceiling kept the space nice and bright. At the far end, the floor looked like it had a hole in it, and the reflections on the ceiling made me pretty sure there was water in said hole. There wasn't any furniture in the place, but a fair amount of junk was spread around. Boxes, crates, quite a few swords, different kinds of armor in different piles, all over the floor. There were also a few piles of what looked like white rocks from the doorway.

Red marched straight towards the end of the room with purpose and drive and a complete disregard for anything else.

I stopped at the entrance because something felt off. Wrong. This didn't make sense.

As if to drive home the point, now I could see a vague shimmering in between Red and the pool.

I called out to the man, but, as before, the assbutt ignored me.

The shimmering overtook the man, and held him in mid-air. Red started screaming.

I swore I heard someone else yell. But like, in my head, not out loud.

"What the fuck was that?" I asked no one in particular.

I got no answer.

I walked closer, moving slowly, sword held in front of me until I was about three feet from Red.

His eyes were wide. He looked at me, imploring for help.

"Hold tight there, buddy," I said, looking at the, for lack of a better word, jelly that had trapped him.

I poked it with my sword.

The jelly didn't like that, and did its best to dodge me, shifting a bit back. It was big, all the way to the ceiling and roughly cuboid. It seemed like it had been constrained by the ceiling and floor, and so it had a bulging middle and some rounded corners.

Just then, an arm-like thing came out of the jelly, angling towards me as if to grab me.

Because it looked exactly like a clear version of the stuff that'd been shoved down my throat as a kid by well-meaning but unimaginative foster parents, I couldn't stop hearing the voice of Bill Cosby echoing around in my head.

More by instinct than anything else, I swung the sword across my body, slicing the gelatinous protrusion off.

"H-E-L-L-no, motherfucker," I snapped.

The jelly shied back while thick viscous liquid poured forth and splashed on the ground.

I swung Dagobert's longsword back and forth, hacking chunks off the jelly. More and more of the liquid spewed out, oozing all over the floor.

The jelly made another swipe for me, managing to get its pseudo-arm around my left wrist. A quick slash solved the problem.

I shook my wrist out and realized the clear liquid had some sort of paralytic effect. And since I was an idiot who didn't wear shoes, my feet were getting numb. I was quickly losing any speed advantage I had over the jelly.

Slice and cut and jab and slice. Over and over again until the jelly lost most of its shape, no longer pressing tight against the ceiling. Finally, we seemed to hit a threshold where the jelly could no longer hold itself together. As if a small and disgusting dam burst, all the fluid spilled at once, flowing out across the stone floor.

Red flopped to the ground, sputtering and coughing.

I grabbed the man and pulled him out of the goo. I did my best to wipe the slime off of the poor dude, even going so far as to stick my hand into his mouth, to pull it out.

He finished coughing, and just kind of leaned on me. I let him, and even gave him a thump or two on the back for good measure.

"What happened?" he asked.

"You tell me," I said.

"I... I do not know who you are?"

"Makes two of us. They say life is a journey of self-discovery."

"I was breaking the wall, but then I was being eaten by an ooze. Which is real. I had never thought—"

"Do you think we can get the fuck out of here now?" I interrupted. "Side question, you know what the thing was?"

"Jellied Demon?"

"Not what I would have guessed," I said, peering at the translucent mess around us. "Motherfucker certainly lived up to its name. Speaking of names, I'm Montana. You are?"

"I am—" his eyes glazed over just a bit, and his head dropped. "— Excuse me."

He started back towards the pool at the far end.

"Wait a fucking minute," I said, and grabbed at him.

Red tried to hit back and push me off of him, but the guy basically felt like a child in terms of strength.

I tightened my grip, and pulled him along with me as I walked back along the path we'd come in on, a process made easier by the mild lubricating properties of the Jelly's Goop. I just sort of dragged the jackass along behind me.

He wasn't giving up though. He bit me.

Which pissed me off, so I hauled off and slugged him.

Pow.

Red folded like a cheap suit, and I was left holding him up completely with one arm.

Maybe I was putting a few too many points into strength.

I resolved to go back upstairs, let Nikolai know what was down here, and then leave it up to someone else to explore this weird place that somehow took over people's minds. Hell, I just wanted to get out of the area before something took over my brain.

Back in the lounge room, I noticed one thing that was very off. The door we walked into was shut. I leaned Red up against the wall, but he promptly fell over to the side.

I pulled on the door, but to no effect. The thing was

locked tight. I kicked it. Nothing. Sword, axe, nothing made the door budge in the slightest.

"Well, fuck," I said, looking around the room, wondering what the fuck would happen next.

Turns out, that's something I should stop doing, because that's when the *other* doors opened.

43

Obviously, the doors didn't just open. Things started coming through them. Humanoid things, with completely black, latex-like skin. And devoid of things like genitals or, you know, defining facial features. Their hands were especially nasty, with fingers as long as my forearms hanging down. And just to make sure I'd have nightmares about them for the rest of my life, they had slack jaws filled with far too many teeth and sunken hollows where their eyes should've been.

"Oh hey," I said, "just took a wrong turn, looking for the exit. You know where that might be?"

They made a guttural keening, and approached en masse, six of them.

I slid the axe off my back, and reminded myself of the low ceiling. I'd need to make horizontal swings.

While watching the creatures, I really wished I knew a way to get more information about my opponents. Something tugged at the back of my brain, and I suddenly remembered the goblins. That I had a fucking spell to identify things. I shot the spell off over to them, and got back:

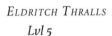

Eldritch Thralls
Lvl 5

Okay then. Probably not particularly friendly.

The closest one reached out for me, its stupid long fingers crackling with iridescent purple electricity.

"Let's not play this game, boys," I said, and swung for the fences.

Straight through the thing. Axe beats thrall.

It was almost too easy. I'd been expecting more resistance, so I was a bit overextended, and the next thrall in line just reached out and wailed on my side. Its fingers just went straight through the chainmail and seemed to rip my insides.

I screamed and kicked out, connecting with the thrall and causing it to tumble back and stumble into its brethren.

Two got tangled together, and I brought the axe into them both, double-kill style. I left the axe there and rushed at the remaining thralls, a move they weren't expecting. I ripped the sword from my belt and sliced across, right through the head of one.

Learning from my mistakes for once, I danced back and got out of range of their hands. A bit more of a backpedal gave me working room, and let me see something demoralizing.

I thought I'd killed four of the six, but now only one looked dead. The one I'd bisected was crawling towards me. Just the torso, sure, but the torso was pulling itself across the floor towards me.

Two were struggling to pull the axe out of each other, so while they weren't dead, they were out of the fight for a moment.

Half-head seemed to be the only one to stay deceased.

"Red," I said to the unconscious lump of jerkbutt I was still trying to save, "could've told me to go for the head."

I faked to the left, then jumped up and stomped both feet down on the crawler. Thrall head versus Montana feet ended with explosion, and gross thrall goo spewed all over my legs.

I went over for a snap thrust, and both the axe buddies went limp.

The rest of the thralls were short work. Leaking, but dead. Or re-dead. I wasn't sure where Eldritch Thralls fell on the whole undead versus alive scale here.

I wiped a bit of sweat from my face, but ended up spreading both cube goo and thrall goo across my hair and beard. I needed to get a handle on what was happening around me.

The door hadn't unlocked. Or moved.

I was still trapped.

In a lounge.

With an unconscious man who seemed strangely determined to drown himself. I think.

I left Red where he was and ran into the store room. The gelatinous remnants were slowly leaking into the water pool at the back of the room. I swore I saw something moving there, but when I got close enough to look into the water, it was just darkness below.

A little search of the room turned up some rope. I mean, there was a ton of other stuff there, but the rope was the stuff I was looking for. I used it to tie Red to one of the comfy chairs in the lounge. I'd gone through too much trouble saving the man already just to have him wander off and die while I finished getting us out of the mess he'd gotten us in.

Asshole.

I went through the doors the thralls had come from, which lead to another hallway. This one had three doors along each side and one at the end. Eight in total, counting the one I came through.

One door was just a hair open, so I edged it all the way with the point of my sword.

A bedroom, like something you'd find in a dorm. But I guess considering the time period I was in, it was a barracks. Small bed, wool blanket. Chest at the foot, small desk, small wardrobe. Crystal up top to light the room.

I poked through the chest. It was mostly sundry items, but everything was very old. Cloth falling apart, yellowing paper, and a jar of something that might have once been food. I slipped the jar in my pouch — could be interesting later. Finally, I found a small bag of coins from the bottom, buried under the rotten cotton, and grabbed it.

The wardrobe held a similar story, except no gold. I did find a pair of shoes though. There was also a little bit of jewelry in a small box. The box went into my bag — being in a game world meant that loot was important. And anyway, I had to refill my purse, considering I'd been so cavalier with money.

The next three rooms were functionally identical. Different clothing styles and sizes, different sizes of purses, but basically everything else was the same. Nothing of note.

The fifth room's chest had a false bottom. I probably wouldn't have noticed except that I'd just looked at four identical chests, and so the depth seemed off. I felt around the edges, played with the latches, and finally felt a little hole. I used the pin of a broach and stuck it through. There was an audible click, and the bottom of the chest came loose.

I pulled it up, and sucked in my breath.

Loot.

Stacks of gold coins, a bejeweled dagger, a handful of books, and a small golden box. All went into my bag. I'd sort the shit out later.

I was almost excited to get to the sixth room. But that's where everything changed.

I opened the door to see an old man standing on his bed, a dagger out and pointed in my direction.

44

We stood there for a moment, neither moving, both of us trying to get a read on the situation.

"Evening," I said.

"I, uh," the old guy's voice was *rough*. Like he'd been smoking and not speaking for a decade. "Who are you? How did you get in here?"

"Do you need saving?" I asked. "Or do you know how to unlock the door out of here?"

"You just stumbled into here?" he asked.

"Accurate description, oddly enough."

"What year is it?"

"I don't know."

"Has the world fallen so far we cannot keep track of years?"

"I'm kind of, I mean, I'm an idiot? I guess? I don't pay attention to that sort of stuff. But I'm a bit weirded out by this place. What is this?"

"But a corruption of what it once was. A folly of—"

"Come on dude, cease the poetics. Where are we?"

"A place of study. A laboratory."

"So you're a scientist."

"I am a wizard," he replied, haughty as fuck. "Once I was known and feared in all the realms. I was courted by kings and—"

"Let's tone it down just a tad, hoss," I said. "No need for horn-tootin.'"

"Horn tooting?"

"And isn't magic kind of outlawed in the Empire?"

"Precisely why I am down here in the bowels of an accursed mountain. We were forced to hide from the fools and charlatans who make rules based on ignorance and fear."

"I mean, not for nothing, but maybe there's something to the rules, considering you were trapped down here, and there's a bunch of nasty stuff walking around. "

"You have fought the thralls?"

"Yeah. I did, and—"

"Did you suffer wounds?"

"A little one, just—"

"Where? Show me."

He dropped his dagger and hopped off the bed. I had to catch the old dude and put him back on his feet.

I held up my mail and pointed to my side.

"Gods," he whispered. I could feel his ancient fingers prodding my side.

I looked down and was shocked. Black flesh pulsated right under my skin, spreading out from the point of contact almost.

"The danger with thralls is not what they are able to do in the moment," the old man said, focused on the wound while he spoke to me. "They have little strength and little speed. It is more what they do should they infect you."

"Which is?"

"Transform you into one of them."

"Okay, that's not good. Can you—"

"I am doing it now. Be quiet."

He muttered something while squeezing and prodding at me. I saw glowing symbols emerge in the air, swirl around, and then shoot into my body.

My side burned, like fire was straight cooking out my innards. I was about to yell when the old man slapped his hand over my mouth, and pulled me down to his level until we were looking eye to eye.

"Apologies for the pain," he said. "Magic is often painful."

The burning started to subside.

"You think you could teach me something?"

"Are you able to wield mystic arts?"

"Yeah, can some people not?"

"Not all are gifted with the—"

"That's lame."

"'Tis the will of the Gods."

"Okay, well, I have the ways and means to throw down the magic. I just need some more learning."

He just gave me a wry smile, then let me stand up while he examined my side again. I looked down and saw just my abdomen. No blackness.

"You must keep an eye on this area," he said with a rather hard poke. "It may not have gone away completely."

I nodded. "Maybe you can teach me that spell then."

He raised an eyebrow at me. "I doubt you have the experiences for that."

"Oh?"

"What spells have you already?"

"Heal others."

"Good for a level one mage. Very useful. Makes people love you in groups. What else?"

"Humus."

"I'm sorry?"

I reached for the spell, then felt the magic flow through my hand. A cubic foot of dirt appeared at the base of his bed, then spread out.

"Summon dirt?" the old man said. "I did not even know it was a spell. But I suppose there might be a use for it."

"Then I've got two identify spells."

"Now what is your Choice?"

"Uh, well—"

"Perhaps I should do a little identification on you, should you not mind."

"Uh, no. Sure, go ahead."

The man put his hand on my head and muttered a few words. I felt a rush of warmth. The old man pulled his hand back and looked at me with a raised eyebrow.

"I am intrigued," he said. "I have yet to hear of your race. Fallen, what is that?"

"I don't know."

"I, uh, how do you not know?"

"I just don't."

He scratched his head, then sat down at his desk. "And a nothing — do you know why you have chosen this as your Choice?"

"I don't know what a Choice is."

"You are a most interesting subject. Should we remain trapped here, and you survive, I would be most curious to study you."

"Weirdest flirtation ever. And what do you mean trapped? How long have you been down here?"

"Ever since the days the Emperor's edict was announced.

We lived in relative seclusion in our lab, and we were making progress like we never had before—"

"Sorry to interrupt, but who is the we? I've only found you down here so far."

"I suppose I am all that's left if you have encountered and defeated the thralls."

"Yeah, they're mostly just goo in the lounge now. And the door in there, the one to the castle, it's locked up tight now."

"The locking would be his interference, I suppose."

"His?"

"Everything changed when he arrived. We had a pool, you see. Connecting to the lake, and we would get fish and algae through there. Quite a bit of our food came from there. Some, obviously, from our greenhouse, but most from the pool. We wanted no one to know we were here, mind you, so we were living fully supplied by resources below the surface. Had we known of the monster the lake held, we would have made other arrangements, I promise you that."

"You sound defensive," I said.

"Some, in the past, have accused us of being willing to traffic with terrible monsters to gain additional powers. But this was not the case here. He came and we—"

"Any chance you're referring to a Jellied Demon?"

He chuckled. "I wish it were that simple. The he I reference is an Agachnern."

"Bless you?"

"Save your blessings. I have been cursed already; it is too late for me. You know nothing of the Agachnern, then."

"Nope, never heard of it."

"The Agachnern are deadly foes. Very intelligent. Powerful psychics. Some say that people are only around because the Agachnern remain in the waters. This one, he swam in, and took us over one by one. He played us as fiddles, turning us against each other until we were fighting and not paying attention. By the time I realized what had happened, it was too late. He forced my hand, and…"

The old man stopped talking. He looked down at his hands, tears tumbling down his face and beard.

Immediately, I knew what he'd done and how terrible he felt.

"I always was the strongest," he said, his voice small and weak, "and I thought I had kept myself in check. But my hubris caught me, and Koth M'gog, the Agachnern struck. We were all stuck in here, but my friends expired. Then it was only me, the Agachnern, and his minions. Since then, I have been forced to do his bidding. To put my research to his ends. I have lost all sense of time. Of everything, really."

"Okay, so there's a big mean bastard called an Agachoo, and we need to kick his ass and then you're free."

"If it were only that simple."

"Pretty sure that it *is* that simple, dude."

"You cannot simply use your oversized axe to cut the creature apart."

"Why?"

"Beyond the Agachnern being underwater and your axe not able to swing there?"

"Minor issue."

"He is smarter than you. Smarter than me. He has met my attempts at rebellion and dissent at every turn, and he has won. I am little better than his slave."

"There's two of us now."

"I admire your optimism, but—"

"But nothing. You got a name?"

"Morcant Treweek."

"Montana," I said, holding my hand out and then

clasping his wrist when he didn't make a move to grab mine. "Now, Morcant, here's the deal: you can choose to remain a slave, and you'll probably live, well, forever. Or you can come with me and fight. You might live, you might die. But you'll be free either way."

He paused, and seemed to give my plagiarized speech a moment's thought, so I decided to keep going.

"Say you stay, and live. Laying in your bed many years from now, would you be willing to trade all the days from this day for one chance, just one chance to—"

"Save the cheap rhetoric for the plebeians and fools, Montana. I see what you attempt to do. I accept your offer to free me, and I will fight with you."

Morcant Treweek has offered you a QUEST!

Freedoooom!

Morcant Treweek has been trapped by a horrific monster for more decades than you've been alive. Or even considered thinking about. Even though you weren't able to complete William Wallace's speech, will you free him from the evil clutches of the Agachnern?

Reward: [unknown]

Yes/No

I THOUGHT, *yes* to accept the quest.

"Great!" I said, clapping my hands together. "Now teach me some magic."

The old man shook his head with a wry smile.

"There are three means to learning magic, young

Montana," he said. "First, learning the hard way. You study the concepts of magic, you understand the core rules of the universe and you bend the universe to your will in the manner you wish. This is the most powerful way to learn, as you can tailor the magic to do whatever it is you would like, rather than memorizing individual spells. Second, you find a book, a magical item in and of itself, and you read the book. In doing so, you gain the potential to learn the spell."

"It's not guaranteed?"

"No. Not in the slightest. It is predicated entirely on your magical capabilities and affinities. If you cannot learn the spell, you will be subjected to quite intense pain. Even death if the spell is substantially over your means."

"And the easy way?"

"I give you all the spells I have."

"I'll take door three please."

"With the giving of spells, there are serious issues to take into consideration. One, I must give *all* my spells to you at once."

"Got it."

"Which means you must be able to take them all. It is an immense amount of pain for your body to handle and for your brain to process. Two, it means I no longer have access to any of those spells. I must relearn them all."

"Noted. Door three, not an option. Got any of those books?"

"I do. But the spell books I own will not likely help us against Koth M'gog. I only made such books for potential lab assistants, so regretfully, I have no offensive spell books."

"Okay," I said. "No new spells for me. So, let's go find M'gog. Ideas?"

"He is likely searching for food. There has been little these days, and he is constantly hungry. He was overzealous eating the tribe early on, and now they are a fraction of what he had originally, and he needs them to get more food for him."

"There's a tribe? Are they, uh, loyal?"

"Nothing is truly loyal to an Agachnern. Koth M'gog uses the tribe as vessels. He takes them over, and forces the tribe members to do his wishes. Likely, you will be forced to kill many of them before you even get a chance to confront M'gog. He is, at heart, a coward. All Agachnern are. They are virtually immortal, immune to the ravages of old age, and they will always run away rather than fight a battle they might lose."

"These things sound like ultimate assholes."

"They are vile."

"He definitely took over the guy I was with, but he's tied up now. So, hopefully we don't need to worry about him. Now, you said you got a lab?"

"Yes."

"Can I see it?"

He hesitated a moment, then shrugged, and led me out the door.

We went back down the hall and into the lounge, where Red was awake and struggling with his bonds. Morcant led me through another door, which led into *another* fucking hallway. There were two doors in this hallway, the further one open a bit. I could see the reflection of the glow crystals off of the water, which made me think that had to be the pool room.

The door in the middle of the hallway led into a massive rooms that looked pretty close to a modern laboratory. There were heavy stone desks spread around, and shelves and closets lined the walls. Notably, one corner of the room held a pool of water, large, dark, disturbing.

"Our library is in the far room there, and the magical item storage is there," Morcant pointed to another door.

"The pool?" I asked.

"An addition for Koth M'gog. The Agachnern cannot be out of water. Thus, he wanted a means to see me and talk to me in every room save my bedroom."

"So there are tunnels?"

"Yes, they lead all around us. To each and every room."

"Why doesn't M'gog leave and go back to the lake?"

"In our fighting, one of my brother-wizards collapsed the tunnel to the lake. He believed he would be able to starve the rest of us, and he would be the only one left alive."

"Same guy made the tunnels to each room?"

"Under control of the Koth M'gog, yes. The collapse of the connection to the lake happened later. Up to that point, we all thought Bern had just grown attached to the idea of burrowing and making tunnels."

"Not a spell you know?"

"I have little affinity for the magics twisting earth and rock."

The surface of the water in the pool rippled, and I couldn't help myself, I walked closer.

But it was so dark inside, I couldn't see a damn thing.

"Morcant," I said, "these crystal lights, can they be moved?"

"Yes."

"Can you toss one in the water?"

I wasn't watching Morcant, so I don't know how he did it, but a crystal sailed over my head, plopped into the water, and shone a light on hell.

45

"Holy fucking shit," I shouted, and scrambled back from the pool as fast as my trembling arms and legs would carry me.

The Agachnern sprung out of the water, spraying liquid everywhere as mass of toothy tentacles lunged for me.

One grabbed my leg, but luckily it was still covered in jellied demon goop. The tentacle flexed to solidify its hold, but my leg slipped free, and I scrambled out of reach.

I felt a great pressure around my head, as if my skull was caught in a vise that someone was wrenching shut. I curled myself into a ball, holding my head, instinctively trying to protect myself. The pressure increased, shrinking the world around me until it was just the space inside my skull. Slowly, from deep inside, I felt my reptilian brain awakening, pushing back. It roared, screaming that we were powerful, we were strong, and we weren't to be fucked around with. So a little human survival instinct and a healthy dash of American Exceptionalism allowed me to open my eyes through the pain.

Koth M'gog glared at me with far too many eyes, all glowing a hideous deep vermillion red.

I staggered to my feet, glaring right back at the calamari-lookin' motherfucker.

Now, bear in mind, Agachnern don't have much in the way of human features. Multiple eyes, tentacles coming out of where his face should be, a massive bulging body with fins. And just to make it all weird, they have two big fuck-off arms with massive claws on the ends of their three four-jointed fingers. That said, pretty sure he wasn't expecting me to stand up.

And he definitely wasn't expecting me to draw my axe.

I spun the weapon in my hands once. Then, fast as I could, hurled it horizontally at the Agachnern.

The axe practically whistled through the air, but the Agachnern wasn't a dummy, dropping into the water, and out of the way as my best weapon made a massive splash before sinking under the rippling surface.

I could probably swim down and grab it, but I knew going anywhere near his territory would just be the end of me. For the time being, I was down to the stolen sword.

"Impressive," Morcant said from behind me.

"I'm sorry?" I asked, turning to face the little old man.

"You survived your first meeting with Koth M'gog."

"Didn't seem that hard, really."

"Most any sentient creature would have walked willingly into his mouth."

"Which brings up a good question: why haven't you?"

Morcant brought up a pendant from beneath his ratty shirt. "I was wearing this at the time he arrived, and I have yet to remove it. Protects me from psychic attacks."

"Useful."

"It is likely the only thing that has kept me alive."

Given his tone, I could tell he was about to launch into his life story again. I was growing weary of his stories, especially since the more that I listened to the tail of Koth M'gog and The Wizard Friends, the less it made sense. Like, if Morcant was never under the sway of Koth, why had he been fighting so hard with his buddies?

I figured I could waste a lot of energy trying to figure out the story, or I could just kill the Agachnern asshole and get back into the rest of the world.

"Okay, so that's the agachnern," I said. "Strong."

"Very," agreed Morcant.

"Fast."

"Reasonably."

"And you said cowardly."

"After a fashion. He will not go to a stand-up fight, if that is what you are thinking. He will wait you out. Ambush you. Find you at your weakest and then take you."

"Okay, so we have to bring the fight to him. Can he hear us right now?"

"That I do not know."

"But we can expect his tribe to attack us?"

"They will likely attack you. I am not sure how Koth sees me at the moment. If he is willing to sacrifice my ability to research for him just because I might assist you."

"Got it. So these tribesmen, are they big and fast?"

"No. They are small, and mind-controlled."

"And I'm guessing ol' M'Gog doesn't exactly have the best fighting skills on land."

"I have yet to be impressed with his land skills. And outside of his control, the tribe are innocent and rather delightful—"

"Focus, buddy. Let's get back to the fight. Any chance

you've got some big fuck-off spear somewhere in the building?"

"It is possible there is something that matches your eloquent description in the store room. I fear I did not work with weapons much."

He waited there for a moment, and then I gestured that he should lead because, well, I had no fucking idea where anything in the damn underground bunker might be. Morcant led me over to a door, which I opened, and saw a room full of shelves and chests. No racks of weapons.

I sighed, and started pawing through everything, looking for anything useful. Bonus, I had to ask Morcant what nearly everything was because each time I picked up a magic item and tried to identify it, I got:

You've found a [????]. Identify the item to learn more.

Super useful.

There was a ton of random crap in the room. The bulk of it seemed as if came from people experimenting on items with no real direction, academic interest with no real-world uses. So you know, mostly esoteric eccentric nonsense. Earrings to let you speak with ants. A monkey paw that was still alive and working despite the rest of the monkey being, well, missing. A journal that could record events as it saw them, which meant it was full of descriptions of the box and the shelf where it was stored. A helm of encouragement. And so on.

There were also failed experiments, my favorite of which

was the anti-arrow armor. The armor turned ethereal when hit by an arrow, so the arrow passes straight through the armor into the flesh of the person wearing it.

Brilliant.

I leaned against the wall and stared at the ceiling.

"Maybe if you tell me what you might need," Morcant said, "I could help you find something."

Before I said anything, I peered around the edges of the room to make sure there wasn't a pool. That there wasn't a way for the agachnern to potentially eavesdrop.

"I need a speargun," I said, but immediately dismissed that. If Koth was a coward, he wasn't going to come at me if I had a weapon like that.

"Koth thinks he's smart," I continued. "Right?"

"He is very intelligent."

"But does he think he's smarter than you?"

"I think he is smarter than me. As far as I know, he believes he is smarter than everyone."

"Okay, step one in our plan: he needs to think I'm stupid."

"Not too hard to sell that."

I frowned at the man.

He shrugged back.

"So," I said, "now that we've established I look like a moron, what would a moron do?"

"Suit up in full plate armor, a sword, and a ring of water-breathing?" Morcant offered.

"Do you have those?"

Morcant nodded, but kept a rather morose and confused look on his face. "I am sure we have those. But you will not survive against him. I have seen his teeth puncture iron and steel. Even red gold."

"Red gold?" I asked.

"It is—"

"It's not germane is it? We gotta focus. Koth is badass. I need him to think I'm going to try and fight him so he comes to me."

"And then?"

"Then I blow him up."

"I am afraid I have lost your meaning."

"Big explosion."

He looked at me for a minute, blinked a few times, then said, "I believe that would end you as well."

"Maybe?"

"Your sacrifice would be appreciated, but it presents another immediate problem. I know of nothing which will explode underwater."

"Fireball."

"Fireballs and water have strange interminglings. As far as I know, they do not work underwater."

"You haven't tried?"

"I have not, no, but my colleagues did. They fizzled."

"No big boom?"

"None."

"Okay. Dynamite? Gunpowder?"

"Regretfully, I must admit ignorance of those words."

"Not a thing, don't worry about it. Blackpowder?"

"Again—"

"No worries," I said. I walked down one of the aisles looking at crates and crates of crap. "Well fuck."

I continued along the perimeter of the room, hoping pacing would bring forth an idea. Dynamite fishing was what I'd wanted to go for, but there was no way to make dynamite. Not to mention the small detail that I had no idea what dynamite was made up of.

Explosions. Underwater. That made me think of a

YouTube vid I'd seen where this oil company used an airgun to make a cavitation bubble underwater. The bubble's inevitable collapse would cause an explosion with as much force as dynamite. Or more even. They'd use the shockwave from the bubble to look for oil. So now I needed to figure out how to make a collapsing bubble underwater. How could I insert a—

"Morcant," I asked, realizing that I might have found a way to make an explosion and not get caught in the damage, "is teleportation possible?"

"We experimented with it," he replied, "and we discovered it was possible in a fashion."

"What does that mean?"

"Limited success."

"What does limited mean? Give me a little more here."

"We were never able to get it to safely work. There were always issues getting to the exact desired target."

"I feel there's a but."

"We did manage to make a one-time use tool, which, when broken in half, allowed a user to teleport to the other. But it has quite a limited range."

"Again, what does limited mean? Ten feet? Ten yards? Ten miles?"

"Fifty feet."

"That'll probably work. Any of those left?"

"Several," he said, already moving. He pulled a small box off a shelf and held it out to me. Inside were small grey discs with a shallow line carved through the middle. He held one out to me. "You break it in half, and leave the left half where you wish to go. When you eat the right half—"

"Eat?"

"You must crush it in your teeth. Then it will teleport your body to the other."

"How much of your body?"

"All of it."

"Armor?"

"Yes. Anything that would be part of you would teleport."

"Buddy," I said with a big smile, "I think we're gonna get out of this one."

"Who is Buddy?"

46

We walked out of the store room, and right into an ambush.

I finally got to meet the tribe Morcant kept talking about. Well, four of them at least.

The tribe wasn't exactly what I was expecting though. They weren't human, that's for sure.

They were, um, otters.

Just larger than any otters I'd seen before, and ones that stood upright and wore clothes and had weapons.

The tribe attacked en masse. Four stone spearheads jabbed into my midsection, pushing against the chain mail, but not going through.

Rage blossomed inside my chest, my instinctual response to being attacked. But a thought trickled down from my head, pointing out that these creatures were being used by the Agachnern, and that killing them wasn't the right thing to do. Not the good thing, at least. And if I was going to be a good guy, then I couldn't just pull out my sword and go ham on the little guys.

Instead, I swept my arm across my torso to get all the

spears off me. Then I reached out to grab the closest otter and toss him far down the hall.

The other three responded by using their spear shafts to club me. I could sense what Morcant had said: Koth M'gog just didn't have a ton of experience moving or fighting on land. He seemed to be struggling controlling three different creatures — they were all working in sync, but not making any different movements.

I grabbed a second one and pushed him to the side, tripping him with my foot.

"Rope," I shouted to Morcant, "get me rope."

Morcant scurried back through the door to the storeroom.

The two upright otters moved to either side of me.

They charged at the same time. If I just stepped back, they'd end up stabbing each other. But I didn't want that to happen.

Instead, I wanted to put on a good martial show for Koth, so he would believe that I believed I'd be able to take him on in the water. With a sword.

I drew my blade and swung up, so both spears went over my head. Then I stepped into left otter, pushing him back, while snapping the flat of my blade out and into the side of right otter's head.

Just as both otters hit the ground, Morcant returned with the rope. Now it was just a matter of grabbing otters and tying them up. The otters on the floor were very groggy, looking both confused and afraid. Which meant, to me at least, that Koth M'Gog dropped possession of the otters as soon as he felt they were even slightly incapacitated.

We put the otters in the lounge, filling up more of the comfy chairs. Red stared at me with fear in his eyes. Fear and confusion.

"Dude, just wait," I said. "You need to relax and let me handle this. And no I won't untie you. But you're probably totally safe here, okay?"

The weird grunts that came from the boy told me he had zero confidence in anything I'd just said.

Then, Morcant and I headed to the room with the jellied demon, on the hunt for weapons and armor.

47

I kitted myself out like an alpha male douchebag's wet dream. There was a surprising amount of that gear tucked in the dead jellied demon room. Pouring over the gack in the room netted a ton of crap to put on. A full set of posh clothes, leather armor on top of that, chain on top of that, full plate on top of that. I then found the largest chest I could and chained it to my front, and tied a fucking wardrobe to my back. Glow crystals were tucked in everywhere, so light basically poured out of me. To complete my ensemble of stupid, I got the biggest weapon I could find:

Mammoth-Greatsword

Item Type: Uncommon
Item Class: Two-handed Melee
Material: Steel
Damage: 80-120 (Slashing)
Durability: 80/80
Weight: 52 lbs

Requirements: Str 30

Description: Built by giants, for giants, the mammoth sword is used for the hunting and killing of mammoths. Some fools use them as ostentatious decorations, but none but giants ever wield them in combat. Even among giants, they are often seen as ridiculous.

Ten solid feet of steel nearly two feet wide. I waddled through the room, snapped the teleportation disc, and popped one half in my mouth and tossed the other to the ground.

A bit more waddling, and I was at the edge of the water. The surface was completely still, and completely black.

I looked over at Morcant.

He merely shrugged. It was pretty clear he had zero confidence in my plan.

I took a deep breath, and hopped in.

Even through all the gear, the water was frigid. My muscles locked up and I wanted to scream out. But I held it in, not trusting the water-breathing ring stuck on my thumb.

The crystals turned the black water into a gross green, but I could see. Not that there was much down there, just rough-carved rock walls. Given the pounds and pounds of steel on me, I sunk like a fucking rock, moving fast down the shaft of the pool until I hit the bottom. Silt exploded out from my feet.

In front of me was a horizontal tunnel, roughly twenty feet wide. It extended out past the crystal's light.

Being underwater and weighted down with a ton of gear, I didn't exactly move quickly. I lumbered down the tunnel, heading in the only direction available to me. I wanted to get deeper in to make sure the cavitation bubble's collapses made as tight an explosion as possible. I ran my tongue over the teleportation half-disc in my mouth, and wondered why I hadn't bothered to do a test run. Why had I just taken Morcant's word for it? I was about as stupid as the Agachnern thought.

I headed down the tunnel, making plenty of noise as I moved, clanking and banging like I had no idea what I was doing in the amor. Not that far from the truth, really. I gave the sword a few swings, at least to the extent that I could in the tunnel, and did my best to appear as if I was gunning for a stand-up fight with the beast.

"Ah, lunch has arrived," a voice echoed out.

I paused, confused. He wasn't making the noise in the water — he was projecting it into my mind.

"You talking to me?" I thought, doing my best to project the thought in the direction I imagined Koth M'gog.

"Oh," the voice replied in mock surprise, "lunch speaks. How novel."

His voice was slimy. I felt gross just hearing it.

"But I *am* quite hungry," Koth continued, "so please, keep the struggle to a minimum. Drop your blade, and I will kill you before I eat you. Otherwise, well, I have heard my digestion system is rather slow. Tortuously sluggish even."

"I'd rather just stab the ever-loving fuck out of you."

"So be it."

God, the arrogance in the voice was overwhelming. It just fueled my desire to make the asshole pay.

Thing was, as soon as the echo of his last word finished reverberating in my head, he attacked. It was fast, coming out of nowhere. He dropped at an angle from the ceiling of the tunnel, his two hands grabbing my arms and crushing the steel armor with his fingers. Laughably easy. His tentacles slapped all over me, their teeth puncturing everywhere at once. I could feel an intense wave of pain washing over me.

I struggled, unable to move. I had a single move to play, but I wanted the agachnern to get closer. I wanted to make sure he was going to get the full brunt of the blow. So I kept struggling, more and more until I heard the fucker laughing in my head. I could see his maw opening up to take a bite.

Tightening my grip on the sword, I bit down on the teleportation disc, feeling the crunch in my mouth, the gritty rock texture and the horrific taste.

And then nothing happened.

For a heartbeat.

Then there was a brilliant light, and I was standing upstairs, dripping water and blood, a litany of wounds practically pouring the red stuff out of me.

Below, there was a deep and resonant boom, loud enough and strong enough that dust shook off the ceiling. A shriek went through my head, a death rattle of sorts, and the agachnern died.

I know because I immediately checked the notification.

~

GG! You've killed an Agachnern (lvl 43 Defiler).

You've earned 5900 xp! What a mighty hero you are.

~

"Holy shit," I said. "That's a lot of XP."

"You killed him?" Morcant asked.

I noticed he was standing with his back against the wall, a short sword held in his trembling hands.

"I did," I replied, tossing a crystal into the pool. The water had turned a thick red, and bits of flesh popped up to the surface.

48

I pulled at a latch, and the chest and wardrobe dropped off me. Then I snatched up a spear and dove back in the water. I wanted to check for loot.

Swimming down was the easy part. It was also the disgusting part, since I was paddling through the liquified remains of the monster formerly known as Koth M'gog. Something at the bottom of the tunnel glowed ever so slightly. I kicked down, and saw small iridescent rocks all across the bottom. I grabbed a handful, and immediately got the notification:

You have found one (15) Agachnern Teeth. You have the feeling this might be useful for [unknown].

Huh. I took a moment and scooped up as many of the teeth

as I could, and then swam back up, something which was made decidedly unpleasant given the armor I wore.

I dragged myself out of the water, and Morcant stood above me, mouth agape, sword held against his leg. I gestured for help, but he just stared at the bloody water. I had to roll myself out of the water, and get up using my knees. But I did get a notification.

Congratulations! You've completed a QUEST

Freedoooom!

You have freed Morcant Treweek from the horrible clutches of the agachnern Koth M'gog. You have also completed the optional secret criteria, harm none of the tribe.

Reward: 6600 XP and [unknown] and [unknown]

"Dude," I said, "welcome to freedom."

Morcant shook his head. "I had no confidence you would pull this off."

"It's okay. I get that a lot."

I struggled with my soggy armor for a bit, until Morcant finally stopped staring at the mess and helped. It was rather painful getting the armor off, requiring a pry-bar at several points. Agachnern were strong as fuck, and I totally won though sheer trickery.

Once everything was off, Morcant pulled out a cool spell that doused me with clean water. I got dry clothes out of my pack and pulled them on. Finally, I shook out the chainmail and pulled that on as well. I was back to normal.

I had a ton of notifications to go through, but it just

didn't seem prudent to go through them until I was back in a safer place, no matter what Nikolai thought. Certainly not in the middle of the this weird dungeon lab with a wizard who'd definitely turned all his former friends into weird gooey zombie-type things.

I got to my feet, snagged my sword off the floor, and headed over to the lounge. I wasn't ready to let Red go just yet. Instead, I turned my attention to the otters. I got them untied and on their feet.

Morcant and the otters led me through the compound, until I was in a room with a massive open pool. It was about a hundred yards across, perhaps two hundred long, roughly round and dug out of the mountain itself. On the far side, there was a bit of a lip and a few tents around small fires. The tribe's home.

Otters were everywhere, all of them standing up on their back feet, all wearing clothes, some with spears, some with leather armor.

The otters who came with me immediately hopped in the water and swam across. I didn't get a chance to talk to them, not that they'd been particularly chatty beforehand.

"Are they otters?" I asked.

"No, otters are just animals," Morcant said. "These are sentient beings, just as you and I."

"Okay, but they're also otters."

"Perhaps they resemble otters, but they are known as Lutra. They are a civilized race, though with a shorter known history than some."

"Are they native to this area?"

"As far as I know, they are spread throughout the lands."

Several of the Lutra dove in the water and zoomed over, and popped up straight to standing.

Looking at them up close, you know, when they weren't

busy being possessed by some bizarre, terrifying creature and trying to kill me, they still really looked like otters. These guys were between three and four feet tall, and heavily muscled with super thick fur. They had small faces with almost unnaturally vibrant eyes, more so than any I'd ever seen on a human. Cute nose, set back small ears that moved about to catch sound, and bigger teeth than I was expecting. Long whiskers came out of their snout, though not quite as thick as a mustache.

"What is this?" the front otter said, his voice gruff.

"This is the man who saved you," Morcant said.

All eyes were on me.

A cry came out from the other side, and all of a sudden, a massive wave of Lutra crossed the water. They all hopped out and crowded around me, their tiny hands reaching out to touch me. I even had tiny baby Lutra lifted up and presented to me. There was crying and all sorts of emotion. I was completely overwhelmed.

I started to back up, the press of the little guys intensifying. But then I realized one of the otters was getting stepped on.

"Hey!" I shouted. All movement stopped. I pushed a few of the Lutra out of the way, and helped the trampled one to his feet.

He nodded at me in thanks.

"Okay," I said, "I appreciate all this, you know, adulation. But how about we all get out of this shit hole and find a nicer place to, you know, talk about what happened, okay?"

The Lutra (although I was definitely having trouble calling them that in my head), looked to one another, then at me, then all started nodding. They all jumped into the water. I guessed they either needed to pack, or, well, knew some other way out.

Morcant looked at me with a bemused expression.

"You have an odd manner of talking," he said.

"Yeah," I replied, "you sound pretty weird to me too."

He nodded slightly. "Perchance I have been down here just a bit too long. The world has moved on I suppose."

"That, I can't tell you."

He rubbed his head, his wispy hair going every which way at once. "I would like to offer you a reward, a thanks for what you have done."

"I appreciate that."

"Follow," he said, "if you will."

Then he started walking out of the pool room. The Lutra all watched as I left. It was a weird feeling, as if they were, I don't know, keeping tabs on me.

Morcant muttered to himself all the way through the compound until we came to the storeroom. He led me back to a metal door I hadn't noticed in my previous search of the place.

"Was that always here?" I asked.

"No," Morcant replied in a flippant way that suggested such a question was silly, and I was silly for bothering him with it. He did a little thing with his hand, and arcane symbols appeared out of thin air, glowing for a moment before sliding in and around the door.

There was a loud ka-thunk, and the door opened ever so slightly.

"Our repository," Morcant said. "Items we planned to sell in order to continue our work.

It was a smaller room, perhaps ten feet long and five or six feet wide. Shelves lined the walls, but were at different levels to allow for larger items to go on certain shelves. There was, however, barely anything there.

"I, uh," he stammered, "apparently I forgot the, uh, that

we already sold many things from here. I fear there is not much I can offer. I would give you healing potions," he pointed to a series of vials with red liquid, "but—"

"I'll take 'em," I said.

That got a half-smile from the old man, and he set them on one end. Then he grabbed the one good-looking item left, a leather bag sitting on the bottom shelf. It had two straps on one side, just like a modern backpack, and a massive opening to shove stuff inside. The mouth looked like it could be rolled up as if it were a waterproof bag, and a thick leather flap covered most everything. Extra cover. It was a natural leather color, and looked really nice, overall.

"A rather useful thing," he said, "it is a—"

"Bag of holding?" I asked, very excited.

"Ooh, I do wish I had thought of that — much better name."

"What did you call it?"

"The Unfillable Knapsack."

"Bit of a mouthful," I said.

"Yes, well, magic is my forte. I did not spend much time on creative pursuits."

"What does it do?"

"It holds everything you want it to."

"How much will it hold?"

"We never found a limit, though I am sure there is one."

"That's amazing. Thank you."

YOU HAVE FOUND A UNIQUE ITEM, ***The Unfillable Knapsack.***

The Unfillable Knapsack

Item Type: Epic

Item Class: Magic Bag

Material: Leather
Durability: unbreakable
Weight: 8 lbs
Requirements: None

Description: Totally not a bag of holding, this bag with extra-dimensional space inside, is capable of carrying an indeterminate amount of material. Might as well test it and see how much crap you can fit inside, you hoarder. As long as you can fit it through the mouth, it can be stored inside.

~

MORCANT GAVE ME A WAN SMILE, and I gave him a hug. He got very uncomfortable very fast.

"Do you mind if I clean out your store room?" I asked. "Is there anything you need here? I mean, are you coming with us?"

"I feel, perhaps, I might stay here," he said. "I fear the Empire is not quite the place I want to be in yet."

"Okay, but—"

"Please," he said with a smile, "take everything you would like."

I gave him a big clap on the shoulder, and then headed back into the store room to test the limits of my new bag. I shoved virtually every piece of weaponry, armor, and even some of the shelves into the bag. It all kept disappearing inside. It was beyond my wildest RPG dreams. It did get a bit heavier and I wondered if it would have any impact on the straps. Would the bag ever break? Just one more thing to test.

49

I got Red, untied him, and explained the whole situation. Just as I was about to walk out the door with him, the entire tribe showed up, standing expectantly in front of the exit.

"Uh, Red," I said, "here's the tribe. Tribe, here's Red."

Awkward silence.

The door opened right up, no problem, and I came face-to-face with Nikolai.

"Evening," I said.

He grabbed my shoulders and looked me in the eyes. Then he looked me up and down, finally he released me.

"You look fine," he said.

"Feeling a bit tired," I replied, "but otherwise fine."

"He saved us," one of the Lutra piped up. Then it was like a dam broke, and all of the otter-like creatures swarmed past me, running up the stairs. I mean, I got it. It's not like I'd want to spend any more time in the place I'd been a slave either.

Nikolai gave me one raised eyebrow, and then he turned and walked up the stairs.

Once we got back to the entrance of the castle, I ran through the whole story for him, going through the assault, the girls upstairs, the prisoners downstairs, and the agachnern.

Nikolai listened, nodding here and there, but otherwise remaining silent. When I finished, he slapped me across the face.

"You are a brave idiot," he said. "Do not be so foolish in the future."

"No offense," I countered, "but I only did what you told me to do."

"Partially."

"I was totally on my own here—"

"I was watching the entire time. Only once you went through the magic door were you on your own."

"I didn't know it was magical."

"It is something you should have checked."

"Okay, lesson learned."

"Almost good work," he said, and started walking. "We must hurry back to town, or we will ruin the schedule."

"I'm sorry?"

"Cleeve has a schedule to keep."

"I need to grab my boots and stuff," I said.

"Hurry," he said, and walked out.

I flipped him off, and then ran up the stairs. Then I began really testing the limits of the bag, looting like a madman, even pulling the four-poster bed apart and shoving that shit in there.

50

It was daylight out, and the weather was absolutely delightful. Sun shining, birds chirping, a beautiful view of the lake and surrounding countryside. We headed out down the mountain, and once again, I got to haul a wagon.

The prisoners I'd rescued from the basement had gone through all the materials piled in the courtyard and recovered most of their trade goods. We loaded up a wagon, and Nikolai volunteered me to pull it. It wasn't exactly my first choice, but I didn't want all these people to be broke and shit. So there I was, strolling down a mountain path as if on a leisurely hike. With a wagon on my back.

Naturally, because I was little more than a beast of burden, I used the time to go through the nearly countless notifications I'd gotten.

~

Cool Beans, you've learned the skill ***Stealth****. Be sneaky! Move around in silence! Tip-toe up to giants and dragons. You're totally* *going to start stealing stuff now, aren't you? +10% harder to detect.*

~

Congratulations, you've discovered an ability: ***Make An Entrance.*** *You really know how to enter a room. Once per day, you may use your ability to make a grand entrance such that those on the other side of the portal are stunned!*

~

Cool Beans, you've learned the skill ***Improvised Weaponry.*** *You can make a weapon out of anything. Say, a dwarf stabbed to a chair. +5% dmg when using made-up things as weapons.*

~

Cool Beans, you've learned the innate skill ***Swimming (LVL 9).*** *You can move through water without drowning. +9% movement speed in water.*

~

I also gained one level in weapon throwing, two in swords, and one in axes. Plus I killed a bunch of things and completed a big ol' quest, so I got a buttload of xp.

Boom:

~

Huzzah! Against all odds, you have reached ***Level 5!*** *You receive 6 attribute points to distribute in the next 36 hours or you lose* *them. Dare to believe you can survive, and achieve greatness. Or don't.*

~

HUZZAH! Against all odds, you have reached **Level 6**! *You receive 6 attribute points to distribute in the next 36 hours or you lose them. Dare to believe you can survive, and achieve greatness. Or don't.*

~

HUZZAH! Against all odds, you have reached **Level 7**! *You receive 6 attribute points to distribute in the next 36 hours or you lose them. Dare to believe you can survive, and achieve greatness. Or don't.*

~

HUZZAH! Against all odds, you have reached **Level 8**! *You receive 6 attribute points to distribute in the next 36 hours or you lose them. Dare to believe you can survive, and achieve greatness. Or don't.*

~

HUZZAH! Against all odds, you have reached **Level 9**! *You receive 6 attribute points to distribute in the next 36 hours or you lose them. Dare to believe you can survive, and achieve greatness. Or don't.*

~

I HAD a bunch of points to dole out — 30 to be exact — but I wanted to ask Nikolai about them. He put me through all that shit to get the levels, so I wanted his advice on what to do. I was tired of floundering, and I knew just dumping more and more points into strength would be pointless. Though at the same time, that would certainly be interesting. The dude was marching at the front of the group though, and I was in the back. Given the pace, and the way the Lutra swarmed around me, it didn't seem like there'd be a chance for me to get up to him. Also, that'd mean running with the wagon.

Instead, I settled into a pleasant hike down the mountain, where I had to make zero decisions about anything. I just took a moment to enjoy the new world. Take in the clean air, and just be.

As we approached Saumiers, I could see the town had its gates closed, and the guards were at attention. It made sense; our caravan was certainly odd, and we weren't exactly hard to see. But as soon as we got close enough, several of the rescued prisoners and nearly all the Lutra all broke into a run, sprinting for the city.

The gates opened up, townsfolk poured out, and there was a lovely moment of reunion. I couldn't help but smile broadly.

Nikolai and I just sort of slowly walked towards the town, letting the moment happen. We slipped through the gate mostly unnoticed. I left the wagon near the entrance, just inside the gates but not blocking the road, and used the mild chaos to disappear through the crowd. Nikolai and I made our way to the inn.

I was happy to not be a part of the crowds, never being particularly great with things like accepting gratitude or anything like it.

Kind of out of nowhere, as Nikolai stepped into the tavern area of the inn, a notification popped up. Since I had nothing else going on, I didn't ignore it.

~

CONGRATULATIONS! *You've completed a QUEST!*

The Saumiers Rescue

Villagers from Saumiers have been kidnapped in the night and were taken into the wilds by slaving bandits. You managed to bring them home safely, with barely a scratch shared among them.

In addition, you completed the secret objective, saving the traders and their goods. This gives you a bonus reward.

AND, the super secret objective was completed, and you managed to bring the long-lost Lutra back to their families, giving you an additional bonus reward.

Reward: Increased standing with the town of Saumiers, 4000 xp, [unknown] and [unknown].

~

CONGRATULATIONS! *You've completed a QUEST!*

A Bandit Problem

You have successfully cleared the bandits from the ruins above the Royal Road with extreme prejudice.

Reward: Increased standing with the town of Saumiers, increased standing with the Empire of Glaton, 2500 xp, 40 gold and a gift from the mayor of Saumiers.

~

"HUH," I said, "odd timing on those."

Nikolai nodded, then added, "Likely they only felt truly safe once back within the walls of Saumiers."

"And the bandits?"

"Perhaps the mayor needed to see the job done before the quest completed.'

"There's a lot I don't understand about this world."

Nikolai just shook his head. "You have so little knowledge, it is as if a babe is playing with dolls."

"Nikolai," I said, "you gotta work on your phrasing."

"Eat food," he replied, "rest. Do not leave."

Owen, the innkeeper, raised a hand to Nikolai. Nikolai nodded and walked off through a door.

I stood there like a fool for a moment, because I got some more news.

HUZZAH! Against all odds, you have reached ***Level 10****! You receive 6 attribute points to distribute in the next 36 hours or you lose them. Prepare for your Choice. Dare to believe you can survive, and achieve greatness. Or don't.*

LEVEL 10. Nice. I guess. Now I had 36 attribute points to spend. I had the feeling the game's math was off somewhere — I seemed to be drowning in fucking attribute points. But if it was unbalanced in my favor, why rock that boat? I decided to follow Nikolai's orders, and I sat down at the bar. "Got any food cooking?"

Owen just smiled.

51

Owen brought out a large bowl of potatoes, fried again, Gods bless 'em, and a massive slab of steak, the marbled fat still sizzling. There was a tureen of gravy and a tall mug of milk. I could get used to life in Saumiers.

While I ate, I chose, pointedly, to not pay much attention to the world around me. Sure, I took a look whenever someone would come inside, but for the most part, I kept my focus on the food, doing my utmost to present the visage of a man who didn't want to be spoken to.

Hence why I was totally surprised when someone came up right behind me.

"This him?" a voice asked.

"Ayup," Owen replied.

I turned around and saw an older man, balding with a trim beard, a little portly, and looking like it'd been a looong time since he'd had a good night's sleep.

Involuntarily, I gripped my knife, not at all sure what was about to happen. I swallowed the urge to say something about not knowing it was his daughter.

The older man stepped closer to me, and pulled a huge sheathed sword out form under his cloak. Then he bent his head and held the weapon out to me.

"You managed to return my future to me," the man said, face still down, looking at the ground as if he was afraid of looking me in the eye, "yet all I have to offer in return is something of my past."

He pulled the sword just a little from the sheath, revealing the metal had a bit of sparkle and glow to it.

"Man," I said, hands up after I let go of the knife. "I'm not sure what it is I did for you—"

"You returned my daughters to me."

"It's fine, I—" I started to say, but I felt a hand on my shoulder, and Owen pulled me close to him so he could whisper in my ear.

"'Tis a mighty bad idea to refuse a gift here," Owen said softly, but in the manner where I knew it was a stern warning.

I really wanted to ask why, but with everyone in the tavern looking at me and watching this interchange, a tavern that seemed to be overflowing with all sorts of folk looking at me, I had no option but to slap a big silly grin my face.

"You are too kind," I said, "but I accept your generous gift. Thank you."

With just a tiny bit of a bow, I took the sword.

~

You have been given the greatsword: ***HELLREAVER***

Greatsword

Item Type: Rare

Item Class: Two-handed Melee

Material: Fletium

Damage: 20-45 (Slashing)

Durability: 1845/2000

Weight: 24 lbs

Requirements: Str 18

Effects: +2 Damage on each strike, +10 Damage against any evil character.

Description: A large straight-bladed sword having a cruciform hilt with a grip for two-handed use.

~

MY FIRST MAGICAL WEAPON.

"Thank you," I said. "Really."

He nodded. "When I was your age, I thought a magical sword was something worth having. But when you get a bit older, you will see it is nothing compared to having yer family."

I wasn't exactly sure how to respond. The man nodded once, his eyes brimming with tears, and then left the tavern.

I just sat there, most of my food gone, holding a massive sword. Seriously, the thing was like, practically six feet long. Beautiful too. The hilt was wrapped in a supple leather with a big ol' pommel, and the sheath was a strange red leather I'd never seen before. Everything about it was just super cool. Except that I had no where to put it. I mean, sure, I could slide it into my bag of holding, but that meant the entire town would know I *had* ta bag of holding. I figured that would be better kept a secret.

Thankfully, just as I realized more than one of the ladies in the room were making serious eyes at me, Nikolai came out of a door in the back and whistled. He made a sharp gesture, indicating I should already be following him, and then turned around.

I gave a half-hearted wave to the gathered townsfolk, and followed Nikolai on the double.

He led me to a small room with an even smaller table and three chairs. Cleeve sat in one of them; the other two were empty. Three mugs took up most of the table, all filled with a foamy liquid, either beer or mead. Either one good with me.

Cleeve pointed at the seat directly across from him, and though I expected Nikolai to join us, he merely shut the door and leaned against it, his arms crossed over his chest.

I sat.

"You are a mighty strange man," Cleeve said.

"Thanks?" I replied.

"Take it however you like, for 'tis a truth. These past few days I have spent many an hour trying to figure you out, trying to understand who you are. All I have is that you are...different."

"Hell man, I've spent my whole life trying to figure me out.'

"And you have no answers?"

"Not yet."

"See, that is the thing," Cleeve said, pointing at me, "you do not say, 'no.' You choose, 'not yet'. Hopeful. You do not shy away from violence. Even if it is extreme and brutal. You make a choice to defend those you believe are innocent. These are uncommon traits in this land."

"Really? Doesn't seem that way to me."

"I gave you a job," Cleeve replied, "But I expected you might die. I chose to hire you, not give you anything."

"You trained me."

"Because I wanted you to protect my goods and my people."

I frowned, taking a moment to think over my life. Which was easy because, at that point, it was only a few weeks long.

"I've had good luck with innkeepers," I finally said. "But I've barely scratched the surface of this world. I don't know the people here."

"It is a hard world," Cleeve said. "Violent. People do not live long here. They protect their own and rarely go beyond that. You had no reason to do what you did in the ruins—"

"Wait a minute — I had to complete the quest."

"You did, but I refer to when you followed the young man into the dungeon below. You could have walked away at that point, left the young man to his own devices."

"Dude had no idea what he was doing! He was what, under control of the aschenfucker thing."

"Agachnern," Nikolai offered from behind.

"Bless you," I said, but no one else got the joke. "Yeah, that thing."

"You had no idea, at the time, that the creature was controlling the man. You just went after him. I want to know why."

I leaned back in my chair, looking from Cleeve to Nikolai and back.

"No offense,"I said, "but why the fuck does it matter why I did it?"

"Because I am curious."

My hackles were raised. Why did he want to know — what was he curious about? And why did it matter why I did anything?

I took a deep breath and let it out nice and slow, doing my best to release my paranoia with the air. My original self, he was a creature of fear and paranoia. I often acted in a way I thought might protect me, just in case. That hadn't worked out well. Here, I had the means mostly to protect myself from essentially anything that might serve to hurt me. Maybe it was time to trust.

"Ah hell, man, it just seemed like the right thing to do," I said, swallowing my attitude. "Dude seemed in over his head, and he seemed like he was going somewhere he shouldn't. There hadn't been a single thing good in the whole castle. No way was it going to start in the basement.

"You didn't think about a reward?" Cleeve asked.

"He tried to deny the reward," Nikolai said. "Owen had to offer a little advice."

"Bad idea to refuse a gift," Cleeve said with a nod.

"Look, man," I said, trying to get both men in view so they'd understand I was talking to them both, "there's too many rules for this fucking world. Why? What does it matter if I accept the gift or not?"

"In the same manner you are given a quest, there are those who offer the reward. If they are unable to give the reward, they will suffer. As you must fulfill certain parameters to be successful, so must this father fill his. At a guess, this man promised something to the gods if they would bring his daughters back. The gods, hearing this, made the quest."

"So he had to give me the sword because he said he would?"

"Likely."

"So," I pointed to Nikolai, "how did he get the quest? Did a god just wing it on down to him?"

"The man found me in the tavern in the morning," Nikolai said.

"So he—"

"You are becoming mired down again," Cleeve said. "The world works in a certain way because the gods deem it so. You may question it, but the questions will never have concrete answers. It is better if you merely accept the manner in which the world works, and figure out how to best operate within it."

I shook my head. "I don't think that's something I can ever fully do. I've always tried to understand things. I need to figure out how they work."

Cleeve rubbed his this beard, and ever so slightly raised an eyebrow in Nikolai's direction.

"Has your opinion changed?" Cleeve asked.

Nikolai scratched his chin. He looked at his nails, then at me.

"He is a bit of an idiot," he said. "You know this, right?"

Cleeve just smiled as an answer.

"Hey," I said.

"But other than that," Nikolai said, "he fits the criteria you set."

"Ah," Cleeve replied, "but notice how you have yet to answer the question. How do you feel about him?"

"Couldn't this have been done when I was out there eating?" I asked.

"Dye," Nikolai said, "I do not think—"

"I asked you. I want an answer."

"It does not matter what I think—"

"It will."

There was a hard silence between the men, as if Cleeve had just said something intense. But I had no idea what that could possibly have been.

Nikolai stepped to the table, reached over me and grabbed his mug. He took a deep pull, then looked over at Cleeve.

"Yes," Nikolai finally said. "I have changed my position on him."

"Capital," Cleeve said with a clap.

"I think I'm missing something," I said.

"Always are," Nikolai quipped.

"Well," Cleeve said, pulling out a piece of paper and smoothing it out on the table. "I am preparing to adopt you as my heir, Montana of no house at all. That is, of course, if you would like to be a Duke in the near future."

CPSIA information can be obtained
at www.ICGtesting.com
Printed in the USA
BVHW040905100522
636508BV00048B/367

9 781945 346088